Through the Mists OF TIME

ORACLE
DREAMS
TRILOGY
BOOK 1

TERI BARNETT

Through the Mists of Time
Oracle Dreams Trilogy: Book 1
Published Internationally by Teri Barnett
USA
Copyright © 2019 Teri Barnett
teribarnett.com
Lucky Crow Press

Previously published as Through the Mists of Time
by LBF Books (an imprint of Lachesis Publishing Inc.)
© 2005 Teri Barnett
Significantly revised and re-released as Through the Mists of Time
by Lucky Crow Press © 2019

Editor: Joanna D'Angelo
Exclusive cover design © 2023 Joanna D'Angelo
Interior design © 2023 Indie Book Designer

PRINT ISBN 978-1-7328138-2-3
EBOOK ISBN 978-1-7328138-3-0

For my brother, Frank Barnett Jr.
1949 - 1981

"If you were the one
suffering the fires of love,
you would be in
more of a hurry
to see Venus.
I love a young
and handsome boy;
I beg you,
spur on your mules.
You've finished your drink,
let's go;
take up the reins
and shake them.
Take me to Pompeii
where my sweet love
is waiting."

~ graffiti found during the excavation of Pompeii

CONTENTS

Prologue	1
Chapter 1	5
Chapter 2	11
Chapter 3	17
Chapter 4	23
Chapter 5	29
Chapter 6	33
Chapter 7	41
Chapter 8	49
Chapter 9	55
Chapter 10	59
Chapter 11	61
Chapter 12	69
Chapter 13	77
Chapter 14	83
Chapter 15	91
Chapter 16	97
Chapter 17	105
Chapter 18	115
Chapter 19	121
Chapter 20	133
Chapter 21	141
Chapter 22	147
Chapter 23	151
Chapter 24	159
Chapter 25	167
Chapter 26	173
Chapter 27	177
Chapter 28	183
Chapter 29	189
Chapter 30	193
Chapter 31	199
Chapter 32	205
Chapter 33	213
Epilogue	219

A Note from the Author   221
Sneak Peek: Shadow Dreams   223
About the Author   227
Teri Barnett Complete Book List   229

PROLOGUE

Pompeii, Italy
79 A.D.

The soft breeze entered through the bedchamber window and moved like a lover over Christos's naked body. A low moan escaped his lips as he turned onto his stomach. The breeze continued upward, over his thighs, and across his shoulders, stopping to tease the thick black hair curled at the nape of his neck.

Christos stirred, kicking away his rumpled bedding. He turned his face toward the window. Could it be? Was she here again? He opened his eyes drowsily. Ah, yes. She was here.

The finely woven linen curtains flanking the window danced around her where she stood, casting an ethereal quality to her form. How she came to be in his room, night after night, he had no idea, but she continued to appear before him just the same. Always when he was asleep, always when he was alone.

Long dark hair, the color of roasted chestnuts, cascaded to her hips. The luscious waves, covered her naked form, tempting his gaze to travel farther down to the darker curls shielding her womanhood. Ah, but he was hard-pressed to tear his gaze from the delicate beauty of her face. Her bright green eyes reflected the glow of a large, teardrop emerald, nestled between her moonlit breasts. Smaller emeralds dangled from her ears, sparkling through the dark, silky strands of hair.

Her own gaze gleamed in the moonlight, teasing him, daring him –
to come closer.

He ached with desire as he marveled at her beauty. He would have
reached for her, but it would have done no good. When he tried to
embrace her on previous nocturnal visits, she always flitted away
from him.

Christos's eyes drifted closed for a moment and the breeze tickled
his skin again. When he opened them, he realized it wasn't the breeze,
but the woman's fingers moving over him.

She drew closer, hovering above him, her hair brushing against his
skin as she delicately ran her nails down his chest and thighs. Oh, but
she was a treasure, this woman of the night. He sighed, savoring the
delicious feel of her touch. He'd stopped asking long ago from whence
she came and now simply enjoyed her nearness.

Once more she drifted away from him. Knowing it would be futile,
he still reached for the beautiful spirit who'd been haunting him for
weeks. But all he caught was the night air as she floated toward the
window. What was this game she played?

"Please—wait!" he whispered. "You must tell me this time. Who are
you?"

She turned to him and smiled. His chest tightened at the tenderness
in those emerald eyes, now darkened by the shadows of the room. "I
am yours," she answered simply. Her voice echoed the sound of
garden chimes in summer, soothing the feverish yearning inside him.

Christos let his breath out slowly. "You say you are mine, and yet
you are leaving me again." He pushed a damp lock of black hair off his
forehead and sighed. "Will you ever stay or will you forever pass
through my chambers on your nightly journeys?"

"The next time you see me will be in the flesh," she murmured.
"You have my word."

He watched in silence as she turned to face the window. Her body,
bathed in the silvery moonlight, glowed for a moment, then vanished
into the darkness—

Christos's eyes flew open. "By the gods," he cursed under his
breath, the tension tight in his belly. How long would he continue to

dream of her, this beautiful, nameless being who followed him into the arms of Morpheus? Was it possible to desire a ghost?

"How soon 'til you return to me, my sweet one?" He closed his eyes, his words a soft prayer. "How soon?"

CHAPTER ONE

London, England
April 1865

"Why dost thou cry?"

Her tears clung to her long dark lashes for a brief moment before spilling down her soft cheeks. *"I cry because there is no love in my world."*

He cupped her chin, forcing her to look into his deep brown eyes. "Nay. 'Tis not so. One as gentle and beautiful as thee will always be loved."

"And who shall love me?" Even as she asked the question, she knew she was being much too bold, much too daring. Her heart threatened to break under the burden of her sorrow.

He smiled warmly. "Can thou sayest with all honesty that thou dost not know?"

"I must hear the words aloud, so my heart will know 'tis not a lie."

"Then thou must listen carefully, for there shall be no misunderstandings between us." He traced the outline of her lips with his eyes. "I love thee, Caroline, and will spend the remainder of my days making thee happy."

Caroline caught her breath as he pulled her close, his strong arms locking around her. "And I love thee, Damon," she whispered against his lips as they pressed their bodies together.

VALERIE SHERWOOD BROOKS fell back against the soft goose down pillows, sighing as they enveloped her within their soothing embrace.

5

She held the book up in the air, just above her face, and reread the last line again and again until she could close her eyes and see the words still pictured in her mind.

"And I love thee, Damon."

Valerie closed the novel and hugged it against her chest as if it would steady the rapid beating of her heart. Oh, but these new romantic novels were just marvelous with their tales of love and passion. A woman would be truly blessed to be loved by such a man.

She lifted the gold watch suspended from a delicate chain around her neck. Noting the time, she sighed. It was getting late. Valerie leaned over the side of her bed and with one last, longing look at the novel, tucked it between the bed frame and thick feather mattress. She pushed the book as far as she could, past the seam of the snowy white linens folded around the striped ticking. She was careful not to bend its red chipboard cover or wrinkle its heavy pages.

For an instant, guilt grabbed at Valerie's conscience. If Mama should find out what she was reading she'd be in trouble for certain. She shook her head, dismissing the thought. No, she wouldn't let herself even consider the consequences. After all, she was nineteen and more than old enough to know of the private things between a man and a woman. She straightened her shoulders. Old enough to already be married with a child of her own, for heaven's sake!

The last thought clutched at her stomach and her shoulders slumped. Valerie took a deep breath, forcing the melancholy back to the hidden depths of her mind. Never mind Mama or marriage. Tonight, she would not allow such thoughts to upset her good humor. She'd just finished reading a perfectly marvelous romantic story and she would take the lovers' reunion into her dreams.

Rising up on her elbow, Valerie lifted the globe from the clear glass hurricane lamp on her night table. Being careful to shield the flame with her left hand, she blew out the fire and replaced the globe with a quiet clink and scrape of metal against glass. She settled back onto the pillows and pulled the creamy satin comforter up around her neck, shifting about until she was comfortable.

A voice bellowed from the street below, breaking the stillness of the night. Valerie realized too late she had left the window ajar. She tossed back the covers and pushed herself to the edge of the bed, first one foot, and then the other, hit the thick needlepoint wool rug with a muffled thump. She reached for the dark English oak cane, propped against the rose velvet side chair and grasped it with her left hand, the top well-worn and comfortable in her grip. Valerie took a step with her right foot, then dragged the lame left foot behind her, leaning on the cane for support. Reaching the window, she leaned the cane against the wall. She grasped the lip of the window frame with both hands and pulled it down, shutting out the night sounds from the street below.

Once back in bed, Valerie again placed the cane against the chair and let her body sink into the mattress. She snuggled as far down as she could under the covers and closed her eyes. As her breathing grew steady, Valerie drifted into a deep sleep, images of a man with curly black hair and ebony eyes filling her dreams.

"VALERIE! VALERIE!"

The high-pitched screech broke the heavy veil of sleep and rang in her ears. Valerie cracked her eyes open only to find her little brother standing beside her bed, his face so close she could see where the sleep still clung to his dark lashes.

"What in heaven's name do you want?" she grumbled.

"Mama said it's time for you to get up. She said you're a sleepy head and I should come and get you for breakfast," he declared.

"Please, Reggie. I'm not ready to wake up just yet. Tell Mama I don't want any breakfast this morning." Valerie rolled over to face the wall, pulling the comforter up over her shoulders.

A soft thud sounded followed by a delighted gasp.

"Oho!" Reggie opened the book and began to read aloud. "Damon, my love, when will I see you again?" He slammed the tome shut. "Papa's going to beat you for certain!"

The book! It must have fallen out.

Valerie flung back the covers and whirled around. "Give that to me!" she demanded, grabbing for him. But he was too fast for her and darted toward the door, stopping just short of exiting her bedroom.

Her eyes focused on Reggie. Flustered, Valerie fumbled for her cane. "I said give that back to me, you little lizard! You have no right coming into my room and taking my things!"

"What's going on here?" Jacqueline Brooks, their mother, stepped into Valerie's room. "What have you got there, Reg?" she asked, ruffling his dark red hair. Victorious, Reggie handed the book to his mother. He wrinkled his freckled nose and stuck his tongue out at Valerie.

Valerie glared at her brother as she stepped carefully over the pile of tossed bedding. "It's nothing, Mama. Just a book." She reached for it, but Jacqueline already had the book open. Valerie sighed, rolling her eyes.

This isn't going to be easy.

"I can see that. But what sort of book would have you calling your brother names?" Jacqueline flipped through the pages, her eyes widening. She shut the book and handed it back to Valerie. "Really, dear you shouldn't be wasting your time reading such nonsense."

"Yes, Val, you shouldn't be wasting your time reading such nonsense." Reggie mimicked his mother, in a decidedly haughtier tone.

Both women turned to the boy and glared at him. He took a step backward. "I—um, I think I'll go get dressed now." Reggie turned and scampered down the hallway, his white cotton nightshirt flapping behind him.

Valerie shared a smile with her mother. "The little lizard." She walked back to her bed and sat on the edge. Jacqueline sat beside her.

"You should be concentrating on your studies," her mother gently chided, patting Valerie's hand. "Now that you've decided to get your teaching certificate, you need to be sharp for your entrance exam to Queen's College."

Valerie stood and went to the window, pulling back the heavy burgundy velvet curtains. She fingered the long single braid that hung over her shoulder.

Staring at the street below, she noted the early morning rush of merchants setting up their wares for the day and the patrons already lining up to make their purchases. How quickly they moved, compared to her. Valerie took a deep breath and let it out slowly. "Please, Mama, reading romantic novels will not interfere with my schoolwork in any way. It's just… I know I won't ever marry—" Valerie glanced over her shoulder at her mother's gasp. "I'm not blind, Mama. I know people stare at me…How men look at me. Truth is, I've thought about little else for quite some time now. And I believe I've made peace with it." She hugged her arms about her. "But it's lovely to dream a little."

Her mother stood and went to Valerie, wrapping her arms around her. "Well, then, you have my permission, as long as your studies don't falter," she said in a husky voice.

Valerie smiled. "They won't. I promise."

Jacqueline pulled away and smoothed the wrinkles from her cotton day dress. "And whatever you do, don't leave that book out for your father to see. He'll be beside himself if he finds out what you've been reading."

"I assure you I'll keep it out of arm's reach from now on." She narrowed her eyes. "Short and stubby ten-year-old boy arms' reach to be exact."

Her mother chuckled as she walked to the bedroom door. "Now, don't dawdle getting ready for breakfast," she called over her shoulder. "Your father wants to talk to the entire family before leaving for the bank today."

"Did he say what it was about?"

"You know your father, Valerie. Everything's a big mystery until he decides to reveal it." She paused, her hand on the doorknob. "I will tell you one thing, though. He hasn't stopped smiling since he came home last night."

CHAPTER TWO

Valerie pulled open the doors of her large oak armoire and rummaged through the rack of dresses. Stopping at a blue moiré, she pulled it off its wood hanger and, balancing on her right foot, slipped it on. She struggled to button the back, reaching first one arm, then the other, arching in innumerable contortions. She stopped for a moment and leaned on her cane, out of breath.

"Here now, Miss Valerie, let me help ye."

Valerie straightened, then rubbed her shoulders where they were beginning to ache from the strain. "Thank you, Lucy. I fear I would have twisted my arms from their sockets had you not shown up just now."

"Ye should have called fer me," the housekeeper scolded. "I was jest helpin' yer brother get himself ready fer the mornin' meal."

Lucy, ever present for as long as Valerie could remember, always came to her rescue. The petite older woman buttoned the cuffs of the dress then stopped.

"What's this all about?" She nodded toward a stiff pile of fabric on the floor. "It best not be what I'm thinkin' it is," the older lady warned.

Valerie's eyes met the housekeeper's in the mirror. "You'll not lecture me today, Lucy. I've had quite enough of those contraptions." Valerie glared at the heavy, whale-boned corset. "I am certain a man invented those bloody things. A woman would never think of putting herself into something like that. Why, I wouldn't be a bit surprised to discover it was used as some sort of medieval torture device."

Lucy gasped, her finely lined skin paling. "Miss Valerie! Yer language!" She drew herself up and wagged a bony finger in Valerie's face. "I won't have ye talkin' like that, I won't! Why, I've raised ye since ye were but a wee babe and never thought I'd live to hear such an outrageous thing."

Valerie raised a hand in surrender. "Forgive me, Lucy. I apologize for my language."

Lucy raised an eyebrow.

Valerie squirmed under the scrutiny, though her eyes sparkled with amusement. It wasn't the first time she'd been scolded by the older woman and likely not the last.. "But I still won't wear it." Valerie stuck out her bottom lip.

"It's just not proper," Lucy muttered as her aged but still deft hands looped each tiny button marching up the back of the Valerie's dress. "Not proper at all not to wear yer corset. What's to become of the world if young girls quit wearin' under things? I'll be havin' a talk with yer mum, I will." She finished fastening the dress and took a step back. "There, now. Ye're as pretty as a picture."

"Thank you, Lucy." Valerie leaned on her cane, considering the image she presented in the mirror. Pity she hadn't been born a man. Walking sticks were all the rage right now and she'd fit right in. She turned around. "Of course, you're right, Lucy." Her eyes filled with humor. "What ever could I have been thinking?"

"Gather 'round, family. Gather 'round," Frederick Brooks instructed as he summoned everyone to their places. He stood at the head of the table, one hand tucked into his weskit pocket while the other tapped on his crystal water glass with a small silver butter knife. He watched with pride as they seated themselves. Jacqueline to his left, Valerie to his right and Reggie at the opposite end of the long narrow table. Such a fine family indeed. An adoring wife, a healthy son to carry on the family name, and a daughter who was as intelligent as she was beautiful. He drew himself up and cleared his throat, running a finger along the stiff celluloid collar.

What's this?

His fine family continued to chatter around him. Why, they weren't paying him the least bit of attention. Well, this wouldn't do. No, it would not. Frederick cleared his throat again, only louder this time. He tugged at his suit jacket anxiously.

This wasn't going at all according to plan. Not at all. His family was supposed to be transfixed by his presence, in awe of the head of the household. At least, that's what all the gentlemen's journals said.

Frederick cleared his throat a third and final time. "See here, all of you. I would like your attention. That is, I demand your attention."

Jacqueline patted his hand where it rested on the edge of the table and smiled benignly. "Why don't you sit down, Freddie? Your tea is getting cold."

"What is it, Papa?" Valerie said. "Mama said earlier you had something you wanted to discuss."

"Yes, Papa," Reggie chimed in. "Why haven't you told us yet?"

Frederick rolled his eyes and pulled a neatly folded sheet of paper out of his inside pocket. Unfolding it, he held it up. It was a boarding notice for the *Fast Alice*. A clipper ship currently docked on the Thames River, it would be sailing for China in less than a week.

"Are we going to China, Papa?" Valerie whispered.

"China?!" Reggie hooted and jumped out of his chair. "Please say we're going to China, Papa! I want to see me a real live panda bear!"

"China, Frederick?" Jacqueline asked, her eyes widening. "Is this the surprise?" Her hand flew to her chest.

"No, no. You've got it all wrong." Frederick took a deep breath then let it out. "No one said anything about China. Did you hear me mention the word at all?"

"Well, no, Papa. But you did tell us you had a an important announcement and then you pulled out that sheet of paper," Valerie ventured. "And it is a boarding notice for China."

"Indeed, I did hold up this very piece of paper. However, we are not going to China." He sat on his chair, unfolded a linen napkin, laid it on his lap, and looked around the table. "We are going to Italy."

"Italy?" Jacqueline rubbed her forehead. "This is all too confusing, Frederick. Please, just tell us exactly what you have in mind."

Frederick scanned the faces around him. "As you all are aware, I have several important clients at the bank. One of them in particular, Sir David Smythe, has various vested interests outside of England. He would like the bank's support to pursue those interests. In order to do this, I need to investigate his proposal to determine whether or not I should grant him a loan."

"Yes, dear, but what does this have to do with Italy?"

"Smythe's latest interest is archeology. Seems he'd like to help finance the excavations at Pompeii. News of it has been in all the papers lately." He took a bite of his sweet roll, glanced at Valerie, and winked. "Surely you've heard of it."

POMPEII!

Oh, Papa was teasing her. Of course he knew she had heard of it, even before Master Hobbs had taught them ancient history. *Pompeii...* Just the word itself conjured up images of elegantly robed men and women strolling ancient streets lined with fluted columns; a forum marketplace filled with vendors of sundry items; the gods and goddesses of Rome sitting high on Mount Olympus as they played games with the fates of mere mortals.

"Pompeii," Valerie breathed. Most of her studies had been directed toward antiquities, but to get a chance to actually visit the site of one of the places she'd only read about, would be a dream come true. She smiled at her father. "You're playing with me, Papa."

Reggie cleared his throat and declared, "I don't want to go to Italy or this Pompy place. If I can't see a panda bear, I'd rather spend summer at Grandmother's village, like we always do."

Valerie's eyes widened, and she chewed her bottom lip, worried that Reggie's comment would make their father change his mind.

After what seemed an eternity, Frederick spoke. "No, Reggie, we won't be visiting Grandmother this summer. Smythe's business is much too important to ignore. He owns a clipper ship and has already made arrangements for it to make a detour to the Bay of Naples for us."

"You know the ocean makes me nervous, Freddie," Jaqueline said, fidgeting with the edge of the white linen tablecloth.

He reached for her hand. "I have every confidence you'll do just fine, dear. As a matter of fact, I'm certain you'll all make fine sailors." Frederick regarded Valerie. "You've been much too quiet about all of this, my dear. I'd have thought you'd have plenty to say on the subject, given your interests."

Valerie opened her mouth, then closed it as tears pricked her eyes. To be presented with this opportunity was the greatest gift her father could have ever given her.

She stood and, using the chairs around the table for support, made her way to her father. Reaching him, she threw her arms around his neck. "Thank you so much, Papa. I can't wait to leave!"

CHAPTER THREE

"Is this really necessary, Mama?" Valerie winced as the seamstress missed the fabric of the dress and poked her instead.

"Well of course it is, dear. We can't arrive in Italy in last season's clothing, now can we?" Jacqueline took a step backward and admired the fine picture her daughter presented. The gown's apricot satin complemented Valerie's fair complexion, while the cut nipped in at the waist and billowed out, drawing attention to Valerie's slender curves, "Besides, we're fortunate this shop offers ready-made gowns—given your father's short notice, we would have never made it in time, if we'd ordered custom-made.

Jacqueline pulled a bolt of lace down from the trimmings shelf as she went on. "Here now, don't forget to add this to the cuffs. It's just the touch this dress needs," Jacqueline told the shopkeeper.

"Yes, mum." The woman curtsied and took the creamy, tatted fabric. "I'll make sure Susie doesn't forget to sew it on the dress." She tucked it into a large willow basket filled with mother-of-pearl buttons, silver and gold thread, and crocheted gloves Jacqueline had already selected for alterations.

"Might I say, mum, your daughter is the picture of loveliness." She frowned and lowered her voice. "Pity about her leg though, isn't it? Was she born that way?"

Valerie stiffened. Jacqueline's eyes caught hers in the mirror's reflection. Jacqueline wished she could take away the pain in her daughter's eyes each time someone made a so-called well-meaning remark.

Jacqueline had blamed herself for the accident, all those years ago. Valerie was only six years old when it happened and the 'if onlys' haunted her for years. If only she hadn't taken Valerie to the shop that day. If only she hadn't stopped to chat with another young mother. If only the group of giggling young women hadn't come in and left the door open. If only her daughter hadn't dashed out. If only the carriage hadn't rumbled by… The doctors said Valerie would never walk again, but her daughter was brave as well as stubborn and walk she did…

"My daughter was involved in an accident. But she gets along just fine, thank you." She picked up a soft yellow dress made of finely woven cotton from where it lay on a side chair.

"What do you think about this one, Valerie?" she asked.

"It'll be fine, Mama," Valerie said with a smile.

Jacqueline smiled back at her daughter, her beautiful and brave daughter. "Very well, Jacqueline said softly. She turned to the shopkeeper. "We'll take these two as well as the green damask and the dark red one as well."

The shopkeeper curtsied again. "Yes, mum. How soon did you say you'd need these to be ready?"

"No later than Saturday." Jacqueline put on her bonnet and tied the ribbons in a neat side bow. "Do you think you can have them in time? We'll be leaving for Italy on Sunday."

The woman drew herself up and smiled broadly. "Why, I'll have them to you on Friday if you'll tell your friends about me."

"IT'S ALMOST TEA TIME," Valerie said. "What do you say we stop at Rennie's and have a cup?" She gestured toward the wood and leaded glass entry next to the dress shop.

But before Jacqueline could reply, Valerie steered her through the door of the teashop and to a table near the front window.

"My goodness, Val, let me catch my breath!" Jacqueline chuckled.

"I'm sorry, Mama. You looked like you might say no." Valerie sighed. "I just needed a moment to collect myself and thought this would be the perfect place."

"My darling, I am sorry about the dressmaker." Jacqueline patted Valeries's hand.

"It's all right, Mama." She plucked at the tablecloth and glanced around the room. Sitting down she was like everyone else. Almost all of the small round tables were filled with patrons. Mauve cabbage roses decorated the golden-fringed tablecloths. Watercolor pastorals hung in groupings on the wall. Their gilded frames reflected the light from candles on each table, lending the room a warm, welcoming glow.

They ordered tea and cakes. Jacqueline poured each of them a cup and Valerie took a sip of the strong brew. It was good and hot and warmed her insides.

She gazed out the window at the passersby, bustling down the street. No need for a cane. No hint of a limp.

She sighed and shook off her melancholy. She wouldn't trade places with any of those people. In a few days' time she would be on a ship, bound for Italy…

"Tell your future, young miss?"

Shaken out of her reverie, Valerie glanced up. An old gypsy fortuneteller was standing beside their table. Though Valerie had seen her in Rennie's, reading for other patrons, the woman had never approached her. She stood quietly with a smile on her weathered face, fingering the beaded fringe of her bright red shawl.

"No, thank you," Jacqueline said in a firm tone.

Valerie leaned across the table. "Please, Mama. It'll be fun."

"You've been reading too many of those novels., They have filled your head with silly notions."

"Please… Just this once, Mama?"

Jacqueline nodded. "All right, if it means that much to you."

The old woman's face creased into a broad smile as she pulled a chair to their table and settled between Valerie and her mother. At Valerie's nod, the gnarled hands reached for the teacup. The gypsy swirled the contents around and around and then poured them back into the pot. Jacqueline grimaced, but the old lady ignored her, peering into the bottom of the cup. "Look there!" she exclaimed.

Valerie leaned closer and frowned as she studied the residue. "All I see are some tea leaves."

"It's not just tea leaves, miss. It's the way they're arranged in the cup that's important."

"Really? Tell me what it says."

"I see a ship. You'll be takin' a journey soon."

"How did you know that?" Valerie asked, her eyes wide.

"I wouldn't be much of a fortuneteller if I didn't know such things, would I?" The gypsy nodded, making her large gold hoop earrings bob up and down. The woman's earlobes were stretched beyond repair by the heavy jewelry and Valerie feared they'd break through the thin layer of skin holding them in place.

"Hmmm. Well now. This is good. I also see a heart—the symbol of love." She winked at Valerie. "Ah, but there's something else…"

"What else do you see?" A shiver ran up Valerie's spine.

"There's a lightning bolt—here—runnin' through the heart. It means a love that'll break your heart." The gypsy looked up, her coal-black eyes filled with sadness. "I'm sorry, little one."

Valerie leaned back in her chair, considering what the woman had just said.

A love that will break my heart—?

At least there would be a love. "Can you tell me more?"

"Aye, well… 'tis strange indeed… Somethin' I heard of, but never seen myself." The gypsy tilted the cup for Valerie to see. "See that line going through the ship?" Her gnarled finger pointed to the symbol and Valerie nodded. "There's more than one journey in store for you, child. A crossin' of some great chasm." She shook her head. "Like I said, I never seen nothin' like it before. Only heard stories from fortunetellers long dead now."

"Is there anything else about love?" Valerie asked, more intrigued by that prospect than another voyage.

The gypsy put the cup down. "I see nothin' more today." She reached for Valerie's hand, clutching it. "Be careful and may the gods keep you safe."

Unnerved by the gypsy's abrupt warning, and tight grip, Valerie withdrew her hand. "Thank you for the reading, ma'am."

Jacqueline laid a shilling down on the table. "I believe that will be all."

The old woman picked up the coin and turned it over and over in her palm, the metal gleaming from the flickering candlelight. "Do ye wish to know what the leaves say for you, dear lady?" she asked.

"Thank you, but no. I already know what the fates hold for me. You see, I'm married and have a wonderful family." She reached across the table and squeezed Valerie's hand. "I've realized my dreams. It's now my daughter's turn to realize hers."

CHAPTER FOUR

Valerie stood in awe as the early morning mist began to dissipate along the banks of the Thames. Her breath caught at the sight of the *Fast Alice*. Sunlight gilded the entire ship in a golden glow.

Crew members were scaling the masts and rigging as they hoisted the billowing white sails.

Here is the chariot that will transport us to Pompeii…

Valerie made her way up the gangplank, gripping the thick rope handrail for support and being careful not to catch the tip of her cane in one of the gaps between the weathered boards.

"Valerie!" Reggie ran up beside her.

"Do you always have to scream when you talk, Reg?" Valerie asked. "You scared me half to death."

"No one listens to me if I don't," he reasoned.

"Trust me, we'll listen just as well, if not better."

"Well, I'll think about it." He skipped along beside Valerie and the walkway listed first to the right, then to the left. "We are going to have the most wonderful adventure, aren't we?"

"I certainly hope so. Please, stop shaking the walk. You'll send me tumbling head first into the Thames for certain."

"I'm sorry, Val," Reggie said as he slowed down. "Tell me, do you think the volcano – what's its name? Suvio? – will interrupt while we're visiting?"

Valerie laughed. "First of all, it's called Vesuvius. And second, it hasn't *erupted* since 1794. So, I think we'll be quite safe."

"Welcome aboard, Miss." The captain stood at the ship's rail and bowed low, his neatly combed and parted gray beard touching his chest. "It's a pleasure to have you aboard my Alice. I'm Captain James

Marcus." He held out his hand and assisted Valerie onto the deck, Reggie scrambling up behind her. "Johnny – he's the steward here – he'll show you and your family to their cabins." He gestured to the small, bird-like man with salt-and-pepper hair, to his right, then extended his hand to assist Jacqueline and Frederick as well.

Lucy hung back, staring at the ship with a growing uncertainty. "What's the matter, Lucy?" Valerie called to her.

The older woman frowned. "Never left the land afore. Not sure I wants to now." She sniffed.

"Don't be a goose, Lucy. This ship is perfectly safe." Valerie flexed her knees, pretending to bounce up and down. "See? I haven't fallen through."

Lucy carefully handed the carpet bags she was carrying onto the deck. She crossed herself, took a deep breath, and stepped over the low railing. The steward took her hand.

"I'm very happy to have you aboard, Miss."

Lucy's eyes widened then she giggled in reply.

Valerie bit back a smile. She could hardly believe it, nor would she have if she hadn't heard it herself. She watched in quiet amusement as Johnny charmed the usually dour housekeeper.

"It's not often we get such lovely ladies of your maturity and bearing on board. I look forward to conversing with you throughout the voyage." He bowed low.

Lucy placed a gloved hand on her chest. "Why, Mr. Johnny, ye do go on, don't ye?"

The captain stepped forward, carefully elbowing Johnny out of the way. "I hope all of you will join me for dinner at my table tonight."

Frederick shook Marcus' hand. "Thank you, Captain. We'd be honored. You haven't seen Sir David Smythe yet, have you? We're to be traveling with him."

"Yes. As a matter of fact, he and his son are on the other side of the deck, seeing to some last-minute details." Marcus pointed to his right.

"Jacqueline my dear, if you and the children will excuse me, I must discuss a few matters with Smythe. I'll join you all later." He turned to the steward. "I'd like you to go ahead and take my family to their quarters."

24

With a smart bow, Johnny scooped up Lucy's baggage. "Be careful with it," she wagged a finger in his face. "The lady's beauty cream is packed tight in there along with a few other things I shan't be discussin' in mixed company."

"Ah, but I can see you won't be needing any beauty cream your-self." Johnny winked, then motioned with a nod. "Please follow me. We'll go down the booby hatch to the suites."

"Booby hatch?" Reggie giggled.

"Yes-sir-ree. That's what we call that hole in the deck. It's where the stairs leading to the lower levels are. Stick by me, boy, and I'll have you talking like a real sailor in no time."

"You will? May I, Mama?"

Jacqueline eyed the hatch carefully. "Um, well, I suppose it wouldn't do any harm."

Reggie jumped and hurried to the hatch, scrambling down the heavy teak steps. Jacqueline went next, followed by Lucy. Valerie stood poised at the opening, not certain what to do next. She sighed. She was thankful her family didn't treat her as an invalid, but at times like this, they always seemed to forget that she might need a hand. True, she had to maneuver up and down stairs every day at home, but they weren't nearly as steep as these were.

"Mama? Lucy? I could use some assistance," she called, but they had already walked on ahead.

Hesitantly, she placed her right foot on the first step. Next, she lowered the cane, pulling her left foot down behind it. Valerie smiled, victorious. She tried it again, only this time, she lost her footing and started to stumble. Her mouth opened in a scream just as a strong hand caught her arm.

"Careful, Miss. You could have broken your neck."

Valerie turned around and looked up. A man stood above her, but she couldn't make out his face. The sun shone brightly behind him, creating a golden halo around his head.

A god. That's what he is. A great Roman god.

"Can I help you to your quarters?" the god asked, his hand still on her arm.

Valerie quickly composed herself. "Uh, no. No, of course not. We haven't been properly introduced." She glanced down. "But I do appreciate your help."

The stairs were wide enough that he was able to move past her down to the next step. She was able to see his features more clearly. A strong, square chin, deep, blue eyes, dark-blond hair. Why, he looked just like she'd imagined Damon, the hero in *Carolyn's Dream*, her romantic novel, would have appeared!

"Would it make a difference if I said your father sent me over here to help you?"

"I beg your pardon?"

"I'm Thomas Smythe, Sir David Smythe's son. I was talking with Sir Frederick when he saw your distress. He asked that I lend you a hand."

"I–I see. I suppose it would be acceptable for you to help me then." She let him guide her down another step. "I'm Valerie Brooks," she whispered.

Thomas smiled, and his teeth shone white against his tanned skin. Valerie took a deep breath and her heart skipped a beat. "How did you ever hurt your ankle?" he asked politely as he continued to help her down the stairs.

Hurt my ankle? she repeated the words in her mind. For heaven's sake, he didn't know about her foot. A whole new world of possibilities opened before her. "It, uh, it was a riding accident," she lied. "My horse, Rexford, threw me."

"Your horse threw you? Well, then, I'd say you were lucky to only have injured your foot."

"Very lucky," Valerie answered with a nod. "Rexford is too wild for his own good."

"There, now. You've made it down the stairs." Thomas gave her arm a little squeeze before releasing her, sending a shiver through Valerie at the intimate gesture.

"Valerie! Where have you been?" Reggie ran toward her, screaming as usual.

"Go away, you little lizard," she muttered under her breath.

"And who might this young man be?" Thomas asked.

Reggie grinned, drawing himself up. "I am Reginald James Brooks, at your service, Sir."

"Well, it's a pleasure to make your acquaintance." Thomas shook Reggie's hand.

"Mama said it's time for you to unpack, Val."

"I'll be along soon," she replied with a smile, her eyes imploring Reggie to scamper off. A deep chuckle came from the Roman god. Her eyes met Thomas's, a warm gleam was reflected in his gaze.

"Mama said you have to come now!" He stomped his foot. "I'm not going to go back there without you. I'll get into trouble for sure if I don't have you with me."

"Sounds to me as if you should be going now, Miss Brooks. Will I see you at dinner?"

"Perhaps. We'll be seated at the Captain's table. Do you know where you will be?"

Thomas smiled again. "At the captain's table as well."

Valerie blushed. Of course, he'd be at the captain's table. After all, his family owned the ship. "I'm sorry. I should have known."

"Nonsense. I wouldn't expect someone as lovely as you to litter your brain with trivial matters." He took her hand and kissed the back of it lightly. "Until we meet again."

Reggie tugged on Valerie's skirt and she reluctantly pulled her fingers out of Thomas's strong lean ones. She turned and let her brother lead her to their suite, taking each step carefully for fear Thomas would realize his mistake. She gripped the cane tightly, her hand still tingling where he had pressed his lips against her fingers.

Valerie fought the urge to turn around and look at him one more time. She knew with certainty that she could lose herself in those deep blue eyes. What was it the gypsy had said? A love that would break her heart? Well, as far as she was concerned, that prophecy would not come true. She absolutely wouldn't allow any heartbreak on this voyage.

CHAPTER FIVE

Making her way to the trunk in her cabin, Valerie unlatched the lock and heaved back the heavy lid. There, wrapped in delicate, white tissue paper, were the new ready-made creations. "Which dress do you think I should wear tonight? Mr. Smythe—did I tell you he's Sir David's son? — will be dining at the captain's table as well." Valerie had told her mother about her fortuitous encounter with young Mr. Smythe.

"Ah, the plot thickens," Jacqueline commented. "No, darling, you failed to mention he's the son of our host."

Valerie held up the dark red satin dress against her and studied her reflection in the mirror. Wrinkling her nose, she hung the dress on a wooden hook and pulled out the green one. "What do you think, Mama?"

Jacqueline's eyes met Valerie's in the mirror. "What I think is that my daughter has grown into a lovely young woman."

"Oh, Mama—" Valerie smiled, grateful for her mother's love.

Jacqueline smoothed Valerie's long, chestnut locks. "And I told you there would be a nice young man out there for you. You only had to give it some time."

Valerie's smile faded and she lowered the dress.

"What's the matter?" Jacqueline asked.

Valerie turned to face her mother. "Well, there's something I need to ask of you. You and Papa. Can we sit on the bed?" Jacqueline moved to loop her arm through Valerie's, but Valerie shook her head and limped to the bed, a task belabored by the sway of the ship as it made its way out of the Thames and into the Sargasso Sea. The ship's horn bellowed, and the cabin vibrated with the sound.

Jacqueline sat beside Valerie, a question in her eyes.

Valerie plucked at the coverlet as she chose her words. "You see, I have a bit of a dilemma. Mr. Smythe doesn't know about my foot. At least not entirely…I told him I sprained it, falling off a horse. A horse named Rexford, to be exact." Valerie lowered her eyes, guilt began to churn in her belly. The horn blew again, the sound mocking to her ears. She'd never really lied before, except to Reggie and usually in jest. But, of course, he didn't count.

"Listen to me, Valerie—"

Valerie raised a hand, interrupting her mother. "I know, Mama. I shouldn't have done it, but it was his idea. What I mean is, he assumed it was just a temporary injury. The thought that I was—permanently different—never entered his mind."

Cripple. The word is cripple.

Strange how one word could carry so much hurt. When the accident first happened, friends came to visit and check on her, bringing small gifts. But as she got older, and it was apparent she'd never walk properly again, they stopped coming.

It was lonely.

She learned to show strength on the outside, but on the inside, her heart broke a little each time a friend said, "She'd be a beautiful girl if not for that horrible limp." And it would hurt even more when a mean stranger said, "Get off the street, you. You're shameful to watch."

She shook her head. "I couldn't bring myself to tell him the truth. I wanted him to think I was like every other young woman my age."

"You shouldn't have lied, Val. If he is as special as you believe him to be, he'll accept you as you are. I wish you would believe me."

"Mama, I know you feel that way, but you need to understand that I see a different story in every young man's eyes I meet."

Valerie stood and smoothed her dress. She walked toward the mirror again, carrying her green dress over her right arm. Lifting the hem of her skirt, she stuck her left foot out. As long as she kept her shoes on, no one could really tell what was wrong. They couldn't see the misshapen toes or her twisted heel.

Jacqueline wrapped her arms around Valerie and held her tight for a moment.

"Please, Mama," Valerie whispered against her mother's shoulder. "You have to promise me you won't say anything,"

"I won't lie for you, Val," she said quietly. "If he asks me, I'll tell him, and so will your father." She leaned back and tilted Valerie's chin up. "But, if the subject isn't broached, then there will be nothing to say, will there?"

Valerie beamed at her mother. "And you'll tell Lucy to mind her own business?"

"Lucy? Mind her own business?" Jacqueline chuckled. "And where did you get the notion Lucy would ever mind her own business where you—or any of us for that matter—are concerned?"

Valerie sighed. "I see your point. Well, I'll just have to make certain the two of them are never alone together."

"You know you'll have to tell Mr. Smythe yourself sometime, don't you, Val?" Jacqueline asked, tucking an errant lock behind her ear.

"I know. And I will, when the time is right." Valerie took a deep breath and let it out slowly as the events of the day caught up with her.

Why is life so complicated?

As though her mother had heard her thought, she tightened her arms around Valerie. Mama was warm and soft and smelled of lavender, like all mothers should. And she wouldn't tell if she wasn't asked. It might buy her some time at least.

CHAPTER SIX

L ucy darted back and forth between the adjoining door to her cabin and Valerie's. "The curlin' iron's heatin' up in the coal bucket in the hallway. Can ye imagine they have a man who's tendin' it fer ye? Somethin' to do with not wantin' anyone to burn the ship down." Lucy shook her head. "Such luxuries! It'll be ready in just a minute, miss."

Scooping up a several thick locks of hair from Valerie's head, Lucy twisted each section to the scalp, holding it in place with a hairpin. Hurrying back out she returned with the curling iron. Grabbing the end of each lock, she deftly wound it around the iron and held it for a moment before releasing a plump curl.

"There, now, ye're as pretty as a spring bloom." Lucy admired her handiwork, fussing over a loose bit here and there. The elegant upsweep was accented with a pearl comb in the back, pushing long corkscrew curls over to dangle impishly beside Valerie's green eyes.

Valerie smiled as she looked at her reflection. "You do fine work, Lucy. It looks just like this magazine picture." She held the illustration next to her face, so she could compare herself to it, pursing her lips into an exaggerated pout like the woman in the portrait.

Lucy peered at the magazine and tutted. "Yer far prettier than that lass. And ye don't need to compare yerself t'others. Now it's time to get ye in yer corset." Lucy lifted the heavy garment from the berth.

Valerie groaned as her eyes swept over the dreaded garment. She didn't argue, though. She had to look her best for Thomas Smythe and if it meant wearing a corset, so be it. Valerie stood and held her arms above her head. "Do what you will with that cursed thing," she muttered, taking a deep breath and holding it.

Lucy stared at Valerie for a moment, clucking her tongue. "I told ye mind that language, didn't I?"

Valerie didn't answer, pretending her attention was diverted by some commotion outside the cabin's porthole window.

Lucy shook her head and wrapped the corset around Valerie's midsection, pulling the ties tightly in back. With a sigh of satisfaction that the laces were just as they should be, and a perfect hourglass shape was achieved, she worked the strings into several small knots, tucking the ends into the top. "There. Ye can breathe now."

"Thank goodness." Valerie exhaled loudly. But, as soon as she relaxed her stomach muscles, a sharp whalebone poked her in the side. "No wonder fainting couches are so fashionable these days." She squirmed. "The corset all but guarantees a woman will faint dead away at the slightest agitation." Valerie tugged at the top, pulling it into place around her breasts. "I suppose it's a good thing that I'm not quite as well-endowed as other women. I fear this hideous garment would greatly decrease the chances of feeding my children should I ever be blessed with any."

"Miss Valerie, I have heard just about everythin' from yer mouth. I don't know where ye've been learnin' to talk so, but I won't tell ye again to stop it." Lucy shook her finger. "A proper lady wears her undergarments without complainin', even if she finds them uncomfortable. As a matter of fact, proper young ladies do everythin' without complainin'."

She held out the steel hooped crinoline and pulled it into place as Valerie stepped into it. "I'll be havin' a talk with yer mother if ye give me any more trouble about it." She lifted the bottle green silk dress from its hook and slipped it over Valerie's head, being careful not to damage her coif. The dress fell into place in a soft cloud. "Am I makin' myself clear?"

"Lucy, after all the years you've been with this family, I never thought I'd see the day you'd threaten to run to Mama about me." Valerie shimmied into the dress, pushing her arms into the long, fitted sleeves. "I must say I'm surprised at you."

Lucy's eyes widened. "Ye're surprised at me?"

"That's what I said." Valerie presented her back to the older woman, a smile tipping her lips. Lucy couldn't stand it when Valerie acted like she was disappointed in her.

It serves her right for making me wear this bloody corset and birdcage.

"If ye just do as ye're told, I'll not be needin' to pull yer mother into this. To tell the truth, I'd rather not since she's not feelin' well anyway." Lucy spoke quietly as she fastened the buttons of the dress. "So, it'll be yer conscience that'll be the worse off if'n I have to disturb yer mother, not mine." She turned Valerie looking her over with a practiced eye. "Ah yes, ye look just like yer mother did when she was yer age. And a bonnie lass she was. Yer father was right lucky to have caught her."

Lucy reached for a rectangular antimony jewelry box tucked into a railed shelf. She removed an intricately woven gold chain with a round cabochon emerald hanging from it. An antique piece, Valerie's father had given it to her for her sixteenth birthday. "I think this will look real fine. What do ye think?"

Valerie gave the servant a quick hug.

Lucy puffed herself up, straightening her crisp white apron. "What was that fuss all about?"

"For asking me what I thought. I do believe it's the first time you ever did." Beaming, Valerie turned so Lucy could hook the pendant around her neck.

Next, she took a pair of matching earrings from the box and clipped one to each earlobe. "I can see ye'll be havin' yer hands full with the young swains this night." Lucy smiled and handed Valerie her best cane, the ebony one with the carved silver grip.

"Maybe I shouldn't use this cane. I wouldn't want it to get damaged." Valerie reached for her old cane leaning against the bureau. Thomas may wonder why she had such a nice cane for a temporary injury.

"Nonsense. Ye're much too dressy to be carryin' that old thing. Besides, ye'll be needin' all the help ye can get to chase away the hordes of men. They'll all be a-courtin' ye before the evenin's over. Providin' ye mind yer tongue, that is," Lucy said as she began to straighten the cabin. "Gentlemen don't take kindly to opinionated women."

Valerie smiled as the image of dozens of men standing in line to speak with her filled her mind. She forgot about the cane as a rush of anticipation ran through her with the memory of Thomas Smythe's lips pressed against her fingers. Of course, it didn't matter how many men there were around her tonight, Thomas was the only one she was interested in. She twirled the cane in her hand. "We shall see, Lucy. We shall see."

THE BROOKS FAMILY made their way single-file down the narrow, wood-paneled corridor leading from their quarters to the main reception area below deck. Frederick was in the lead, followed by Jacqueline, then Valerie, with Reggie skipping along behind them all.

"Hurry up!" Reggie demanded. "I'm starving!" He shoved at Valerie's backside, pushing her into their mother.

"Stop it, Reggie. You'll knock us all down," Jacqueline scolded. "It's hard enough to maneuver through this narrow passage with the sway of the ship let alone you causing more trouble."

Valerie swung her skirts behind her, running the stiff steel crinoline into Reggie's shin. He fell flat on his bottom and Valerie giggled. "Lizard."

Reggie jumped up and started for Valerie just as they arrived at the grand salon. At the sight of the massive room, he froze in his tracks, as did they all.

Here, the narrow passage opened into a large expanse, opulently furnished with upholstered banquettes and heavy velvet curtains. Valerie's gaze absorbed each and every detail. The walls were painted a streaked dark red overlaid with fantasy scenes of King Neptune and his court. Mermaids and dolphins in shimmery shades of green and gold seemed to float right off the wall and into the room itself. She took a step forward and ran her hand along the back of one of the blue, tapestry-covered chairs wrapped around a support column and cleverly arranged into small conversation groups, from one end of the vast salon to the other.

Reggie ran over to one of the chairs and all but leaped into it, bouncing on the firm cushion.

"Here now, Reg. Take it easy son," Frederick admonished. "You'll crash the seat right through to the hull."

"Do you really think I could, Papa?" Reggie asked, his eyes gleamed with mischief. He scrambled off the chair and gripped his arms to heft himself onto the seat again. "Hey! This chair doesn't move." He tugged at it, but it wouldn't budge.

"Of course, it doesn't move. The seating is fastened in place in case of rocky waters or a storm," his father explained.

Valerie wandered to one of the murals, her cane thumping softly against the carpeted deck. She studied the representation of the birth of Venus, a typical rendering of the maid arriving on a mollusk shell, escorted from the sea by several angels.

"Beautiful, isn't it?" The deep voice startled her, making her breath catch.

Valerie turned and smiled at the picture of masculine elegance standing before her. The fine, white-linen shirt and creamy ascot was striking against the crisp, black suit. "Yes, it is. Good evening, Mr. Smythe."

Thomas inclined his head, a grin on his lips. For a brief moment, he reminded Valerie of a cat who was about to corner its prey, then she shook the picture from her mind, her musings interrupted by her father's voice.

"Good evening, David, old man."

Valerie turned her attention to the gentleman Frederick was greeting. He looked exactly like an older version of Thomas.

"There's my father," Thomas said. "Come, I'll introduce you." Valerie slipped her gloved hand around his arm as he led her toward the gathering. He leaned near her as they walked. "I must say I'm grateful to Father for forcing me on this trip. If I hadn't come, I never would have met you."

A blush heated Valerie's cheek. Never in her life had a man paid such close attention to her or said something so daring.

"Valerie, come here, child," her father bade, smiling. "I'd like you to meet someone." Frederick drew Valerie to his side. "Sir David, this is my lovely daughter, Valerie."

Valerie curtsied as best she could, catching a slight frown on the elder Smythe's face as she did.

"That's not really necessary, young lady. I can see it takes a great deal of effort for you."

She froze, embarrassed he would call attention to her malady, then straightened. "It's a pleasure to make your acquaintance, Sir David," she offered with a tight smile.

He nodded. "I see you've already met my son," he observed. "Have you two been properly introduced or did he simply force his company on you?"

"Actually, Sir David, Papa sent him to my aide earlier today when I required assistance on the stairwell."

"Well, that's just like him," the elder Smythe murmured. "A perfect knight in shining armor."

Valerie was about to agree when a man wearing a short white jacket entered the salon. He cleared his throat loudly and announced, "Dinner is served."

There weren't many passengers on the ship, as its main purpose was to carry cargo from England to China, but the ones who were there crowded toward the dining room. Smythe caught his son's arm, then motioned for Frederick and his family to go ahead without them. "We'll catch up with you in a moment," he explained. Frederick nodded and tucked Valerie's arm into his as he led her into the dining room.

Valerie peeked over her shoulder to catch one more glimpse of Thomas and smiled as her eyes met his.

As soon as the Brooks were out of sight, Smythe leaned toward his son. "See here, boy. I'll not have you spoiling this business deal by compromising Brooks' daughter. This loan is too important to the expedition."

Thomas looked at his father, feigning innocence. "Be assured, Father, I haven't a clue as to what you're talking about."

"Oh, you know perfectly well what I'm talking about. I won't have a repeat of that scene you caused back in Liverpool after your dalliance with the Count's girl. Besides," he began, his eyes following Valerie's painful trek to the dining room, "the girl's got something wrong with her."

Thomas rolled his eyes. "It's only a sprain. Do you really think I'd waste my time on a cripple?" His eyes met his father's. "You taught me better than that."

Smythe's face hardened. "I suppose you are much too vain to be seen with a permanently damaged woman. Mark my words, though, you lose this loan for me because of your behavior and I'll take the money out of your sorry hide."

CHAPTER SEVEN

V alerie was utterly amazed by the ingenuity of the shipbuilders as she entered the dining room. Wide velvet covered booths were built into both sides of the clipper under a double row of narrow windows. In place between them were dining tables long enough to seat eight to ten people. Anchored to the table legs and opposite the booth was an upholstered bench, all fastened neatly in place in case of a choppy crossing. Over the tables hung heavy, dark-oak racks designed to hold wine glasses and bottles. Every last detail of the room, down to the pristine-white tablecloths, assured a satisfying meal, no matter the weather.

Frederick stopped one of the waiters. "We're to sit at the captain's table this evening. Can you point us in the right direction?"

"Certainly, sir. It's the large one at the other end of the room."

"Come along, family." Frederick motioned with a wave of his hand. "The table's over here." He straightened his jacket and squared his shoulders proudly as he led his brood past the other passengers.

"What's Papa doing?" Valerie whispered to her mother. "He acts as if he's in command of Her Majesty's army."

Jacqueline chuckled "Frederick is just showing pride in his family." She put her hand on Valerie's arm. "Tell me, Val, was the fair-haired young man you were speaking to the same gentleman who came to your assistance?"

Valerie nodded, a smile curving her lips. "What did you think of him? Wasn't he everything I said he was? Why, even his own father called him a knight in shining armor."

"Indeed, he did…" Jacqueline frowned. "I've noticed there are plenty of young men on board, though. Perhaps your father can arrange for you to meet another gentleman?"

"I don't think that would be appropriate, Mr. Smythe might be put out if other men show me any attention."

"Valerie, don't you think—"

"Good evening, ladies," Captain Marcus interrupted. "So happy you could join me this evening."

The steward peered out from behind the captain, his long gray hair tucked neatly into a queue. "Where is that lovely Lucy of yours? Will she be joining us?"

"I'm sorry Johnny," Jacqueline replied. "Lucy is dining in the kitchen with the staff."

"Well, if you'll all excuse me, I'll go see to her comfort."

"That is very kind of you," Jacqueline offered as the Captain helped her to a chair.

Johnny smiled, turned to the captain, and saluted him, then executed a smart turn and marched out of the dining room.

The captain *harrumphed* as he seated Valerie a few seats away from her mother. "Well, it appears my steward is smitten with your maid." He motioned to Frederick. "Sir Frederick, won't you sit next to me? I've reserved the seat on the other side for Sir David. I understand you two are business acquaintances?"

"We are. Reggie here can sit on my right if you don't mind. I think it's time for him to start learning a bit about the banking trade, so he can follow in his father's footsteps one day." Frederick smiled and rumpled Reggie's hair as the boy took his seat.

"Of course, of course." The captain caught sight of Thomas and his father. "Over here, gentlemen," he gestured as they approached. "Young Mr. Smythe, I'd like you to seat yourself next to this lovely young lady, if you don't mind."

Thomas smiled at Valerie. "I'd be honored."

"And you, Sir David, please take the seat at my left." The captain claimed his seat between Frederick and David. "There, now." He scanned the faces at the table. "Everyone's hungry, I pray?"

"Yes, sir!" Reggie answered enthusiastically. "I'm always hungry." He leaned back in the booth with a grin, satisfied he'd made his presence known to all. He caught Valerie looking at him, stuck his tongue out at her. She rolled her eyes then turned her attention to Thomas.

"So, will you be visiting Pompeii with us, Mr. Smythe?" Valerie asked as the server poured her a glass of red Bordeaux. She took a small sip of the vintage and coughed, not accustomed to the wine. She held her napkin to her mouth, then wiped the tear from her eye. "Excuse me, it must have gone down the wrong way."

"No excuse needed." He leaned forward and whispered, "The tear in your eye makes their green depths glimmer with a vibrancy to rival the emerald you're wearing."

In the center of the table, the server placed a tureen of seafood chowder. He dipped a silver ladle into the thick, creamy soup and, starting with the ladies, offered each a half-bowl full. After everyone was served, Reggie peered into his bowl. "How come it's not filled all the way to the top?"

"If we happened to hit choppy waters, and your bowl was filled to the brim, it would spill all over you," the captain explained with a wink.

Reggie scrunched his eyes in thought. Then, with a satisfied nod, he scooped up some soup and slurped it off the spoon, loudly smacking his lips.

"Really, Reggie," Jacqueline scolded. "Show your manners, son."

Reggie grinned, a chunk of potato caught in the space previously occupied by one of his front teeth. "Sorry, Mama."

Once everyone was finished, the server cleared the table and served the main course leg of mutton and beefsteak pie along with mustard potatoes, creamed onions, and sliced loaves of steaming hot bread. The aromas wafted around them.

"It—looks—wonderful," Jacqueline whispered, her face paling.

"Are you all right, Mama?" Valerie asked.

Jacqueline lifted a hand to her mouth. "I think I'll be fine in a moment. Just a touch of *mal de mer*. That's all."

"Perhaps you should lie down, dear," Frederick offered. "I can have Lucy bring you a plate later. You may feel like eating after you've had a nap."

"Well, if you wouldn't mind?" She glanced around the table.

"Of course, we don't mind," Captain Marcus said. "I'll have one of my stewards escort you." He gestured to one of his men. "Sea sickness is, unfortunately, a common occurrence among our passengers. You go on ahead and I'll personally make sure your maid gets you a plate."

"Thank you, Captain. I do appreciate your gracious hospitality." Jacqueline stood and excused herself from the table, but not before sending a "behave yourself" glance Valerie's way.

"It'll be good to be back in Italy. I so enjoy the countryside," David Smythe began. "The area around the site is spectacular."

"Do you travel to Italy often?" Valerie asked, forgetting her dinner in favor of information concerning their destination.

"Not nearly enough. For the time being, I only go when necessary to visit the excavation. There's a gentleman in charge there whom I keep in contact with, Fiorelli's his name," Smythe explained. "Fascinating chap. Two years ago, he devised a clever method of preserving the discovered remains of the ancient peoples who perished in the eruption."

"I've never heard of such a thing," Valerie interjected. "How in the world could someone do that?" She looked at everyone. "After all, the eruption occurred almost eighteen hundred years ago."

Smythe took a drink of wine. " I felt the same way until I saw it myself last year. During the digging, when the workers hit a hollow spot in the ground, a small opening is made, and plaster is poured into it. The next day, the volcanic ash is chipped away, usually revealing a perfect cast of the object that had once occupied the space under it – be it man or beast. Even casts of food and furnishings have been taken." He shook his head. "The detail is so great, you can see the poor souls' expressions as they lie dying, captured forever in a plaster statue."

Valerie leaned back into her chair. A chance to see what the Pompeiians looked like would be a tremendous opportunity for her education. Had they been tall? Did they have classic Roman features, as she had seen illustrated in books, or were they different? "Can you imagine what it would be like to have actually lived during the time before the eruption?"

David chuckled and glanced at Frederick. "Your daughter has quite an appetite for knowledge, doesn't she, Brooks."

"Yes, she has. The girl has always shown a keen interest in the antiquities and hopes to teach—"

"Teaching?" David interrupted. "Frederick, my good man, certainly a man of your stature wouldn't allow his child to work."

Frederick straightened. "It's Valerie's choice."

"Valerie's choice?" David countered. "Well, I can see you're much more modern in your thinking than I. If it were my daughter, I'd be busy finding a husband for her."

Valerie's eyes darted back and forth between the men. She twisted her napkin under the table.

Please don't say anything, Papa. They don't need to know the truth.

Smythe wiped his mouth with his napkin and leaned towards Frederick. "Besides, whoever said a female should be making her own choices? They just don't have the capacity for serious thought."

"Now see here, David," Frederick began, "there are obvious reasons at play as to why my daughter wishes to teach."

Valerie blanched. Dear Lord, he was going to spill the story about the accident and the doctors and her foot. She set her hands on the table and was about to push herself up to leave when Thomas touched his hand to hers.

Once more the young man saved her from a fall—this time from grace. "I'm certain Miss Brooks can accomplish whatever she puts her mind to. Besides, we were enjoying our conversation."

Valerie let her breath out slowly and relaxed back in her seat.

That was much too close.

Papa might have explained everything about her right then and there. Thank goodness Sir David decided to change the subject. Perhaps if she left, they'd forget all about the conversation. "Papa, I'm feeling a bit under the weather, too. Would you mind if I excused myself?"

"Certainly not, dear. Will you be all right?" he asked.

"I'll be fine in the morning. It's just been a long day." She placed her hands on the table for support, but was assisted once more by Thomas who stood and moved her chair back.

"Sir Frederick, would you allow me to escort Miss Valerie to her room?"

"Well, if it wouldn't be any trouble?"

"No. None at all." Thomas turned to Smythe senior, who gave him a curt nod. "No need to worry, Father. I'll be back in a few moments." Thomas tucked Valerie's hand into the crook of his arm and led her from the dining room.

The cool night air blew in through the open windows of the grand salon as they made their way to the corridor. Valerie shivered, and Thomas drew her even closer. His body felt firm and warm through the silk of her dress.

"You didn't really need to leave the table, Mr. Smythe. Although I do appreciate your help, Reggie could have taken me to my room." Valerie glanced at him out of the corner of her eye.

Oh, but he is quite smashing indeed, my knight in shining armor.

"Nonsense. I would have insisted, in any case." He held her hand as she stepped over the threshold and continued to hold it as he walked in front of her along the narrow passage.

"Here's my room." Valerie reluctantly let go of Thomas' hand and pulled the key out of her reticule. She handed it to him and, as he took it, his fingers caressed hers and she shivered again. He pushed the door open, then bowed low.

Valerie inclined her head as a blush warmed her cheeks. "Thank you, Mr. Smythe. I do so appreciate your kindness."

"I have to admit it was entirely selfish on my part." He lightly caressed her cheek with the back of his hand. "I wanted to spend a few moments alone with you."

"Mr. Smythe. I—I don't know what to say," Valerie murmured.

"You needn't say a word, for if you did, you may choose to deny me the sweet pleasure of your lips." Before Valerie could speak, he pulled her to him and lowered his mouth to hers.

His lips were hot and moist. Valerie knew she should push him away, but the delicious tingle stirring in her belly was too wonderful to let go.

Slowly, he raised his head. "Forgive me. I'm a cad."

"Yes, you are," she replied, her voice low. With a smile, she stepped into her cabin and gently closed the door behind her. She leaned back against it and hugged her arms around her waist.

My first kiss!

And it was everything she had ever imagined it to be, and more.

"Heaven help me," she whispered to the darkness. "I think I may be falling in love."

CHAPTER EIGHT

Valerie sat with her family in the grand salon of the *Fast Alice* and watched as the passengers began to gather for their last dinner together before reaching shore. The past three weeks had flown by so quickly, she hadn't had a chance to catch her breath, let alone tell Thomas the truth about her foot.

Her days had been filled with Thomas' company. Attentive and kind, he'd stolen a few more kisses when no one was looking. Valerie touched a finger to her lips and smiled.

Well, maybe stolen isn't exactly the right word.

"I see that young man of yours coming this way," Jacqueline whispered. She was still pale and gaunt from sea sickness but had insisted on joining everyone for their last night aboard ship.

Thomas approached and bowed low to the ladies. "Good evening, everyone." He straightened and adjusted his jacket. "May I say both mother and daughter are looking quite ravishing this night?"

Valerie giggled at his lavish compliment.

Is this what it's like to be in love?

Valerie rose from the chair with Thomas' gallant support. "Mama? Papa? Do you mind if we get some punch before supper?"

Frederick glanced up from his book. "Jacqueline, my dear, would you like some punch?"

"Oh, yes Freddie. Thank would be wonderful."

"Very well, then. Valerie, I'll join you." He removed his spectacles and tucked them inside his jacket pocket.

At the refreshment table, Thomas poured each of them a glass of the fruity concoction and a fourth for Jacqueline. Valerie took a sip, enjoying the sweet beverage.

"Good evening, everyone," Sir David said as he joined them. He shook Frederick's hand and sketched a shallow bow toward Valerie. After their first meeting, Valerie decided she would forego curtsying and offered a polite nod instead.

"Good evening, Sir David," she bade.

Smythe picked up a glass of punch and took a long drink. "So, tell me Frederick, have you managed to find the girl a husband on board?"

Valerie all but sputtered her punch. "I—I beg your pardon?" she choked out.

Frederick chuckled. "Well, it would seem this son of yours has monopolized all of her time." He nodded toward Thomas. "I don't believe there's been a chance of anyone else getting to know her." He smiled at Valerie. "I must say, though, it's been wonderful for her confidence to have young Thomas pay such close attention to her."

"Really, Papa. We don't need to discuss this, do we?" she pleaded.

"She has trouble finding suitors, does she?" Smythe's eyes swept over her. "As comely as she is, I would think you'd have to keep the doors barred against the men."

"Well, no one else has seemed able to look past her injury like Thomas here has," Frederick explained.

Valerie's gaze bounced from her father to Smythe to Thomas. This wasn't going well at all. If she didn't do something fast, Papa was going to explain about her foot right here in front of everyone—in front of Thomas. She *had* intended to tell him the truth, but it just never seemed to be the right time. And she certainly didn't want it blurted out by her father.

"Thomas, I'm not feeling very well," she whispered, placing her hand on his arm. "Would you mind escorting me above deck for a breath of fresh air?"

"Of course." He turned to their fathers. "Miss Brooks has asked me to take her above deck. She's not feeling well," he explained for her. "Would you mind, Sir Frederick?"

Valerie's father waved his hand. "No, go right ahead. But dinner will be served soon. Don't be late."

Valerie allowed herself a small sigh of relief as they made their way up through the hatch and out into the cool night air. With her hand on

Thomas' arm, they strolled to the front of the ship and watched the glistening spray as it shot up near the bow of the clipper.

The half-moon cast its glow on the water and it rippled with the movement of the dark, shadowy waves. Valerie leaned on the railing, her curls blowing off her face. "It's so beautiful out here, isn't it?"

"Mmmm. It certainly is."

A kaleidoscope of butterflies began to gather in her stomach. Thomas was so close, his breath tickled the back of her neck, and sent a shiver down her spine. She turned to face him.

Thomas lifted a hand and caressed Valerie's cheek. He let it drop to the back of her head and gently pulled her to him.

"Mr. Smythe, are you attempting to take advantage of me while we're alone?" she asked, breathless.

"Absolutely." He grinned, moving ever closer. Gently, he tipped her chin until her eyes met his. "I fear I'll never grow tired of your sweet, sweet kisses."

Thomas' lips touched hers and she melted against him. The butterflies in her stomach fluttered in unison. Certain she would faint at any moment, Valerie leaned into Thomas for support. His kiss grew more insistent as is hands slid over her shoulders and down her arms.

Her skin tingled, everywhere he touched her. His hands caressed, moving upward over the thick whalebone that shaped her waist, and stopped at the edge of the square cut neckline. Thomas let his fingers tease the lace edge and dip beneath the fabric.

Valerie stiffened. "Thomas. Please. You mustn't."

"Don't tell me this isn't what you've been wanting because I won't believe a word of it," he whispered into her ear. "This is why you really asked me up here, isn't it?"

Valerie's mind whirled at the accusation. What in heaven's name was he implying? That she somehow was to blame for his behavior?

Thomas' voice turned raspy. "Your lips were made for mine, Valerie. Let them do what they will." He kissed her ear, then her chin, then his mouth followed the path his fingers had just taken and moved along the sensitive skin of her décolletage.

This wasn't right. Everything was happening much too fast. Valerie struggled to catch her breath.

"Valerie!" Reggie scurried across the deck, screeching her name, and ran right into the pair. The momentum knocked Thomas and Valerie apart, and her to the floor. Thanks to the crinoline, her skirt went up over her head. Mortified, she struggled to her feet as Thomas helped her up.

"Sorry, Val, but Papa said I should come and get you. It's time to go in for dinner and he thought maybe I could help you down the stairs."

"I don't need any help, thank you." Valerie ground out the words. "Haven't you helped enough already?"

"But your foot—"

"Shouldn't your foot be almost healed by now?" Thomas asked as he dusted off his trousers. "After all, it has been nearly three weeks."

Breathe. I can't breathe.

"Y–yes, er…about that," she squeaked. She turned to her little brother. "P-please go on ahead Reggie. I'll catch up with you shortly."

"But Val, why would he say that? Your foot isn't going to get better," Reggie said. "The doctor said it wouldn't ever get better."

Valerie closed her eyes and prayed to Heaven. *Please Lord, make it so Thomas didn't hear those words.*

But when she opened her eyes, she knew he had heard all too clearly.

"What is the child talking about, Miss Brooks?" he asked, the warmth in his voice cooling as he spoke. "I thought you said it was only a sprain."

She took a deep breath. "I-I'm sorry I didn't tell you sooner. I should have." She swallowed. "You see, I-I was hit by a carriage when I was very young and my foot was—it was," she cleared her throat. "Damaged."

"Do you mean to say you're a cripple?" His voice had turned frigid.

"Does it m-matter to you?" she whispered.

"Matter? Why should it matter to me?"

She looked at him and read the truth in his eyes. The butterflies had all flown away, leaving nothing but a hollow ache in the pit of her stomach.

"I've asked myself that same question, Mr. Smythe." She turned to her brother and put her hand on his shoulder. She blinked hard as tears stung her eyes. "Reggie, I believe I'd like you to help me down the stairs after all. Would you mind?"

Reggie straightened, as he offered Valerie his arm. "I wouldn't mind at all." Scrunching his face, he stuck his tongue out at Thomas.

Valerie held her head high as she walked alongside her brother. This time, she didn't turn back for one final glance. It didn't matter anymore…Thomas was no longer her knight in shining armor.

CHAPTER NINE

Valerie entered her cabin and closed the door, thankful she had a room separate from her parents. Leaning against the door, she struggled to catch her breath as she fought to keep the sobs from breaking through. It had taken all her willpower to sit through dinner with Thomas ignoring her. What had he been thinking the few times his eyes met hers? Probably how he'd wasted the entire voyage on a *cripple*.

Her gaze skipped haphazardly around the room as she tried to steady her emotions. Valerie straightened and tugged at the back of her dress, all but ripping the buttons from the facing, until the bodice hung down around her waist.

"Damn," she cursed. "Forgot the bloody crinoline." Valerie undid the laces and let the steel cage drop, the dress following closely thereafter. She grabbed her cane and stepped out of the pile of clothing, but her foot caught in the folds of the fabric and she tripped. She stumbled to the floor and didn't even bother to try and get up. Laying down, she gave in to her sorrow.

A few moments later, Lucy appeared at the doorway between their rooms, carrying an oil lamp. "I thought I heard ye come in," she began, her voice trailing off at the sight of Valerie in a heap on the floor, crying, her clothes twisted around her. Lucy put the lamp down, bent over and helped Valerie to her feet.

"What's troublin' ye, child? I've never seen ye carryin' on so." Lucy used the corner of her robe to wipe away Valerie's tears.

"It's n-nothing, Lucy. P-please. Leave me be." Valerie sat on the edge of the bed, tears still streaming down her cheeks.

"I'll not leave while ye're in such a sorry state." Lucy put her hand on the young woman's shoulder, stooping to look her in the eye. "It was that young Mr. Smythe, wasn't it? He's the reason ye're so distressed." Lucy studied her charge. "What'd he do to ye?"

Valerie's eyes flew to Lucy's. "Nothing."

"Ye answered much too fast fer me to believe ye."

"Please, Lucy, just go to bed. I really don't want to talk about it right now."

"Can I get ye a nice cup of tea then? It'll be good for what ails ye."

"No, thank you," Valerie whispered, her throat tight. "I'd just like to get some rest. We can talk in the morning, all right?"

Lucy straightened. "I understand, girl. I'll leave ye be if ye promise ye'll call me if ye need help."

Valerie nodded, wiping her eyes. "Thank you." As Lucy turned to leave, she called after her, "Lucy, please don't say anything to Mama. I don't want to bother her with this." She forced a smile. "Besides, I'm certain I'll be fine in the morning."

"Well, if that's what ye want. But I'm certain, whatever 'tis yer mother'd want to comfort ye."

"Perhaps when her health is better," Valerie offered.

As soon as Lucy was gone, Valerie lay down on the narrow bed. She took a deep breath to steady her nerves and was stuck in the side by a corset stay. Turning this way and that, Valerie wrestled the ties until the offending undergarment finally loosened. Yanking it off, she threw it onto the pile on the floor. "Well, that's the last time I wear a bloody corset for any man," she vowed.

How could I have been such an idiot?

Why had she been foolish enough to believe Thomas would be different from any of the other men she had ever met? For heaven's sake, in her vivid imagination, they were already wed and had a full brood of offspring.

Shame and anger swirled inside her. The gypsy's words echoed in her mind—a love that'll break your heart…

How did she know?

Her heart clenched as fresh sobs escaped her. Valerie rolled over and pulled the pillow close to her chest when her arm brushed against a square object tucked beneath the sheets. She pulled it out and stared at it. The book. The love story of Caroline and Damon. The reason for her false hope about a love of her very own.

Well, there'll be no more of that!

She flung the book across the room where it thumped against the door and landed with a dull thud on the floor.

No longer would she pin her heart on a dream of marriage and children of her very own. Instead, she would focus on her studies. She would use this trip to further her knowledge.

But what about love?

Her heart clenched once more as she pushed the thought away. Love was not for her. She would never put herself in such a vulnerable position again.

CHAPTER TEN

"Let me help you, Miss Brooks," Johnny offered. He held his arm out and Valerie took hold of it. Gently, he assisted her in climbing over the lowered railing and onto the wooden ramp leading from the ship to the shore. Reggie ran up behind them.

"Wait for me, Val!" He tossed a small canvas bag over her head. The bag landed with a loud thud on the walk.

"Careful!" she scolded, ducking just in time. "What have you got in there? Cannonballs?"

"Of course not," he huffed. "Everyone knows cannonballs are much too heavy to be carried around for everyday use." He placed one hand on the rail and, before Valerie could stop him, vaulted over the side and landed next to his belongings.

"What's in it then?" Valerie asked, straightening her skirt.

"Rope and knots and wax and some pitch and—"

Valerie raised a hand and laughed. "Never mind. I get the picture." She stepped off the plank and caught sight of Thomas heading down the walkway. Well, he was the last person she wanted to see! Valerie grabbed Reggie's arm and yanked him along as she picked up her pace.

"Where's Mama and Papa?" she asked, scanning the crowd. She spied Lucy saying goodbye to Johnny. A smile touched Valerie's lips.

At least one of us has found love on this voyage.

"Miss Brooks. How nice to see you today."

She winced and turned toward him. She could hardly avoid a direct greeting in public. She smiled, a hard glint in her eye. "Pity I can't say the same about you."

"I beg your pardon?" Thomas asked.

Good. She'd caught him off guard. "I believe you heard me quite plainly." She thumped her cane hard on the wood walk beneath their feet, then raised it up between them. The carved Jack-in-the-Woods head stared threateningly down at Thomas, its eyes slanted in an evil grin. "We may have to travel together, but if you don't keep your distance, you'll get to know Jack here intimately." Valerie looked him in the eye. "Do we understand each other?"

Thomas straightened, an angry flush covering his cheeks. "I don't see what you're so upset about. After all, you were the one who lied to me."

"Be honest just for a moment, Mr. Smythe," her voice gaining strength as she spoke. "When I revealed the truth about my foot, you called me a *cripple*. Would you have been interested in me if you'd known otherwise?

He shifted his weight from foot to foot, avoiding her gaze. "I see Father up ahead. I have to go now."

Valerie stepped in front of him. "I asked you a question and I believe I deserve an answer."

"You want an answer, do you?" Thomas snorted, shaking his head. "I'm sure you already know the answer to your question. You may be lovely, Valerie Brooks, with your bright green eyes and shining chestnut hair." He lifted a hand as if to touch the curls, then let it drop to his side. "But the simple truth of the matter is that crippled foot of yours makes you—" he cleared his throat, "—undesirable." He shrugged his shoulders. "Blame me, if you want, but that's just the way it is."

Valerie was suddenly grateful for the cool Mediterranean breeze. Tall cypress trees dotted the rocky landscape above the shore, bowing away from the direction of the ship as the wind caught their upper branches. She took a deep breath, tears stinging her eyes. "Thank you for your honesty, Mr. Smythe."

He nodded and walked on. Valerie stood motionless a moment longer as the crowd of passengers pushed past her. A single tear trailed down her cheek. "Thank you very much."

CHAPTER ELEVEN

The long winding road leading inland from the Bay of Naples was well-rutted and strewn with rocks of every size. The carriages carrying the Brooks and Smythe families moved slowly, the drivers taking their time, choosing a careful path to prevent throwing a wheel.

Valerie peered out the small window. The gray dirt of the road contrasted sharply with the cool green of the surrounding countryside. She fell into an almost hypnotic trance as the landscape unfurled before her—groves of silvery olive trees, arbors of grape vines, and scattered ruins of places whose names were long forgotten. Even Pompeii had ceased to be called by its Roman name for a while and was referred to by the locals as only *La Civita*, The City. It wasn't until the excavations had begun at the turn of the century that the original name had been rediscovered.

She caught her breath as her gaze shifted to the horizon. There, in the distance, loomed Mount Vesuvius. Its peak was surrounded by low lying clouds; the sky gray and misty.

"Look, Papa," Valerie whispered. She gestured toward the mountain. " Isn't it magnificent?"

Frederick lifted his head and peeked out the window. "Yes, quite lovely," he mumbled before returning his attention to the account books he had brought along.

How could he be so flippant when presented with such a beautiful sight? "Papa, you didn't even look," she gently scolded.

"Valerie, your father is busy. You mustn't bother him right now." Jacqueline shifted on the hard wood seat and straightened her hat. "Tell me, how are things going with you and young Mr. Smythe?"

Her mother was studying her much too intently. Had Jacqueline surmised that Thomas had kissed and—and touched her? Valerie tamped down the guilt that still gnawed at her for allowing Thomas such liberties and shrugged, schooling her expression into one of mild disdain. "I decided I didn't really care for him after all."

Jacqueline raised an eyebrow. "Really now? What happened to the 'knight in shining armor'? You had me convinced he was the man of your dreams, Val. Why, I even began to wonder if we'd be planning a wedding upon our return home."

Valerie frowned.

I thought the same thing myself, until last night.

"Remember the fortune teller, Mama?" she asked instead.

"You mean at Hazel's?"

Valerie nodded, glancing at Lucy and Reggie out of the corner of her eye. Good. Lucy was asleep and Reggie was occupied practicing the sailors' knots Johnny had taught him. "Do you recall what she said?"

Jacqueline's cheerful expression fell. "'A love that will break your heart'? she whispered.

Valerie nodded and returned to studying the countryside. "Who'd have thought she would be so accurate?"

"I'm so sorry, dear. If only I hadn't been so ill with the *mal de mer*, I would have realized." Jacqueline leaned forward and squeezed Valerie's hand.

"Why don't ye tell yer mother what happened?" Lucy grumbled, cracking open an eyelid. "Ye promised me ye would."

Valerie jumped. "For heaven's sake, Lucy, you scared me half to death. I thought you were sleeping."

Lucy waved her hand. "Just restin' m'eyes, I was."

Jacqueline looked from Lucy to Valerie. "What are you both talking about? What happened?"

"Nothing really, Mama." Valerie forced a smile, leaning back against the cushioned seat. "Lucy happened into my room last night when I was upset, that's all." She shrugged again. "What can I say? Mr. Smythe turned out to be nothing like I had imagined."

"She came to her cabin in tears, she did," Lucy fussed. "Why, I never seen the girl carry on so."

"I want to know exactly what he did to make you cry," Jacqueline demanded. "Frederick, are you listening to this?"

Valerie shot Lucy a narrow-eyed stare. Lucy lifted a brow and wagged a finger at her. Could the woman ever keep a secret? She sighed and answered her own unspoken question. Only when it suited her.

Frederick nodded from behind the bank ledger he was still studying. "Yes, dear."

"Frederick, this is serious. Mr. Smythe may have compromised our daughter."

Frederick slammed the book down on his lap. "What are you talking about?" he bellowed, thumping his fist on the leather volume. "I'll have him flogged!"

Valerie shook her head. Papa only listened when it suited him. "You're jumping to conclusions, Papa."

"No, he's not," Reggie piped up as he tossed the rope aside. "I saw it! He kissed you!"

"He kissed you?" Jacqueline gasped. She pulled off one of her gloves and fanned her face. "Thomas Smythe forced himself on you? What else did he do?"

"Mama, please."

"Don't 'Mama, please' me, young lady. This is serious." She fell back against her seat and the glove dropped to her lap. "Well? Aren't you going to answer any of my questions?"

Four pairs of eyes were upon her.

If only I could just disappear.

"It was just a peck, on the cheek," she sighed. It wasn't a lie really, just a sort of an abbreviated truth. For heaven's sake, if they really knew what had happened, she'd probably be forced to wed the hateful man. "And it was only last night. Reggie came to help me down the stairs for dinner. That's when he saw Thomas kiss me." She looked at Reggie, hoping he'd keep out of the conversation, but he'd already gone back to his rope knots. She sighed again in relief. She loved

Reggie but she didn't need him giving Mama the vapors or putting notions about flogging into Papa's head.

"I certainly hope that's why you decided you didn't like him anymore. The nerve of that man." Jacqueline huffed. She turned to Frederick. "It's our fault, Freddie. We're much too free with the girl."

"Well, I'll be having a talk with Smythe about his son's behavior." Frederick picked up his ledger again. "And I want you to stay away from him from now on, Valerie. Evidently, he's only after one thing."

"Frederick! Don't be crude."

"Well, it's true, dear. I was a young man once myself. I know how single-minded they can be." He returned his attention to Valerie and stared hard at her over the top of his reading glasses. "Is that understood, young lady?"

Valerie let out a sigh of relief. Thank goodness her family was more forward in their thinking than most. They could have decided right then and there to lock her up for the remainder of the trip if they had so desired. "I understand, Papa. I promise it won't happen again."

"Look! There it is!" Reggie yelled.

Valerie awoke from her doze. After the carriage had finally shifted to smoother terrain, the sway of the vehicle had rocked her to sleep. She rubbed her eyes, then peered out the window. There it was. The city of the ancient Romans. Pompeii.

"Beautiful," she whispered. In the near distance, the ruins themselves seemed to rise up from the very ground they had been built on. The site had been excavated off and on for centuries, but not as intently as this most recent expedition. The areas long ago exposed were most likely the ones covered in thick vines and weeds. Crumbling portions of a stone fence, the original paint now peeling and almost indiscernible, sprang up from the earth. Scattered on either side of the road were fragments of fluted columns, some with their decorative capitals still intact. Graceful Ionic, with tight swirls forming all four corners, were the most dominant. Simple Doric, straight and square, also appeared within the architectural mix. Valerie drank it all in, impressing the images on her mind.

As they approached the main entrance gate, they came upon the Necropolis, just as she had seen it illustrated in her history books. Large stone mausoleums, as far as the eye could see, surrounded the town. Built of cool white marble, they sat in stoic silence, the setting sun casting them in a soft, orange glow. Here and there, a bench beckoned from a grotto. *Come. Rest your weary bones and offer up a prayer for the dead.*

Valerie caught her breath as the carriage passed through the stone and iron gate. There, to her left and near the remains of a small building, stood a statue of Dionysus, the god of wine. Balancing on the balls of his feet, he held a goat skin high and gestured as if he were pouring the entire contents down his throat. She studied the small structure next to it and decided the local vintner must have owned it, for he would have been most interested in invoking the help of this particular god.

"Look over here, Val!" Reggie motioned out his window.

She leaned across her father. There, lying in the dust thrown up by the carriage, were the cast images of several people, each preserved in the throes of dying. In one grouping, she could make out the forms of a man, a woman, and a small child. The man was raised up on one elbow, obviously still trying to save his family from the ash and pumice that had pelted the city. Farther along, a solitary woman lay, her head resting on her arms. She appeared to be sleeping, waiting only to be awakened. Valerie wondered how she would have reacted if in the same situation. Would she have died so peacefully?

Though Sir David had explained the process, she had no idea how life-like the statues would appear. The folds of their clothing, the horrified expressions frozen forever in time. Valerie sat back, her eyes damp.

Those poor people must have realized their fate, only too late.

She gazed at the large mountain in the distance. Such awesome power within its core. Vulcan, the god of the volcano, had spoken here almost eighteen hundred years ago, sending thousands of people to their deaths.

THE CARRIAGE PULLED to a jerky halt. Reggie threw open the door and toppled onto the dusty ground. He jumped up, ran over to the remains of a stone house and began to climb up the wall.

Sir David pulled the boy down by his collar. "See here, now. You mustn't be doing that. You'll get hurt or damage the building."

"How can I hurt this place if the volcano didn't?" he asked, his eyes wide.

Frederick walked up to him. "What's the problem here?" he asked.

Smythe cleared his throat. "The boy shouldn't be climbing all over the structures. Some of them may be unsafe."

"Run along, Reg, and help your sister out of the carriage." Frederick ruffled his son's hair. "I need to talk to Sir David in private for a moment."

As Reggie scurried off, Frederick turned to the older man. "Your son seems to have put my daughter in a compromising situation while on ship."

"Wh–what?" Smythe sputtered rubbing the mutton chop whiskers on his cheeks with a shaky hand. "But I warned him—"

"Well, evidently, your warning fell on deaf ears. But I hope my warning is heard loud and clear—keep your son away from my daughter." Frederick straightened to his full six-foot-three-inch height and glared down at the shorter man. "Do we have an understanding here?"

"Of–of course, Brooks. You have my sincerest apologies, and my word. I-I certainly hope this won't affect our business dealings." Smythe's voice took on a desperate plea.

Frederick extended his hand. "I don't see why it should. Business is business."

"Yes indeed. Indeed, it is." Smiling, Smythe shook Frederick's hand.

"I shall send Thomas on ahead to Naples. I've a friend there who can keep an eye on him."

"I think that would be best, considering the situation," Frederick conceded. Smythe nodded and walked back to his carriage.

Frederick smiled as his wife and daughter approached.

"Well, husband, are we to enjoy a peaceful stay in Pompeii?"

"It's all taken care of," he explained, leaning down to kiss his wife's cheek. "Thomas will not be staying here with us." He turned to his daughter. "I'm certain you can explore to your heart's content," he smiled. "Within reason of course."

"Of course, Papa."

CHAPTER TWELVE

She was free!

If Thomas had remained with them, she'd probably be guarded every moment by either Lucy or Mama. With him gone, she could explore Pompeii without being watched over like a chick by a mother hen. She couldn't wait to get started. First on her list—The City of the Dead.

"Sir David. Welcome back to Pompeii." A short, robust man approached the visitors. He shook Smythe's hand, pumping it up and down vigorously.

Valerie peeked over her mother's shoulder. The stranger must be Giuseppe Fiorelli, the man in charge of the expedition.

The man responsible for bringing the dead back to life.

She'd seen lithographs of him working amongst the ruins and had expected someone much taller and younger. She hid a smile. Artists always seemed to have a penchant for re-interpreting reality.

"Good to see you, Giuseppe. This is Sir Frederick Brooks. He'll be extending the loan to keep this little operation of ours running." Smythe grinned as Fiorelli and Frederick shook hands. "If he likes what he sees, that is." He waved his arm behind him. "And this, of course, is Sir Frederick's wife, Mrs. Jacqueline Brooks, and their daughter Valerie, and son Reggie."

Fiorelli bowed low. "So happy to make your acquaintances. Would you like a tour of the site before you get settled?"

Valerie stepped forward. "That would be wonderful."

Jacqueline cleared her throat. Valerie glanced at her mother whose eyes held a warning. "May we go, Mama?" she amended.

Reggie jumped up and down. "I want to see the dead bodies. All of them." He tugged on Fiorelli's sleeve. "Are there any bones or skulls lying around? I'd like to see those too."

Fiorelli chuckled and patted Reggie on the shoulder. "Maybe we can find a few for your inspection."

Jacqueline sighed. "I suppose it would be all right, but don't be gone too long." She looked at the sky. "It'll be dark soon."

Fiorelli whistled and motioned with his hands to the workers. A group of men in pairs each hefted a contraption consisting of a chair fastened to long poles. Setting one of the traveling chairs down in front of Valerie, the two men squatted, balancing the contraption on their backs.

Fiorelli moved to assist her and Reggie before climbing into his own chair." Are you certain you won't join us?" he called to Jacqueline and Frederick.

Frederick waved his hand. "Plenty of time for that later. Smythe and I need to talk business."

"And I need to see to the unpacking," Jacqueline added as she waved at Valerie and Reggie. "Enjoy yourselves but do be careful."

"We will," Valerie and Reggie said in unison.

Heading down the dusty main thoroughfare of what had once been a bustling city, Valerie noted the crumbled remains of ancient homes poking up through the ground. Here and there, bright colors decorated the bits and pieces of the ruins—orange, yellow, blue, green, and a profusion of red. Even a few touches of gold leaf glinted in the waning sunlight.

Pompeii must have been magnificent in its day.

"What's that over there?" Valerie asked, pointing to a large building almost totally unearthed. The entrance was roped off and the newly installed wood door was closed.

"Ah," Fiorelli cleared his throat. "Nothing you need be concerned with."

Valerie leaned forward as the men continued to walk, struggling to interpret the words that covered the walls. "It's not quite Latin, is it?"

"You are correct. Oscan, a sister to Latin, was the language spoken."

"Mamia – is – good – for – sex. Only – twenty – *sesterces*…" Her eyes grew wide as she realized the meaning. "Oh my! " she murmured.

"You have a keen mind, *Signorina*. I'm most impressed. But, as I believe you've just deciphered, we are in the pleasure section of the town. That inscription was mild compared to some. Perhaps you should avoid reading until we have made our way past these buildings." He gestured to the area around them. "Most of the brothels are here, as near as we can tell. And," he looked at her before continuing, "Ladies are not allowed in them."

WITH THE UNPACKING DONE and dinner long over, the small group had finally settled in for the night and rested around a fire.

"Would you like to hear a ghost story?" Fiorelli asked Reggie.

"Yes, sir!" He sat up straight as a board. "Tell us now!"

"When I took over the excavation of Pompeii, there were rumors milling about." He stared hard at the boy. "Rumors that the ancients were rising from the dead."

"Impossible!" Reggie slammed his fist down on his thigh as he had seen Frederick do a hundred times before.

Valerie covered her mouth, suppressing a giggle. "Please go on, *Signor* Fiorelli. What made the people believe this?"

Fiorelli smiled and pulled a cigar out of his jacket pocket. He lit a twig in the fire and held it to the tip. After puffing hard enough to create a sizable cloud around his head, he continued. "Seems an old woman has been seen throughout the city. I've never seen her myself but, others have seen her in the tombs even in the bakery. He leaned forward and tapped the ashes from the cigar. "And she is always dressed in the garments of the Romans."

"Now, Fiorelli, that doesn't prove anything, does it?" Smythe said, with a chortle.

"No, but the workers are superstitious. They tell me she gives them the evil eye. They go around making the sign against the Devil all day long." He held up his right hand with just his forefinger and little finger extended. "Like this."

Reggie held his hand up in front of him and tried to form the gesture. "Look. I did it."

"Good boy," Fiorelli said patting Reggie on the head.

"But she could just be a local playing a prank," Frederick suggested.

Fiorelli shook his head. "According to the men, there have been other signs. Some of the statues we've cast have turned up missing. Why in the world would someone want one? The locals believe they came to life and up and walked away…" Fiorelli's voice faded as a low rumble emanated from deep within the earth.

"What just happened," Reggie whispered.

"I don't know, son," Frederick replied. He exchanged a worried glance with Jacqueline.

"It must just be the ground settling," Smythe said. "Happens all the time doesn't it Fiorelli?"

If that's true why are Mr. Smythe's legs shaking?

Valerie looked at her parents, Lucy and Reggie. Were they about to experience an earthquake?

Smythe continued his babbling about the ground regularly groaning at night, but the Italian raised his hand to silence the older man's chatter.

And then it happened again, only this time the rumble grew louder. The ground began to shake, loosening a large boulder from its perch atop a hill of rocks. The boulder rolled down and stopped a few yards away from the group.

Valerie jumped to her feet, clutching her cane so tightly her hands went numb. "Mama, Papa something is very wrong," she shouted over the rumbling. The ground beneath her feet began to crack and shift as though the very earth was about to open up beneath her.

Jacqueline drew Valerie into her embrace, while Frederick picked up Reggie. The family huddled close together while Smythe waved at his servants for assistance. Only Fiorelli seemed to remain calm. He paced around, examining the fissures, sniffing the air, and listening intently as though the earth was speaking a language only he could understand. After a few moments, the shaking subsided.

"Well, my friends, in case you haven't figured it out, that was an earthquake," Fiorelli explained, his voice quiet. "We've been experiencing them off and on here for the last few months. I fear this site might become buried again before we're able to finish our work."

"Well, that makes the bank's investment precarious as well," Frederick said, setting Reggie down.

"You're talking about work and business when we could have been killed," Jacqueline said pulling Reggie into the protective circle of her arms.

"There was no chance of that," Fiorelli said. "It was very mild." He looked pointedly at Frederick. "We need the funds so we can expedite the digging should a major quake strike in the future."

"I've never felt an earthquake before," Valerie whispered.

Fiorelli chuckled, waving his hand in a wide sweeping motion. "Rest assured. It was nothing like what was experienced by the former inhabitants of this town on that long-ago morning in 79 AD when Vesuvius erupted. I can guarantee you that."

Valerie pulled away from her mother as they all resumed their seats. She gazed into the shadows cast by the waning fire. "How much of the city do you think you've uncovered so far?" she asked.

"I'd say about one third," Fiorelli replied.

"Only a third?" Valerie echoed.

Smythe chuckled. "You must forgive the girl, Fiorelli. She's most inquisitive. I'm afraid Brooks here has allowed her to study the history of the area."

"That explains why she knew much about the site. And Latin as well. Best pronunciation I've ever heard." Fiorelli smiled at Valerie. "As far as I'm concerned, a woman with a keen mind is a sight to behold. Especially one as lovely as yourself, *Signorina*."

Valerie's back stiffened and she sat up straighter. Thomas had also used such pretty words. Of course, Fiorelli seemed genuine. As much as her unfortunate experience had made her wary, she couldn't go through life suspecting every man who paid her a compliment. Besides Fiorelli was considerably older and he already knew about her foot. She relaxed back in her chair. "Thank you, *Signore*."

Reggie yawned and stretched, setting off a chain reaction around the fire. Valerie had just yawned herself when Lucy appeared from the shadows. "Off to bed with the both of ye," she shooed. "The men have yer tents ready and ye need yer rest. Too much excitement for one day. There'll be plenty more nights to sit 'round and talk."

Valerie stood without arguing. She had to admit she was tired and longed to be out of the stiff corset that seemed to find every opportunity to poke her. She and Reggie followed closely behind Lucy as she led them to their sleeping quarters—small structures constructed of canvas, stones, and stripped logs.

Lucy opened the flap to Reggie's tent. "Please let me stay up a bit longer, Lucy," he begged.

"Don't ye be rollin' yer big brown eyes at me like that. Off with ye." She gave him a gentle push.

After Reggie was settled, Lucy escorted Valerie into her quarters. "Let me help ye with that, miss," she offered. Valerie turned around and the older woman began unbuttoning her dress. Next, she helped her out of the crinoline, then the corset, leaving Valerie in her chemise.

"Oh, Lucy, just think about where we are." Valerie hugged her arms about her, rubbing away the goose bumps.

"I know exactly where we be. In the middle of nowhere with the ground ready to shake and rattle," she sniffed. "I don't like it one bit."

Valerie turned around and gave her a teasing smile. "You said the same thing about the ship. That is, until you met Johnny, the steward. I think you're only upset because you had to leave him behind."

Lucy puffed herself up like a pigeon. "I beg yer pardon?"

"I think you heard me quite well." Valerie pulled back the hand-spun wool blanket and sat down on the edge of the simple camp cot. "Do you love him, Lucy?"

"I don't think that'd be any of yer business," Lucy replied haughtily. She folded Valerie's dress and placed it into her trunk at the foot of the bed.

Valerie rested her chin on her hand. "You're not going to tell me, are you?"

"Like I said—"

"I know, I know. It's none of my business." She lay back on the cot with a frown. She wouldn't get any information out of the servant tonight. "Good night, Lucy," she bade.

"Sweet dreams," Lucy whispered with a chuckle, setting Valerie's cane next to her bed. She carried the lantern out of the tent and into her own next door as Valerie drifted off to sleep.

"STOP IT!" Valerie twisted her body first to the left, then to the right. She was surrounded by a crowd of people, all clothed in the robes of the ancient Romans. Their bejeweled fingers glinted in the sunlight, blinding her.

"No!" she screamed as the Romans poked and prodded her.

"What's the matter, child?" Lucy shook her hard. "Come to yer senses!"

Valerie continued to struggle, shoving Lucy away from her, as heavy iron chains were clamped around her feet. She tripped and felt herself falling, falling. For an eternity she was suspended in the air, never touching the ground.

"Valerie! Wake up!" It was Jacqueline this time. "You're having a nightmare."

"Mama?" Valerie asked, her voice hoarse. She pushed herself up. A fine layer of perspiration covered her body and her chemise clung to her. Jacqueline pushed back the stray locks of hair that had escaped Valerie's braid.

"It's all right, dear. It was just a bad dream."

"But they came for me, Mama." Valerie wiped her eyes. "They wanted to take me away."

"Who did?"

"The people. They hated me," Valerie's voice broke as she began to sob. "It was the Romans. They were going to kill me."

Jacqueline pulled Valerie to her, tucking her head against her breast. "I understand now. You spent too much time in the ruins yesterday. Your imagination is acting up." She stroked Valerie's hair in a soothing motion. "No one is going to take you away from us. You're safe now. It was just a bad dream. It's the middle of the night. Come now, I'll stay with you until you fall back asleep."

But the chains had felt so real, so heavy and rough against her skin. Valerie shivered, then began to relax as Jacqueline hummed a lullaby, the same one she sang when Valerie was a little girl.

It was just a dream…

She took a deep breath and closed her eyes.

Just a dream…

CHAPTER THIRTEEN

V alerie dozed fitfully the rest of the night, the disturbing images floating in the darkness around her. She rose early the next morning, aching and tired. Did she dare begin exploring the ruins on her own?

I'm sure Mama was right. I was just reacting to all the events of the day. Oh, I'm such a goose!

She sighed and poured water from a heavy clay pitcher into a bowl on the small table next to her bed. She splashed her face, neck, and arms with the cool water, then twisted her braid into a tight chignon, fastening it into place with a jet and marcasite comb.

The water having revived her spirits, she leaned across the bed and lifted the lid of her trunk with single-minded determination. Digging through the contents, Valerie yanked out her corset. She wrinkled her nose and tossed it aside then found what she was looking for. A simple, white blouse and deep, charcoal skirt was just the thing for exploring the site. The dark color wouldn't show dirt as easily if they permitted her to help with the digging. She stood and dressed, buttoning the high collar shirt, and pulling on the long skirt.

Valerie took a step and almost tripped over the length of the garment. Without crinoline, there was an excess of material along the hem. Recalling the peasant women she'd seen along the road, she pulled the skirt up between her legs and tucked it into the waistband. Carefully, she adjusted the sides until her stockinged legs were discreetly covered. Satisfied with the result, she picked up her cane, and left the tent.

Frederick and Jacqueline were already up and enjoying a hot cup of tea near the fire. The smell of sausage frying reached Valerie's nose and her mouth watered. "Good morning," she bade.

"What have you done to your skirt?" her mother asked, her eyes wide.

Valerie shrugged. "It's something I saw the Italian women do. It makes it easier to walk. I thought it would be more practical for me this way."

"Where's yer crinoline?" Lucy ran up behind her, shaking a finger. "Ye'll not be paradin' around here with yer ankles showin'."

"Mama?" Valerie pleaded.

Jacqueline presented her back to Valerie "Go back and change. If you hope to spend any time outside of that tent today, you'll get yourself properly clothed."

Valerie shook her head. Didn't they understand how difficult it would be for her to manage her skirts over the uneven terrain? Of course, she could use one of Fiorelli's chairs, but that would limit her access to the site. Then, a thought came to her and she hid a smile. "All right. I'll go put the silly thing on." Valerie turned and let Lucy lead her back to the tent. She lifted the hem of her skirt while the other woman fastened the crinoline into place.

"Lucy, I've decided I don't want any breakfast after all. I'm going to begin exploring right away," she said, smoothing her clothes into place.

"Are ye sure ye should be goin' about today? What about them dreams ye had last night?" Lucy asked, worry lining her face.

"Oh, now, I can't be a goose forever. It was just a dream, after all." She tapped her cane on the compacted dirt floor. "Besides, when else will I ever get such a chance to see and touch ruins as old as these? I can't let a nightmare scare me away, can I?"

"Well, I think ye should wait before ye head out. Ye really should eat somethin'." But before Lucy could present any further arguments, Valerie grabbed a hunk of bread left on her nightstand from last night, a canteen of water, and was out the door, her skirt stirring up a cloud of dust as she walked away from the camp.

Valerie picked her way slowly over the raised stepping stones that allowed foot traffic to cross one of the ancient streets and made her way to the other side. Once out of sight, she ducked behind a tumbled down wall and removed the crinoline. Tucking her skirt back between her legs, she smiled triumphantly. "Bloody contraption", she swore as she left it behind the wall. Scanning the area she spied the stone gate she had traveled through the day before. Walking through the portal, she returned to the City of the Dead.

Valerie stepped into the middle of the road and stopped. In the bright light of day, every detail revealed by the archeologist's fine brushes was visible on the stone and marble tombs. Carved friezes of alternating acanthus leaf patterns, images of the gods and goddesses in their finest raiment, and busts that most likely represented those laid to rest within, adorned the alcoves built into the sides of the structures. She turned in a circle…

Where to begin?

To her right stood mausoleums adorned pillars and fountains long dried out. She ran a hand over the carved braided stone edge of one fountain. Scooping up a handful of dirt from the basin, Valerie let it sift through her fingers and blow away with the wind. In front of another tomb was the remnant of a small garden planted centuries ago. Neat rows of rocks sectioned the garden from a sitting area with statues set between them. Here, a visitor could relax and spend time with thoughts and prayers for the deceased.

Valerie took care as she stepped through the garden, losing herself in contemplation of what must have been, at one time, a peaceful place. A creaky sound coming from somewhere behind her, brought her out of her reverie. She took a step forward, then stopped. A movement. Was someone following her? She listened another moment. It sounded more like someone was dragging something.

That little lizard!

Her incorrigible brother was no doubt up to his usual mischief. Expecting to catch Reggie sneaking up on her, she whirled around. With a gasp, she recoiled and stumbled backward. Not ten feet away was an old woman, shriveled and bent with age, clutching her tattered shawl to her breast.

"*Buon giorno,*" the woman called out in a low, raspy voice, as she shuffled toward Valerie. She coughed and a cloud of dust flew up around her. "*Mi auiti per favore?*" She took a few more steps, sidling up closer to Valerie. "*Ho sete.*"

"*M-mi dispiace.* I–I'm sorry. My Italian is not very good. Do you speak Latin?" Valerie asked, not certain what to do. She glanced about her. It was getting hot. The workers must have left for their noon meal. There was no one else around.

"Ah, you *Inglese*?"

"*Si, Inglese.*" Valerie gripped her cane tighter.

"Will you help me?" The woman pointed to herself. "Water, *per favore*?" She motioned to the canteen Valerie had slung over her shoulder.

Valerie nodded and let her breath out slowly. The poor old woman only wanted to quench her thirst. She handed the container to her. "*Mi chiamo* Valerie. Valerie Brooks."

"Hekate."

The old woman wiped her mouth with the back of her hand, leaving a dirty streak across her cheek. Her skin was like tanned leather, lined and tough, and reminded Valerie of the gypsy at Hazel's. Valerie's eyes narrowed. If not for the fact that the gypsy was back home in England, the two women, could've been one and the same.

"I apologize if I'm staring, but you seem familiar. Did you say Hekate? You are named for the goddess of the crossroads?"

Hekate waved off the question. "You been nice to me. I tell your fortune."

Valerie shook her head. Had the old woman read her mind? She raised a hand in protest. "*Grazie*, but no. I've had enough of fortune tellers to last me two lifetimes—"

Valerie's next thought died in her throat as Hekate grabbed her hand. The old woman stared at her for a moment then spat in Valerie's palm and rubbed the saliva around in a circle with her thumb. "You never know what fate throw your way."

Valerie grimaced.

"There's magic in saliva, I tell you." Hekate squinted and turned Valerie's palm toward the sun. She pulled it closer to her eyes. "Ah, long life. You will live long time. Young ladies always want to know *amore*. You the same?" she asked, a sparkle lighting up her brown eyes.

Valerie couldn't help but smile in return. "*Si, amore,*" she replied. "Tell me of love."

"Love," Hekate repeated. But, as she explored the criss-cross of lines and creases, the smile on her face began to fade. "I see you must travel to find your love." Her eyes met Valerie's. "Travel through the mists."

"The mists?" Valerie asked. She looked at her hand. Not one of the lines made any sense to her, but what had she really expected to see? "What do you mean? Where does it say that?"

The old woman shrugged. She squeezed Valerie's hand, then let it drop. "It not for me to tell. You know soon enough. Good luck on journey. I pray for you." She smiled again. Her teeth were startlingly straight and white against her tanned skin. "I pray to Aphrodite, Goddess of Love."

"Aphrodite?" Valerie shook her head, confused by what Hekate had said and confused even more by the woman's very presence. None of it made any sense at all.

Then, a sudden thought came to her. What if this old woman was one of the ancient ones Fiorelli had spoken of during his tales the night before? She pushed down the panic creeping up from her stomach.

For heaven's sake, it was only a ghost story.

Hekate started to shuffle past when Valerie touched the old woman's arm. Shocked at the feathery light texture of her skin. Almost ethereal. "Wait. Can you tell me more?"

She waved a gnarled hand behind her and kept walking as Valerie let her hand drop. "You know soon enough," she repeated. "Soon enough." Her voice trailed off into a cackle as she disappeared in a sudden gust of windy dust.

CHAPTER FOURTEEN

What's wrong with me?

Valerie had pondered for a moment perhaps the old gypsy was actually from another time. One of the ancient ones, indeed. Her imagination was definitely running away from her. It must have been the recent upheaval from the journey and her experience with Thomas.

Sitting on a flat rock, Valerie pulled a small leather-bound notebook out of her skirt pocket and began to sketch the tomb in front of her. Rolling a gum eraser into a small ball, she dabbed at the charcoal until the image of the column had just the right amount of shading to look like the light was reflecting off the marble. Valerie smiled as she put the finishing touches on the drawing.

As she blew on the page to scatter the excess charcoal dust a deep rumble shook the ground where she sat. Valerie stuffed the book back into her pocket, gripped her cane, and stood as the earth shivered around her. The ground began to shift and roll, like waves in the sea. Thick clouds of dust swirled around her, obstructing her sight.

The quake was much stronger than the one from the night before. Frantic, she whipped her head around searching for a safe place to wait it out. Spying a small grotto next to one of the tombs she walked as fast as she could and climbed inside, praying it would provide a refuge from the quake.

Another vibration erupted from the very bowels of the earth pushing up toward the surface. The grotto shook violently, and remnants of volcanic ash lodged in cracks and crevices scattered over her, choking her. Covering her head with her hands, the ground continued to move and shift, listing and rolling like the ocean she had just crossed. A column a few feet away, toppled to the ground with a loud thud.

"Stop!" she screamed as the ash continued to fall, covering everything in a layer of gray dust. Then she heard it. A heavy cracking sound. Looking up she saw the roof beginning to splinter.

Oh, my God. I've got to get out of here.

Valerie got up just as a heavy stone came tumbling down from the roof. She ducked and it missed her, bouncing off the side of a nearby tomb. But another stone soon followed and this time it bounced against the wall of the grotto and, before she could duck, hit her hard on the head. She screamed and fell to the ground, plunging into darkness and then nothing more...

CHRISTOS CAMPANIUS MARCELLUS LAY ABED, scanning the new frescos that covered the walls of his room. The muted colorations and touches of gold were pleasing to him as his gaze moved from one erotic scene to the next. The deep red background was truly a passionate color. A brilliant idea the artist had, painting the progression of the seduction of a young virgin by Zeus.

And what better place to paint it than my bedchamber?

He chuckled, turning onto his stomach. It was getting late in the morning and he should be seeing about his business affairs, but the warmth of the woman next to him was too soft, too alluring to leave behind just yet. Her naked flesh curved around him and he felt his need grow again.

He nuzzled her neck and she giggled "Christos, it is time I left. You know as well as I that the slaves will talk at the market."

"Damn the slaves," he murmured. "Eros has led me down this path, and I will see it fulfilled, Gravia."

The woman arched against him, wrapping her legs about his buttocks as he moved within her. "Oh, Christos," she sighed, "when will you make an honest woman of me?"

"You know as well as I that there's no room for honesty in our rela-tionship," he growled against her lips. Would he ever grow tired of her soft and yielding form? He could lose himself too easily in her welcoming embrace, but he knew that was exactly what Gravia had hoped to accomplish.

He moaned with one final thrust. She panted, calling out his name over and over again. "Christos, my love…"

With a shudder, he tucked her into his embrace, settling a soft kiss on her rosy lips. Spent from their lovemaking, he rolled over and stretched.

Gravia patted him on the arm, then rose and pulled her creamy white *stola* over her head. The fine wool garment fell into soft folds over her well-rounded figure. She cinched the waist with a belt made of heavy links of gold, a gift fashioned by Christos's own hand. "Will I see you tonight?" she asked as she finger combed her dark-blonde hair.

Christos propped himself up against the soft feather pillows. "No, I don't think so."

"And why not?" she pouted. "I will miss not having you by my side in the morning."

"I've warned you before, Gravia. Don't get used to having me around." He ran his free hand through the thick tousle of black curls covering his head, his full lips set in a firm line.

Gravia opened her mouth to protest but was cut short by a loud cry from the street. She hurried to the open window and looked below. "Christos, come see," she called.

"What is it?" he asked, rising wearily. "Another goat loose in the forum?"

"No, I do not think so. Ah, I see the cause." She pointed to the center of the crowd. "There. It is a woman." She leaned over, straining to get a closer look. "What are those ridiculous clothes she is wearing? The top is so tight and the skirt so full. Look how the material drags on the ground behind her. How can she move about? I have never seen one dressed so."

Christos nudged Gravia out of the way. He scanned the crowd until he saw the object of their attention. Just then, the woman in the street looked up and their gazes locked.

Those deep green orbs seared straight through to the depths of his soul.

By the gods, it is she.

The woman from his dreams, the ghostly beauty come to life.

He could place no name to the apparition-turned flesh-and-blood woman. Her skin was the color of apricots, and her chestnut locks glinted with burnished gold strands in the sun.

"I am yours," she had said. Looking up at him now, her emerald eyes were wide with panic.

"Go home, Gravia," he whispered, his voice strained.

"What?"

"I said 'Go home'," he spoke louder this time, his eyes never leaving the prisoner's.

"I will go. But do not expect me to be waiting for you this evening. I believe I will go to Felix's dinner party. You may be interested in knowing he sent me an exclusive invitation…"

He shrugged, and the subsequent door slam barely registered as he continued to watch the young woman in the street below.

Christos's concentration was broken when the crowd grabbed the woman by the shoulders and pushed her on. She stumbled, then got back up. They shouted, "Witch! Witch!"

A witch, eh? Had she enchanted his dreams? Cast a spell in the night while he slept? Is that why he had seen her in spirit before seeing her in the flesh? Christos yelled down to one of the bystanders. "Where are they taking her?"

"To the jail, I think," the man answered.

"Jail?"

"Yes. At least, that's what I heard someone say."

Christos grabbed a short white tunic and tossed it on. He should wear his toga out on the streets, but there was no time to wait for the servants to position the folds just so.

He had to get to her.

Quickly lacing on a pair of brown leather sandals, he rushed down the stairs, through the central atrium of the house, and out the front door. Once on the street, he knocked down a small child in his haste.

He stopped and helped the girl to her feet, taking a moment to wipe away her tears. Then he continued on, following the crowd to the jail.

THE LAST THING Valerie could remember was the violent earthquake. She remembered it shaking the grotto where she had sought refuge. She remembered the ceiling cracking and the rocks falling from above. She recalled being hit on the head. But that's all she could remember…

How did I get here?

When she woke up the ceiling was still intact, and when she climbed down from the grotto, the street around it was neat and tidy, not overgrown with vegetation as it had been when she'd started out that morning. Even odder, the tombs all had fresh flowers.

As she left the tomb, she became even more confused. And more than a little frightened. There were a few people standing nearby, dressed in flowing robes and togas of cream-colored linen and cotton. They immediately stopped talking when she emerged and looked at her strangely, making that odd forked symbol with their fingers Signore Fiorelli had shown Reggie and her last night.

When Valerie tried to speak to them, they hurried away. One of them began to shout in Latin. She'd thought that odd as well. Could they have been actors researching an upcoming play?

She began to walk along the street, hoping to catch up with them, wanting to ask for help. When she turned along a bend in the road, she stopped dead in her tracks. She gasped, her eyes wide, her mouth open.

Pompeii!

The city in all its glory lay before her. Gone were the crumbling ruins with chipped and faded colors. Every building stood erect, the stucco finish pristine, the paint, bright and colorful. Even the iron gate was free of rust and looked to have a fresh coat of black lacquer over the metal. More surprising yet, a group of children clustered around a fountain situated in the fork in the road. They giggled as they splashed in the cool, flowing water.

Am I dreaming?

She placed a hand to her head, wondering if the blow from the falling rock had somehow altered her perception. She took a deep breath and steadied herself. Well, she couldn't stand here all day. She had to find Papa. He'd know what to do. She returned to the grotto, retrieved her cane, and retraced her steps through the city gates.

"*Venefica*! Witch!" a woman shouted. "Look at the strange clothing she wears!"

"We saw her climb out of the tomb," another woman yelled out. Valerie recognized both women from the grotto. She had asked them for help but they had run off. A curious crowd had begun to gather around Valerie, keeping their distance as they did so.

She was trying to raise the dead!" a man declared. Somewhere in the midst of the mob, a small child began to cry.

"No!" Valerie screamed as a man grabbed her. "I'm not a witch! Stop! Please!" she pleaded with him. He kicked her legs out from under her. She fell hard to the ground, her breath whooshing out.

"Did not the senate of Rome counsel we should turn from the menace of witches and sorcerers? Did they not say we should protect the State from their evil influences and magical spells?" He jabbed at Valerie with his toe before turning to face the crowd. "I say we put her in jail."

Valerie rolled to her knees and, planting her cane firmly on the ground, pulled herself up. She didn't understand what was happening or why these people were accusing her of witchcraft, but there was absolutely no way she was going to jail.

Her eyes scanned around, hoping to find a way through the crowd. She had to get away and hide for a while, until she could figure out what had really happened to her.

The man turned to face her again. With a sneer, he took a step closer. Valerie held her cane out in front of her and swung it in a wide arc. It came down hard on the man's shoulder and he stumbled backward.

"*Obsecro*. Please. Let me go!"

His eyes narrowed and he rushed toward her again, this time ripping the cane from her grasp. He slammed it down over his thigh, breaking it in half.

"Now let's see you do your magic without this." He flung the broken pieces to the ground.

"What are you doing?" Valerie screamed. She fell to her knees and retrieved the fragments. Struggling to her feet, she covered her ears at the cruel insults and accusations. Recalling the disturbing images from her dream the night before, she began to tremble.

My nightmare has come true!

Another man came at her, brandishing a pair of shackles. Balancing on her good leg, Valerie kicked at him with her other foot. With little effort, he knocked her to the stone-paved street. She cried out as a sharp rock ripped through her blouse and gouged her skin. Two women held her head down while the men clamped the chains into place around her ankles.

"Why are you doing this?" Valerie cried.

The men yanked Valerie to her feet and dragged her along. Without a cane, she stumbled, and almost fell. Someone laughed and threw a rotten pomegranate at her back, striking her squarely between the shoulders. Valerie spun around, scanning the crowd following her. Everyone jeering, shouting obscenities at her. There was no assistance to be found among them.

Her eyes landed on the statue of Dionysus she'd seen only yesterday, but the building next to it was completely intact.

Realization dawned on her. Unbelievable. Inconceivable. Her head swam as the crowd closed in around her...

My God, how did I come to be in ancient Pompeii?

The people circled Valerie as if she were a wild animal. She stumbled again, her breath coming in short, sharp gasps. Two men grabbed her by the arms just before she hit the ground, forcing her to move along or be trampled. Frantically, she looked about. Was there no one who could help?

And then she saw him.

The man in the window.

Do I know him?

He seemed disturbingly familiar to her in this strange place. Perhaps it was only because his features resembled the patrician busts she'd seen at the museum in London. Straight nose, full lips, heavy-lidded eyes. She'd studied and sketched them for hours on end, every time she'd visited the museum.

But there was something else. The way he watched her. The expression in his deep, ebony eyes. Compassion? Recognition? Would he be the one to stop this madness? She gazed back at him, hoping to convey her need to him.

Just as she was about to call out to him, the crowd pushed her along, breaking the mesmerizing connection. She closed her eyes, praying he would find her.

Help me! Help me, please!

CHAPTER FIFTEEN

Valerie fought back the panic threatening to undo her. The crowd was growing in size, shoving and pressing in upon her, people joining in the march along the streets of Pompeii.

Shouts of *'Witch! Witch! Witch!'* echoed around Valerie as the men dragged her along by the shackles.

Above the din, snatches of conversation floated to her from onlookers following the procession.

"She defied the law!" a man declared.

"What law?" a woman asked.

"The senate passed the decree," he went on. "Anyone who partakes in evil rituals will either be driven away or sold into slavery…"

Two small boys ran up behind Valerie and hit her with a long stick. The thin reed snapped against her skin like a stinging whip. Valerie cried out in pain, struggling to break free, searching her memory for references to witches and sorcerers from that era, desperate to recall any bit of information she could use to release her from this hell.

She tripped over the length of her skirt and the men jerked her back to her feet. Her gaze scanned the horde, anxious for a glimpse of her family or someone she might know. Valerie flung her head back, tossing her long hair away from her face. She tried to lift her hands to wipe the sweat and tears from her eyes so she might see more clearly, but they pulled down on the shackles.

Finally, the procession came to a halt and Valerie realized they had reached the jail. The two men released their hold on her. She took several deep breaths and wiped her sleeve over her face.

Directly in front of her was the squat building that served as a jail. The thick stone walls were covered in all manner of graffiti. It reminded her of the bordello she'd seen when Fiorelli had taken her and Reggie on the tour.

Scanning the various messages, she realized they weren't scandalous but motivated by justice and politics. *Free Honoria, Tiberius is innocent, and I'm voting for Salerno*. If she had read them in her time, she would have had a hundred questions for Fiorelli, but her fear was uppermost in her mind.

One of the men shouted at her to get moving and gave her a shove to make his point. Her exhaustion made her stumble and she tripped over the threshold, falling flat on her face inside the jail.

"What have you brought me now, Lucius?" the jailer asked as he rose lazily from his couch. "Runaway slave?"

"A witch, Maurus," Lucius whispered.

Maurus rolled his eyes and sighed. "Not another one. I wish the damned senate had left well enough alone. We've always had soothsayers and we always will, law or no law."

He poked his head out the door where the surly crowd had begun to chant 'witch, witch, witch' once more.

"These fools need another gladiator competition in the coliseum to whet their appetites." He shook his head. "Go home, all of you. Don't you have anything better to do with your day?" he called to the gathering.

"Banish her!!" a man shouted.

"Kill her!" another man yelled.

Maurus pushed Valerie behind him and planted his meaty hands on his hips. "You superstitious old fools. What makes you think she's a witch?" He glanced over his shoulder. "Why, she looks like a waif. Probably an escaped slave from Oplontis. "I'll see to it she's dealt with properly. Now, go home before I arrest the lot of you." Maurus grunted with satisfaction as the mob began to disperse, their shouts reduced to a few murmurs and grumbles.

Valerie shifted against the wall where she was leaning for support, her shackles clattered against the stone floor.

What is to become of me?

Maurus sat down and crossed his arms over his broad chest. "So, tell me Lucius, what makes you think she's a witch?"

"Why, just look at her!" Lucius grabbed Valerie by the shoulder and drew her forward.

An indignant huff escaped her and she swung at him with her fist. Losing her balance, she missed her mark and fell to her knees.

"Look at those clothes. Only a witch would wear such odd garments." He leaned forward and whispered, "She was seen climbing out of a tomb, carrying a staff for casting spells and raising the dead."

"And where is this magical staff of hers?"

"I broke it myself." Lucius patted his chest proudly. "She hefted the vile thing and was about to curse us all with it, I tell you."

Maurus's gaze traveled over Valerie's form. "Her clothes are strange, I'll give you that." He leaned forward. "What were you doing in the Necropolis, girl?"

Valerie took a deep breath.

What do I say?

Did she dare tell him she was hiding from an earthquake in the year 1865? Would he even believe her if she did? She must be a terrible sight with her dress torn and covered with dirt. As she considered her options, she lifted a hand to smooth her stray locks.

The man called Lucius grabbed her wrist and twisted it behind her back, wrenching a moan of pain from her.

"See? She was going to send a curse your way." His eyes narrowed. "Listen to how she talks. Go ahead, witch." Say something."

Maurus rested his elbows on his knees. "Well?"

Lucius pulled Valerie to her feet and she had to bite her lip to keep from crying out again as the chains dug into the tender skin of her ankles. She continued to stare straight at the jailer as tears streaked her face. It would do no good to explain herself to these two. They had already made up their minds about her.

She squared her shoulders,

I'm damned either way. To the devil with all of them.

"Speak to me, or things will be worse for you," he warned.

Lucius yanked the chain between her legs. Valerie immediately fell once again to the hard tile floor. Her chest heaved as she struggled to catch her breath. Sitting up, she tried to tuck her legs under her and almost gagged at the bloody and bruised mess her legs had become.

In the name of God, what am I doing here? Surely, Papa will march in that door at any moment to take me home. Dear Papa. Isn't he always there to rescue me when I need it most?

"A stubborn one, aren't you? Well, if you won't obey me, there's only one thing left for me to do." Maurus' eyes bore into hers. He grabbed the front of Valerie's blouse and pulled her up until she could feel his hot breath on her face. "Lock you up."

"Lock me up?" Valerie repeated, her voice ragged from the dust of the streets. No sooner had the words spilled out than she put her hand over her mouth, her eyes wide. So much for her resolve.

"You *can* speak." He nodded toward Lucius, his eyes never leaving Valerie's. "You're right. Her voice is different. Definitely not from here." He continued to watch her. "Not a true Roman citizen, anyhow. Do you have proof of freedwoman status?"

Valerie shook her head, a terrible sense of dread building in her. She knew from her studies how important such a piece of documentation was to anyone traveling in a Roman city.

"Well, that leaves me with just one alternative. Since you carry no papers, I must assume you are an escaped slave." He rubbed the back of his neck. "You'll be sold at the market tomorrow morning."

Maurus reached out and roughly handled her breasts. "You're a little too skinny for my tastes, but your curves are all in the right places. I'd say you'll make a fine house slave for some lucky master anyway."

"How dare you touch me?" Valerie took a swing at Maurus as she tried to break free of his grasp.

Maurus laughed, the loud grating sound of bounced off the stone walls and echoed in her head. The pain from his rough handling was compounded by her exhaustion and thirst. She put her hands over her ears, trying to wrench herself free as she fought to stay alert, but it was too much. Her last thoughts were of her family and home as she collapsed to the ground in a heap.

VALERIE CRACKED open her eyes and moaned. She must have fainted. She found herself on the cold, hard floor of the cell. "You must let me out of here," Valerie pleaded, as the heavy iron door was shut. "I've done nothing wrong."

"That's exactly what every criminal I've put in here has had to say," Maurus said through the window. "You should consider yourself lucky." He chuckled. "You only have to stay one night and then you'll be sold. Most of my guests stay much longer and they usually end up getting the lash or the cross.

"Crucifixion?" Valerie whispered brokenly, her face growing pale.

"Ah, so you do know more than you let on. That's what happens to runaway slaves." His eyes narrowed. "Best to keep that in mind, in case you have any other ideas."

Valerie heard Maurus' heavy footsteps fade away, taking the torch with him. If it wasn't for the glow of the moon beaming through the small window, she'd be in total darkness. Without her cane, she had to use the wall for support as she stood and shuffled to the small straw mattress in the corner, the iron shackles grinding against the floor.

I have to stay calm.

She let her breath out slowly, as she eased onto the cot. If she ruminated too much about everything that had happened to her, she'd go mad for certain. Next to the pallet sat a bowl of tepid water and a round loaf of bread. She touched the bread. It was rock hard. Valerie's stomach growled and she put her hand over it.

Why didn't I eat this morning when I had the chance?

Valerie hit the loaf against the wall and a small piece broke off. She dipped it in the water and took a bite. Chewing carefully, she reached down and pulled up her skirt. She coughed and choked on the bread when she saw her legs. The fine woolen stockings were in blood-stained shreds where the shackles were still clamped. Valerie tore off several pieces of her skirt hem and, after wetting them down, tucked them under the bands of iron. She started to take another bite of the bread. Her stomach retched.

To compound her nausea, the sour smell of urine and sweat pervaded the cell and assaulted her senses. Her eyes burned and started to water. She tried so hard not to gag but the combination was too much to withstand. Crawling over to the opposite corner of the cramped cell, her stomach heaved harder this time, dispensing itself of the meager fare she had just consumed. She vomited again and again, until nothing remained in her but the bitter taste of bile.

Dear God, please let me go home...

Valerie wiped her mouth on the sleeve of her torn and dirty blouse. A wave of panic ran through her.

What if I'm stranded here forever?

She shuddered and began to rock back and forth.

Maybe I'm going mad.

She held her head with trembling hands.

Maybe I never left England. Maybe I'm still at home. Maybe Mama and Papa are right here and I just can't see them. "Mama," she whispered, "I'm here." She listened for a moment. There was no response.

An old woman's cackle echoed off the stone walls of the damp jail and jarred her memory. Hekate.

My God. She said I'd have to travel through the mists. Was this what she meant? How could she have known? Why didn't she warn me?

Wearily, Valerie crawled back to the mattress and lay against the hard, cold wall, too exhausted to think anymore.

From somewhere in the darkness of the jail, a thin reedy voice began to sing. The words were slurred and nonsensical, but the melody gave her something to focus on outside of herself. After a few moments, she began to hum along with the other prisoner, finally drifting off to sleep just before dawn.

CHAPTER SIXTEEN

"Wake up," a voice called.

Valerie stirred. "Go away, Reg," she murmured and turned over.

"I said wake up!" the voice shouted this time.

Valerie's eyes flew open, and she sat up. As her sight came into focus, she rubbed her forehead. Maurus was standing on the threshold of the cell.

Dear Lord, I wasn't dreaming.

The night had come and gone and still she was in ancient Pompeii. She struggled to her feet and almost immediately tumbled back down onto the mattress. The chains had done their damage. Her legs were stiff and swollen, even her good foot wouldn't support her.

"I–I can't," she whispered.

"For the love of Zeus," Maurus cursed. He walked up to her, grabbed her arm, and pulled her up. "Now move."

Valerie stumbled and fell against the wall, scraping her cheek. "Please. I need something to lean on while I walk."

Maurus looked at her suspiciously. "What are you talking about?"

She turned around and pressed her back against the wall. The cool stone penetrated her clothing and helped soothe the mad fever building up inside of her. "Your friend Lucius. He broke my cane. I can't walk without it – or something like it," she explained, her voice breathless.

"Well you won't get one." He laughed. "You think I want my head banged in?"

"Then you'll either have to carry me or drag me out of here." She shook her head. "You don't understand, do you? I need it to walk."

Maurus shifted back and forth. "I'm not about to stand here and argue with you, girl." He gestured with his hand. "Now, get moving before we're late."

Valerie took a deep breath, near tears. She swallowed hard as the now familiar taste of bile worked its way up into the back of her throat. She tried to focus on the jailer's face.

I will not give this man the satisfaction of vomiting in front of him.

She took another deep breath. "I'm crippled."

Oh, how I hate to call myself that word.

"Prove it," he ordered.

She sat down and unlaced the black leather shoe and slipped it off. Her stockings were so torn and ripped from the chains, her foot poked through. Valerie raised her left foot slightly. "See?"

Maurus removed the chains and examined the crooked toes and turned heel. "All right." He nodded and left the cell as she put her shoe back on. Returning a few moments later, he handed her a waist high, straight stick of red cedar.

Valerie leaned on it and stood. The wood was rough and aromatic as she ran her hand over it. "Thank you."

He yanked her arm and pulled her through the jail cell door. "Don't even act as if you're going to use that as a weapon or you can crawl the rest of the way to the Forum. Is that understood?"

She nodded, holding her tongue. It would do no good to rile the man any further. She needed the use of a cane if she hoped to escape. Valerie took a step. Her legs felt so light now that they were free of the shackles. She took another and limped ahead of Maurus and out of the jail.

Off to the side of the street, several people had gathered. "She won't bring any money, Maurus," someone observed. "No one wants a witch in their homes."

"Go ahead and put her in a whore house." The woman who spoke followed Valerie's movements. "Looks like she'd do best lying on her back anyway."

Valerie stiffened and squared her shoulders. People were really no different, no matter what era. The Pompeiians talked about her as if she weren't there—the same as the people of her own place and time. "Why are you doing this to me?"

Maurus sighed. "Look, you come into our city and try to raise the dead. I'm duty bound."

"But I didn't—" she interjected.

He threw up his hands. "You were judged by the people. They saw you come out of the tomb. If it had been a month ago, no one would have given it a second thought." He absently gave her arm a tug as she started to fall behind. "But the senate just passed a new law banning the practice of witchcraft. I'm just trying to do my job."

She glanced at the fine stuccoed buildings around her with their tall pillars and elaborate entries. The city had seemed magical when she'd first arrived with her family. Even the ruins, after so many centuries, had called to her. But now, she saw the truth of it. No magic. Just ignorance.

A slave girl carrying a small baby stepped to the side as she and Maurus passed by. Was this to be her fate as well? The girl's gaze met hers. She gave her a small nod and a sad smile as if she'd read Valerie's mind. It would be so.

Maurus snorted, breaking into her thoughts. "I don't agree with those people back there. I think you'll bring a decent price." He looked at her out of the corner of his eye. "A wealthy citizen was already asking after you."

Valerie's heart skipped a beat. Could it be Papa? Had he found a way to rescue her? "What did he look like? Did he say if he was a relative?"

"No." He paused, swatting at a gnat. "It was a statesman." He jerked her arm again and pushed her ahead of him. "Quiet now, I've had enough of your questions."

Valerie raised her eyes as they approached the Forum. Here, all manner of people, both free and slave, passed through the tall, columned entry and into the open, marble-paved center. The massive stone structure occupied several blocks of the city and provided a center for commerce, worship, and meting out judicial decisions.

Passing through the gates, the pair moved slowly through what Valerie guessed to be the marketplace. All around, vendors hawked their wares. The aroma of boiled onions and garlic, mixed with sweat, permeated the humid air.

It really wasn't so different here from the merchant's section of London, except for the clothing of the shoppers and some of the items they bought. Built close to the sea, Pompeii had a vast selection of fish, octopus, even dolphin. She caught the scent of fermented grapes, then spotted a vintner's shop. Tall flasks sat in crevices cut into the counter, ready for anyone to purchase.

Valerie paused, watching as a man sitting on the ground tried to coax a snake out of a woven basket with a subtle movement of his hands. The crowd clapped and gasped as the creature appeared and seemed to dance in the air.

Maurus spun on his heel and caught Valerie by the hair. He whipped her around in front of him and flung her to the ground. He stepped over her, hands on his hips. "Don't wander off like that again. Understand?"

She nodded and pulled herself to her feet. "I didn't do anything wrong."

"You did." Maurus shook her so hard, her teeth rattled.

"P-please," she said, closing her eyes as she fought a wave of dizziness. After a moment, she opened her eyes and wished she had fainted…

There, straight ahead, was the slave market. Wooden stalls, smaller than what horses were kept in back home, lined a long wall. In each stall, the slave stood, scantily clad, while prospective buyers—pinched and poked, looking in mouths and examining teeth.

Nearby a naked man stood on a wood platform, forced to parade back and forth in front of the crowd as bids flew about. Valerie's eyes skittered away from the sight only to land on a woman lying in the straw with a sign around her neck stating she was a thief. The slave sobbed and rocked from side to side.

"Why is she crying?" Valerie asked, her voice strained.

"She knows no one will want a slave that steals. She was a fine lady's servant but will now end up working in the fields for the rest of her life. Unless no one buys her. Then she'll be put to death." Maurus pointed to an empty stall. "There. Take your place."

I have to escape from here.

Valerie scanned the area, spying an alley that led to an exit. As Maurus was intent on unlocking the stall, she began to shuffle away, keeping her eyes on Maurus as she did so. When his back was fully turned away from her, she gripped her cane and with all the strength she had in her, hobbled to the alley.

Just as she was reaching the exit a hand grabbed her on the back of the neck and yanked her up like a rag doll.

Maurus spun her around, his face so close to hers she could smell the stale ale on his breath. "I'll tell you something, girl. I know you're not from this area, so you best be warned. Should you try and escape, you *will* be put to death. I won't even try to sell you."

He gripped her forearm and dragged her into the slave stall. He grabbed a length of rough unbleached wool fabric. "Get rid of those clothes you're wearing."

"I beg your pardon?"

"You heard me. Take them off and wrap this around you." He gestured with his hand. "Tie it on like that woman over there."

Valerie craned her neck around the side wall. The woman Maurus was pointing at had looped the material around her body and over a shoulder. Her knees were barely covered, let alone the rest of her legs. She thrust her chin up. "I refuse to wear that flimsy cloth."

Maurus cursed. He grabbed the front of her blouse and tugged downward. The small pearl buttons flew in every direction, exposing her corset and bosom beneath. Valerie grabbed frantically at the tattered shreds and tried to pull them together.

"What gives you the right?" She spat the words at him, her face flush with anger and embarrassment.

He cupped her chin and forced her to look at him. "I have every right. You are a slave. You best remember your place." He let go of her and she stumbled back. "Change your clothes." Maurus turned his back to her.

Valerie eyed him for a moment, fingering the walking stick. He'd warned her numerous times. So far being defiant had not worked in her favor. No, she's probably would have a better chance of getting away if she pretended to be meek and mild-mannered.

She removed her tattered blouse and unfastened her skirt, letting it slip to the ground. Holding her breath, she twisted around, her arms going to her back to tug at the corset ties. She loosened them enough so that she could slip the undergarment off. Taking deep breaths, she leaned heavily on the cane to keep her balance.

Naked, except for her stockings and pantalets, she picked up the rough cloth and draped it around her shoulders, folding it around her body, as close to the Roman-style as possible.

A loud clapping and deep male chuckle made her look up. Her heart stopped.

The man from the window!

Had he come to help her? Or was he here only to humiliate her like the others?

"A fine show," he commented as he stepped forward, placing a tanned hand on the door of the stall. "I've never seen a woman with so many layers of clothing. Where exactly are you from that they bind you up so?"

Heat suffused Valerie's cheeks. "Y-you saw everything?"

He smiled and winked. "Everything."

"Ah, Patron Christos Campanius Marcellus," he muttered, tossing a red felt hat to Valerie. "This one is not worth your time."

Christos raised a dark eyebrow. "No? You don't believe she's worthy of being a slave?"

"Worthy of being a slave?" Valerie asked, her tone curt. "How exactly is one measured to determine such worthiness?" She waved the hat at Maurus, her eyes narrowed. "What in heaven's name is this ridiculous thing for?"

"Put it on. It'll show everyone you're being sold without a guarantee. As is." He looked at the other man. "See what I mean? She is ill-mannered and ill-tempered. Maybe it would be better to let her go to Livia. She might do better in a brothel."

Valerie swallowed hard. Brothel? She gripped the walking stick until her knuckles turned white.

Over my dead body!

With a grunt, she swung and hit Maurus squarely in the chest. Caught off guard, he fell backward, hitting the hard-packed ground.

The man called Christos threw back his head and roared with laughter.

Furious, Valerie raised the stick again aiming for Christos. Quick as a panther he grabbed her weapon in mid-air. Holding onto the cane, he pulled her to him. His body was hard and unyielding, his muscles taut and lean. "Don't make that mistake again," he warned, his voice low. His ebony eyes were so striking, she almost forgot to breathe. He let his hand drop and Valerie fell back against the wall.

Feet apart, hands on hips, Christos's gaze seared her for a moment, before he turned on his heel and strode away from the stall.

Maurus scrambled to his feet and backhanded her across the face. Valerie tasted the steely warm wetness of blood as it trickled down the corner of her mouth. Clutching the robe to her breast, she slid down the length of the wall and into the moldy hay that covered the floor of the slave market.

CHAPTER SEVENTEEN

This isn't happening. It's just a dream.

Valerie was pulled up the stairs and onto a wooden platform. Below her, spectators gathered, some whistled, while others jeered.

The auctioneer stood before her, a small weasel of a man with a whip tucked under one arm. He reminded her of her schoolteacher, Master Hobbs.

"Greetings people of Pompeii. I am Caias. Let us get in the spirit of the occasion, shall we?" With one sharp tug, he ripped the length of cloth from her shoulder, exposing the soft flesh beneath.

"No!" Valerie gasped. She clutched at the material, trying to wrap it back around her. The hot summer sun beat down on Valerie's head. She'd barely eaten or had any drink in two days. Between the forced march to the jail and the constant hits and slaps from Maurus, she was on the verge of collapse. At least if she passed out, she wouldn't be aware of the shame inflicted upon her…

No! I can't let that happen. If I faint, they can do anything to me!

With renewed determination, she took a deep breath and straightened her shoulders.

"Come on. Off with the rest of it." Caias leaned forward. "Now!" he commanded.

Valerie took a step back, shaking her head. She trembled as she stood firm. Silent tears began to stream down her cheeks.

The auctioneer motioned with his hand. Two oversized giants leaped onto the platform and grabbed her. They stood on either side of Valerie, tossed her cane aside, and held her arms out. She struggled against them, but to no avail. Caias grabbed the cloth and roughly unwound it from her form.

She closed her eyes, her tears squeezing through her lashes, as the last of the fabric fell to the wooden platform.

"What's this?" Caias asked, pointing to the pantalettes. He laughed and several people in the crowd tittered as well. "Only barbarians wear such clothing."

With another tug, the thin cotton undergarments were torn from her as well. Valerie now stood naked before the crowd, wearing only what was left of her stockings, her shoes, and the red felt hat.

Caias approached her and gripped her chin, forcing her to look at him. His eyes moved down her body, coming to rest on her full round breasts.

"Not bad. Not bad at all." He spun around and faced the crowd. "What is my opening bid? Who will take this feisty woman from me?" He scanned the crowd. No one ventured forth with an offer.

Despite the heat of the midday sun on her body, Valerie shuddered. She moved her head from side to side, making her long hair tumble over her shoulders, offering a scant amount of cover.

Oh, please dear Lord. Let me awaken from this nightmare.

She mouthed the prayer, over and over again, swallowing the bitter taste of bile as it rose in her throat once more.

"Look! The witch is casting a spell!" a woman in the crowd shouted. A chorus of gasps rippled through the mob.

"We don't want her in our homes. She'll curse us all!" a man called out.

The auctioneer regarded Valerie with a cold look. "If no one will buy you, I suppose I'll have to turn you over to the whore house." His eyes swept over her again. "Though I can't say that would be a bad thing," he said, his thin lips twisted in a leer.

"I–I don't understand. Can't you just let me go?" she croaked out. To think, only a few days ago, she'd wondered what it would be like to live here, in this time prior to the eruption. Now, she wanted nothing more than to forget she had ever heard of the city of Pompeii.

He laughed. "And how will the jailer be repaid for the lodging and food he offered so generously?"

A murmur went up from the crowd as a tall, ebony-haired man stepped forward. Valerie caught her breath. Christos! Remembering his threats in the stall, she wondered how her first intuition could have been so wrong about him.

She'd glimpsed compassion in his eyes when she'd glanced up to the window as she'd been dragged through the streets.

I couldn't have been more wrong.

He obviously wasn't there to help her. More than likely, he wanted to further humiliate her.

"I'll take the girl," he stated flatly.

Her eyes widened at his declaration.

"No, Marcellus. She'll destroy your house with her black arts," a man urged from behind.

Christos said over his shoulder. "Don't be ridiculous. She's just a girl."

Valerie watched the two men discuss her as though she weren't even there.

At least he doesn't believe I'm a witch.

The crowd seemed to be holding its collective breath, waiting for the outcome.

"Well, then, what will you pay me for her, Patron? She's a fine-looking thing, certain to decorate your household quite nicely." Caias waved his arm and the men holding Valerie forced her forward. They pushed her to her knees and made her lean over the platform, so her face was near Christos's. "What do you think? Is she not pleasant to look at?"

Valerie closed her eyes again. Her face burned as Christos studied her countenance. She jerked back when he ran a finger lightly down her cheek. She opened her eyes only to find him staring intently at her. His eyes never left hers.

"I'll pay you the going rate, Caias, and not a *sesterces* more."

The auctioneer opened his mouth to speak. Christos interrupted him. "Don't even think of trying to get any more from me. She's been cuffed, beaten and appears to be crippled." He continued to stare at Valerie as the two men pulled her to her feet.

She stood with her eyes downcast, no longer fighting, no longer seeing the two men who were haggling her fate.

Valerie had reached her limit. She'd traveled back through the mists of time, only to be arrested as a witch, thrown in jail, beaten, and sold on the auction block.

My fate is sealed...

The shouts and sounds from the market faded away as she retreated into her memories. She imagined herself in a field of amethyst heather, sitting on a blanket and sketching a bluebird perched on the branch of a nearby tree. Reggie giggled as he chased a yellow butterfly. Her parents sat on another blanket, her father reading, her mother doing needlepoint. Lucy was tidying up the remains of their picnic.

She smiled, as a sense of peace and home enveloped her...

"Come on down from there, girl." Christos ordered.

No thank you, I'd rather stay in this lovely field ...

THE GIRL IS MAD.

Her eyes were closed, and a dreamy smile curved her lips.

"I said come here," Christos said in a gentler tone. He climbed the platform steps and picked up the rough cloth Caias had ripped from her. Gently, he wrapped it around her, then handed her the walking stick. The girl trembled as she took hold of the stick, but she kept her eyes closed.

Christos silently berated himself for not following his instincts to bring her home, then and there, when he'd gone to see Maurus last night. The people of Pompeii could be cruel in their rush to judgement and the proof was in this poor one's battered and bruised body. He searched her face, looking for the recognition he'd seen the day before on the street. It was there, under the abuse, and his chest tightened at the injustices she'd suffered.

Caias strutted over and held out his hand. "Payment is due before you take her. You know that." The auctioneer ran a finger down Valerie's spine and she shuddered.

Christos grabbed Caias' hand and held it tight. The other man squirmed with pain. "Touch her again and I'll kill you," Christos growled. "Understand me?" He turned to the crowd. "If one of you raises a hand toward this woman, I'll see you imprisoned. She's mine now and she'll be treated with the dignity afforded my house."

He released Caias and shoved the payment at the other man. Christos turned his attention back to Valerie, this mysterious young woman from his dreams who now belonged to him.

At least she hasn't tried to run away.

He took her by the hand. "Everything will be fine now," Christos whispered. "We're going home."

Home!

How I wish that were true.

The field of heather faded from her mind and she fully opened her eyes.

And gazed into the deepest, darkest eyes she'd ever seen.

Christos held her hand and helped her down the steps. His gentleness surprised her, then again, he had just purchased her. She now belonged to him. He could do whatever he pleased with her...

Everything in her life comforting and familiar was gone, lost to her. She would never see her family again.

In the span of two days, she had been transformed from a young woman who lived a quiet, albeit comfortable life in England with a loving family to a slave of ancient Pompeii, the property of a man named Christos.

She blinked back the tears that pricked her eyes. Her heart pounded in her ears like a drum beat.

A slave.

Her days would be filled with serving her master. She had studied enough to know what the ancients did with – and to – their slaves. Would he abuse her? Or would he be gentle?

With a deep breath, Valerie forced herself to keep up with Christos's long stride. She stared at his back as he walked ahead of her. His bearing was arrogant and spoke of privilege. The taut play of muscles beneath his tunic spoke of a man conditioned for battle. No wonder he had disarmed her so easily when she'd attacked him with her cane in the stall.

There was something so oddly familiar about this Christos. And it wasn't just because he resembled a regal statue from a museum...

I've seen him before, but where?

She recalled snatches of a dream—blurry, like looking through a misty fog—a comforting dream...

Just then, a young boy and girl ran by and threw several rocks at Valerie's back. She cried out in shock and pain.

"Witch. Witch. Witch."

A group had followed them from the slave market. Valerie shook from the pain and humiliation.

When will this end?

Christos spun around, his expression dark. "What's the matter with all of you? Was I not clear in my statement?" he growled at the crowd.

He turned to Valerie and held her gently by the shoulders. He searched her face. "Are you hurt?" he asked.

Valerie shook her head. "Can you make them go away?" she whispered. "Please?" She was tired of having to defend herself. Even the insults she'd experienced as a child had never prepared her this kind of abuse and assault.

"By the gods," he swore loudly. "This woman is not a witch. She is now a slave in my household and I'll not have her abused by any of you."

He glared at each and every person gathered around them. "As I promised at the auction, if anyone ever raises a hand against my property, I'll levy charges against you in the Basilica." He turned to her. "Come along."

Valerie gazed at him. She was his property, she belonged to him.

That's the only reason he protected me

Pain twisted in her breast like a knife but she pushed it away. She pushed away the confusion and hurt, burying the emotions deep in her soul. If she was going to survive in this place and time, she needed to learn everything she could about these people and their culture. To learn as much as she could about this man who called himself her master. She needed to find his weakness, then use it against him to escape—use whatever she could learn to return to her own world.

They walked past a low-roofed building that served as a bakery. One side of the structure was entirely open, exposing large cone-shaped stone ovens. Freshly baked round loaves of bread sat cooling on wood shelves, the yeasty aroma floated out to tickle Valerie's nose. Her mouth watered and her stomach growled in response. Valerie glanced at Christos. He was busy haggling with a seller over a bag of legumes. She was so hungry. What harm would it be to snatch a small roll?

A hand grabbed her by the arm and shook her.

"Don't touch me," she warned, gripping her cane for protection.

"Slaves must stand behind their master," a large burly man breathed in Valerie's ear. "And they only speak if they are spoken to." With a shove, he let her go.

For heaven's sake, how was she supposed to know every rule about slaves? Up until two days ago, she was a proper English young lady. She glared at the hulking brute of a man."

Christos stopped talking and turned around. "You know, I can't quite place that accent of yours," he said to her. "Say something else."

Valerie gaped at him.

The other man thumped her hard on the arm. "Are you deaf? He said something tor him."

Valerie rubbed the spot where he hit her. It was already beginning to turn red and swell. Did this Christos save her from the crowd only to let this man assault her?

She drew herself up, her temper flaring. "Damn you to bloody hell! I've had enough abuse from all of you. Is this how visitors to your *fine* city are treated?" She whacked the heavy cedar cane into the brute's side with such force, it sent her flying backward.

Christos caught Valerie just before she toppled onto the stone pavement.

The large man took a step forward, hand raised. Christos grabbed him by the forearm before he could strike. His eyes bore into the brute's. His voice was low as he spoke. "No, Julius. She's been through enough. Besides, violence only begets violence."

"She deserves a good beating, Christos. Let me teach her a lesson or two." He ran his hand over her breasts, grinning at her gasp of outrage. "I'll break her in real good for you. Make her a slave to be proud of."

Christos shook his head. "Nay, Julius she is not to be abused in that way."

Valerie scowled at the lout. She was tempted to hit him again but knew it would be no use.

Christos turned to Valerie. He cupped her chin in his hand, forcing her to look into his obsidian eyes.

"Julius is my personal guard. He looks out for me. I would not allow the townspeople to harm you, but I would have to let Julius discipline you if make the mistake of striking him again. Do you understand?"

Valerie jerked away from Christos's touch and took a step backward. Her eyes narrowed as she shook her head. "I'll not let any of you touch me again." She squared her shoulders. "Do you understand me?"

Christos threw his head back and roared with laughter. "Sorceress or not, you do have a witch's fire. If you were a free woman, I'd wager Athena, Goddess of War, would be your patron. Or perhaps Diana, Goddess of the Moon."

"More like Kronos, God of Time," Valerie replied with a terse smile as she made circles in the dirt with her cane.

"So, you know of our gods. But your accent is not Roman." He cupped Valerie's chin again, forcing her to look into his eyes. Valerie was tall for a woman, but Christos stood a good head taller than she. The intensity of his stare took her breath away. "Where are you from?" he asked, his voice low.

"Britannia." The ancient Roman word rolled off her tongue like a lover's name and she pushed back thoughts of home. She would only be able to indulge her memories when she was alone.

"Impossible!" Christos laughed and dropped his hand. "I was there with the Roman army and saw nothing but savages; people who wear skins and live in stick and stone hovels."

Valerie needed to hold her own with this man if she hoped for even a small measure of his respect. "I am from the town of Londinium. We are different there."

"Londinium, you say? I was busy fighting in other areas. I never ventured to that particular place." He took a step closer the heat of his body enveloping her. "Tell me. Are the people correct in what they say?" he said in a soft voice. "Are you really a witch?"

Valerie shook her head. "No, not a witch. Just a woman."

"Ah, not just a woman." He leaned forward and his breath caressed her cheek. "You are now the property of Christos Campanius Marcellus." With his thumb, he smeared away some of the dirt that covered her face. "Your skin is soft and unblemished under the filth. I imagine you might be quite lovely after you're cleaned up."

Valerie's head pounded with a dull ache. She tugged at the material wrapped around her. It seemed impossible to keep any modicum of decency with the garment. She almost laughed aloud thinking of how many times she'd battled with Lucy over that blasted crinoline. It was a lifetime ago… "What are you going to do with me?"

Christos turned and started walking. "Can you get around without that stick?" he asked over his shoulder.

"No."

"Then I suppose you'll have to work in the kitchen since it would require the least amount of movement. Besides, Stella's always grumbling she could use some help."

CHAPTER EIGHTEEN

Falling into step between Christos and Julius, Valerie ventured a cautious look about. She was careful not to slow down or appear too interested in any one item, all the while trying to memorize the path they were traveling through the Forum. If she were lucky enough to be allowed to visit here again, she needed to have an escape route planned and ready for use.

"What do we have here, Christos, my love?" asked a petite woman as she approached Christos. Her dark blonde hair was arranged in intricate curls on top of her head and she smelled of expensive perfume. The woman wrinkled her nose in distaste. "My, but she looks like one of those wretched children who live in the caves by the sea. When was the last time you visited the baths?" she asked Valerie.

Valerie drew herself up. Perhaps this woman would like to hear about the less than sanitary conditions in the prison and the deplorable way visitors are treated. She opened her mouth to speak when Christos intervened.

"She's been in jail, Gravia," Christos answered for her. "I bought her at the auction and we're now on our way home."

Recognition lit Gravia's face. "She is the one we saw being dragged through the streets, is she not?"

"She is."

"But, Christos, everyone says she is a witch." Gravia's eyes grew wide. "How could you bring her into our house?" She considered Valerie. "She'll bring the heavens – and the senate – down on our heads. You can't afford to garner the counsel's disfavor."

Our house? Strange, she wouldn't have pictured a man like Christos married to a woman like Gravia. She she seemed close to thirty – not much older than he was, but with her ostentatious jewelry and painted beauty, she resembled a woman who desperately wanted to hold tight to her youth.

"*Our* house, Gravia?" Christos stopped walking and turned to the woman. He rubbed his chin as he spoke, "Just what have you been telling people?"

"Why nothing, Christos. Except that I care for you a great deal." Gravia weaved her arm through his and smiled sweetly up at him. "Can I come over this evening?" she purred into his ear. "You look so tense. I would love to help you relax."

"Mmmm, perhaps."

"Do not tease me," Gravia pouted.

He laughed. "I suppose we could have dinner in my room if you like."

Gravia released his arm and clapped her hands together. "I would like that very much." As she hurried off, she called behind her, "Later, my love."

So, they weren't married after all. "Is she your betrothed?" Valerie asked as she watched Gravia leave.

"What did I tell you about speaking out of turn, girl?" Julius growled.

Valerie shot him a look over her shoulder, her eyes narrowed.

"It's all right, Julius. I don't mind a few questions, as long as they don't become too troublesome."

Christos looked at her, his eyebrows raised. "Well? Was there something you wished to ask me?"

Valerie shrugged as she adjusted the cloth around her shoulders. "It's nothing, really. I only thought she, Gravia that is, was your wife. I guess I was mistaken."

He began walking again. "Gravia and I know too many dark secrets about each other to be married. She is my mistress."

"I–I see," Valerie murmured. In her own time, no gentleman would have admitted so freely to keeping a woman for pleasure only. Then again, these people had an entirely different set of moral standards.

"I don't see why you let her stay around, Christos," Julius said. "She's bad, that one."

Christos laughed. "Julius here doesn't think I should see Gravia. If I didn't know any better, I'd think my friend was jealous."

Julius snorted. "Personally, I wouldn't give her a second look."

"Now I know you're lying. I've seen the way you watch her when she comes to visit." Christos clapped him on the back and sighed. "Like a ram ready to charge."

The two men laughed as the trio turned a corner into a residential district. The houses in this *insula* were built tightly together, each structurally dependent on the other. Valerie sighed. Would she ever fit into this society as neatly?

"I don't understand. If Julius is a slave, why is he allowed to speak so freely?" Valerie asked.

"He isn't a slave at all. Julius was my second in command in the army. When our commissions were completed, he came to work for me. It'll take some time, but you'll eventually understand." He glanced at her. "At least, if you're as intelligent as I believe you to be, you will."

Valerie stopped and stared hard at Christos's back. 'As smart as I believe you to be?' Indeed. He had no idea at all about the type of person she was. Nor did she care for him to find out. She would be long gone from this evil city before he had a chance to really know her. Julius interrupted her thoughts with a push. She hurried to catch up with Christos as he turned another corner.

Stopping in front of an elaborately painted and stuccoed house, Christos reached inside of his tunic and pulled out a key from a gold chain around his neck. He unlocked the heavy wooden door and walked in, leaving it open behind him.

Valerie followed Christos into a narrow hallway flanked by mosaic scenes intricately set into the walls. The ocean at night, with several different types of fish leaping out of the water, reminded Valerie of the mural aboard the *Fast Alice*. She ran her hand along the artwork as she walked, feeling the cool uneven texture of the small tesserae tiles. She came to an abrupt stop as she walked into the open atrium of the house.

Turning slowly around in a circle, Valerie looked up through the middle opening and into the clear azure blue sky above. Beneath the roof, and circling the atrium, was the second level of the home. Tall fluted columns with elaborate Corinthian capitals supported the red clay tile roof, creating a colonnaded corridor in front of several doors. She smiled, delighted, when she spotted the various styles of down-spouts attached to the roof's drainage system – dogs, demons, and gods. From there, she followed the path of the gutters to where they emptied into the central pool built into the floor.

Christos watched in mild amusement as she made her assessment. "Quite different from a house made of sticks and stones, don't you think?"

"It's beautiful. I've never seen anything like it. Did you hire an architect, or did you design it yourself?"

"I designed it, for the most part. This front entry and atrium were original to the house. My father had it built when he settled in Pompeii over forty years ago. After he died, I added on the back portion," Christos explained as he pointed down another long corridor.

Valerie walked to a simple wood frame couch off to the side of the space and ran her hand over the heavy linen upholstery. The afternoon sun reflected off the gold thread woven into the fabric. It sparkled and winked at her. "Beautiful," she breathed.

"*Gratias*." He gestured to Julius who pulled a small bundle out from the folds of his tunic. The other man handed the package to Valerie. "I thought you might like to have these," Christos explained.

She accepted the offering with a mixture of wonder and trepida-tion. What could he possibly be giving her? But her fear turned to joy when she discovered her white blouse and dark charcoal skirt within the package. She hugged the garments to her breast. "Thank you," she whispered as tears welled in her eyes. "You don't know how much I appreciate this."

Christos inclined his head. "Julius, why don't you take her to Stella. She'll have plenty of time to explore her new home later. Tell her to see to the girl's needs." He turned and disappeared down another corridor.

Julius grabbed Valerie by the arm and pulled her toward the back of the house. She yanked her arm free from his grip and walked in silence next to him.

"Who is there?" A woman's voice called from the back of the kitchen and the sound echoed against the stone walls.

Valerie peered around the corner. This room was so plain compared to what she had just seen. The floor was laid of simple red clay tile, the walls left unadorned except for heavy pots and pans hanging from hooks. At the back of the kitchen and standing before a heavy stove built of stone was one of the roundest people she had ever seen.

The woman finished stirring the bronze pot before her, put down the wooden spoon, and turned around. With the back of her hand, she pushed away the wisps of graying hair that clung to her brow. The heat of the room was stifling, and she moved slowly, each motion deliberate. "Well? I asked you a question, girl."

Julius gave Valerie another shove. "This is your new help, Stella."

Stella's eyes narrowed as she looked Valerie over from head to toe. She gestured toward the cane. "What's the matter with her?"

"Don't know." He shrugged. "I think she's a cripple."

Stella threw up her hands. "Well, I've seen everything now. Leave it to the master to bring me half a servant." She shook her head. "He's always bringing in strays off the street. Problem is, they can't hardly do anything. Then who has to do all of the work?" She jabbed a chubby finger at the center of her chest. "Stella, that's who!"

"I don't know what to tell you other than your master says you're to get her cleaned up."

She nodded and winked. She smiled knowingly and her mouth disappeared into the folds of her chin. "Ah, I see. She's to be his enter-tainment, then, is she?"

"Entertainment?" Valerie took a step forward. "What are you talking about?"

"I don't think so," Julius replied. "Gravia is coming over tonight. I think it's like you said. He just felt sorry for her." He turned and left the room.

Valerie swallowed hard and wiped the sweat from her brow. So, he just felt sorry for her. That explained why he made her a gift of her clothes and why he was allowing her to ask questions. She shook her head. Had she really expected to be treated differently by a man who had just bought her? After all, she was no longer the genteel daughter of a gentleman.

I'm now a slave.

Well, it didn't matter, she told herself. She wouldn't be here long enough to worry over it. She would escape as soon as she could. Carefully, she composed her expression into one she hoped would convey calm acceptance and servitude.

"If you would show me to the bath, I would like to get myself washed. Then, if you like, I'll help you prepare the evening meal." Valerie's mind raced, wishing she could retract that last statement. Why had she said it? There must have been something else she could have offered to do. For heaven's sake, she hadn't the faintest idea how to cook anything. Mae always took care of that.

"What exactly do you know how to cook?" Stella asked. It was as if she had read Valerie's thoughts.

Valerie took a deep breath. *Better to be honest than to be proven a liar,* Papa always told her. "Well, you see, I've never actually assembled a dinner. But I'm a fast learner," she added quickly.

Stella sighed and, with a plump hand, fanned herself. "I can't say I'm surprised. What's your name, girl?"

"Valerie. Valerie Sherwood Brooks."

"Never heard a name like that before. Of course, I never heard a voice like yours either." She looked at her. "Where you from?"

"England. I mean, Britannia," she corrected herself.

"Britannia? Never heard of it." Stella lumbered over to the sink and pumped some water into a glazed terra cotta basin painted with wildflowers, the only adornment in the room. She washed her hands and dried them on her white apron. She turned her attention back to Valerie. "All right. I'll give you a chance. But I'm warning you. Let me down just once and I'll see to it you're sent to the vineyards. As far as I'm concerned, it makes no difference to me if you rot in here or out there, in the dirt."

Valerie thought of the woman she had seen lying in the slave stall, crying because she was going to be sent out to farm. She straightened her back. "I assure you, there is no need to be concerned."

Stella shook her head. "We will see. We will see."

CHAPTER NINETEEN

"Clarus!" Stella called out through the back window. "Come here, girl!"

A thin, tow-headed child about nine or ten years old peeked into the room from the kitchen courtyard. She clutched a bunch of lettuce leaves to her breast, squeezing them tightly. "Yes?" she asked, her voice barely a whisper.

"Take this new slave to the bath and make her presentable."

Stella glanced at Valerie and wrinkled her nose.

"And find her something more appropriate to wear. She'll distract everybody trying to keep covered up with that length of cloth."

Clarus dropped the lettuce and fell to her knees, wringing her hands in front of her. "Oh, please, isn't there someone else who can do this?" She raised her eyes to Valerie, then quickly looked away. "She's a witch!"

Valerie sighed and shook her head. "I am not a witch."

Stella stared hard at her. "Keep quiet, you. It makes no difference to me what you are. The master brought you into this house and that's all we need to be concerned with." She drew herself up and shook a finger at Valerie. "But don't even think about practicing your black arts in my kitchen. I find one evil herb here and I won't be held responsible for my actions. I run a good kitchen and I won't have you spoiling it."

"I assure you I haven't the faintest idea what it is you're talking about." Valerie put her hand on her hip and stared back at Stella.

Having spoken her piece, Stella turned her attention back to Clarus. She raised an arm and, before the girl could react, cuffed her on the ear. The child listed to the side, whimpering.

"How could you?" Valerie took a step forward, but Stella stepped in front of her, keeping her eyes on Clarus.

"Now, girl, you will do as you are told with no argument. Is that understood?"

Clarus nodded as tears ran down her cheeks. "I–I'm sorry." She unfolded her gangly legs and stood, unsteady as a newborn colt. Walking past Valerie, she hesitated for only a moment before speaking. "Follow me."

As the pair left the kitchen, Clarus had to fight the urge to turn and stare at the strange woman everyone called a witch. She wished for a moment she had eyes in the back of her head, so she could watch the witch more closely. She shrugged. Nature had not deemed it necessary to her survival. Perhaps if she were more like Athena's wise old owl, she could turn her head all the way around. Yes, she decided, that would work very well.

Oh, why did she have to be the one to tend to the woman? The other servants had warned her about witches and their evil spells. Clarus shook at the very thought of getting close to her. Why couldn't Stella have listened to her for once? Of course, why should today have been any different? No one paid much attention to anything she said.

Clarus, deep in her thoughts, quietly led the woman called Valerie down the long corridor to the back atrium where the house's private bathing area was located.

"Where exactly are you taking me?" Valerie asked, breaking into the Clarus's musings. "Are we going to the Forum?"

"Of course, not." She cast a quick glance over her shoulder. The walking stick was doing just that – helping the witch to walk. At least she wasn't trying to cast a spell. She let her breath out slowly. "Master Christos likes his slaves to keep themselves presentable. Where else would I be taking you but to the bath?"

"But we aren't going outside," Valerie said. "I thought the Roman bath houses were all located in the central part of the city."

Clarus turned around and continued to walk backward. She sighed and threw her hands up, much the same as she had seen Stella do on many an occasion. Didn't this woman know anything? "Master Christos is very wealthy. He doesn't need to go to the public baths. He has one right here, in the house."

"I see," Valerie answered as Clarus spun on her heel and faced forward again.

VALERIE FELT a warm breeze brush against her cheek as they approached the bath. She finally found its source at the end of the passageway, enclosed in a peristyle garden. Here, the construction of the atrium was similar to the front one. Decorative downspouts were located to spew forth rainwater for collection in a well.

"See that small tub in the corner over there?" Clarus asked, pointing. "That one's for the servants. We're only allowed to bathe early in the morning and we can never enter if the Master is in here. Master and his guests use the large tub over there."

"And his guests?" The image of the petite blonde woman crept into Valerie's mind. "Male and – and female?"

"Of course." Clarus turned around. "There is nothing wrong with washing together. Besides," she shrugged, "it saves water during the dry months."

Valerie shook her head. This concept was not new to her and she really shouldn't be in the least bit shocked. In her studies, she had learned that the ancient Romans often shared their bathing rituals with friends and family.

Clarus shifted from foot to foot

"What is it?" Valerie asked, sensing the girl's distress.

"Is it true? Are you really a witch? Will you cast a spell and turn me into a snake if you don't like me?" the girl asked, the questions rushing out of her.

Valerie considered the girl. The poor child looked like a frightened rabbit. "Of course, it isn't true. I'm not a witch, nor do I know how to turn young girls into snakes."

"You don't?"

Valerie chuckled, the sound echoing off the columns. She cupped the girl's shoulders. She wasn't much taller than dear Reggie. "I promise."

Clarus smiled, soothed by Valerie's words. "Please sit here and I'll help you."

Valerie sat on a marble bench near the servant's area. The girl knelt and removed the leather shoes. "I've never seen foot coverings like these before. We'll have to get you some sandals."

"Sandals do sound more practical, but I'm not certain they'll work well with my foot." Valerie crossed her left leg over the right. "See. I don't think I'd be able to keep them on."

"Maybe not. It will depend on the lacings," Clarus said as she helped Valerie out of her stockings. The young girl winced in sympathy at Valerie's gasps as the thin fabric pulled away from where it was stuck to the sores. "I'll ask Stella for some ointment for your legs. They don't look too good where the chains were rubbing against them. Maybe she'll know of someone who can help your foot, also."

"It was damaged when I was very young. There's really nothing that can be done for it. But thank you anyway." Valerie smiled gratefully. "You're quite smart for your age." She watched the tow-headed girl for a moment. "How old are you?"

"I'll soon be eleven." She leaned toward Valerie. "And someday I'm going to marry Master Christos." She sighed. "He is so handsome and kind."

"Does he know of your plans?" Valerie asked, suppressing a smile. The girl was so serious, she didn't want her to think she was making fun of her.

"Well, no. It would not do for a master to marry his slave. But someday, I will buy my freedom. Then I will surprise him with a wedding."

"I see." Valerie tucked a lock of the girl's hair behind her ear. "Has the master ever been married?"

Clarus nodded. "Yes, but his wife died while trying to birth their son. I will be very strong and will bear him many sons without dying. You won't tell, will you?"

Valerie felt a pang of sadness. How terrible to have lost both a wife and a child at the same time. "You don't need to worry, I'll keep your marriage plans a secret."

Clarus smiled, then began humming a simple tune as she helped Valerie out of the sack cloth.

"You get in the bath and I'll get the ointment and some clean clothes," Clarus bade.

Valerie watched as the child left, and then lowered herself into the water. She was surprised to find it was very warm. She leaned over the side and saw where lead pipes were plumbed into the tub itself. Running heated water? In ancient Rome? Most English houses didn't even have such a luxury. Valerie shook her head and eased back with a sigh, allowing the stiffness to soak out of her muscles.

THE TINKLE of a woman's sweet laughter tickled Christos's ears. Following the melodious sound, he leaned over the balcony and peered into the atrium below. Just off to the side, he could see the woman he had bought today. He smiled as dear little Clarus helped her out of her clothing. But his smile quickly faded as the dusky light of evening brushed the woman's form. It touched her full breasts and caressed her buttocks when she turned. He felt a stirring as he watched her settle into the water, her shimmery chestnut hair spreading out around her. Maybe she really was a witch after all.

"Gravia has arrived, Christos."

"Hmmm? Did you say something, Julius?" Christos asked absently, his eyes never leaving Valerie.

Julius looked below and chuckled. "Looks like she's cleaning up quite well," he commented.

"Quite well, indeed." He shook himself free from his thoughts. "I'll meet Gravia in my room. Have the girl bring up our dinner."

"Do you think that's wise? You know how jealous Gravia can be."

Christos smiled crookedly and winked. "I know."

"Now, see if you can balance this tray with one hand." Stella placed the bronze serving platter on Valerie's outstretched hand.

Next, she piled on some bread, honey, and two golden goblets of warm wine. "Can you manage this?"

Valerie took first one tentative step, then another. "I think so."

"All right, then. Go out this doorway and into the atrium. You'll see the stairs. The master's bedroom is upstairs and at the far end of the corridor, near the bath."

Valerie made her way to the stair, then paused, trying to decide exactly how she was going to manage to climb it with cane and tray in hand. Just then, Clarus ran up beside her. "Give me the tray."

"Thank you, Clarus," Valerie said as she handed over the tray. She followed the girl as she made her way to the second story. Once they reached the floor, Clarus handed the tray back to Valerie.

"Don't tell anyone I helped you. I'm not supposed to."

"Why not?"

Clarus shrugged. "We're only to tend to our own tasks, not the tasks of the other servants as well. But I've decided I like you. If you need me, just let me know and I'll see what I can do."

"I appreciate everything you've already done for me," Valerie said. She smiled at the girl and thanked her again for tending her cuts and bruises after the bath. And how, so gently, she had worked the tangles out of her long hair with a wide toothed comb, then braided it for her. "If ever there's anything I can help you with, please ask as well."

Clarus nodded, then scampered back down the stairs.

Valerie walked the remaining distance to the end of the corridor, balancing the tray with one hand and balancing herself with the cane. Glancing over the handrail, she noticed the bathing area was in full view.

Was it possible Christos had seen her?

A woman's laughter broke into her thoughts. Shaking off her musings, she lifted her cane and tapped on the door.

"Enter," the woman called out.

Valerie walked in, careful to keep her eyes lowered as Stella had instructed. She might not like being a slave, but it would be foolish to disobey. She could not afford any more ill treatment. If she was beaten, she would not be able to escape. "Where would you like me to put the tray?"

"Look at me," Christos bade.

Valerie raised her eyes to meet his. The desire she saw in the dark depths completely disarmed her. Never had a man looked at her so. Not even Thomas before he found out the truth about her foot. Thinking of Thomas sobered her. He had called her undesirable. She wasn't appealing to a modern man, so why had the foolish idea so suddenly entered her mind that this man from ancient Pompeii might find her so?

"I'm pleased to see I was right about you. Your appearance has vastly improved now the grime has been scrubbed away," Christos commented.

Her cheeks grew hot as his eyes moved over her body. With cane in hand, she awkwardly tugged at the side of her tunic.

"Put the tray down next to the bed." Gravia gestured imperially with one hand from where she lay on a couch next to Christos.

Christos rose and took the tray from Valerie. She pulled her eyes away from his and ventured a look around the room. Up a few steps and near the center of the expanse was a large bed, carved of ebony, and covered with multi-colored striped bedding. Sheer white silk draped around the bed partially concealing the flicker of the oil lamps positioned near the headboard. She felt her cheeks grow even hotter as she scanned the painted images on the walls of nude men and women engaged in all manner of private activities.

"What is that you're wearing?" Christos asked.

"Is there something wrong with it?" She glanced down at the flowing white fabric. "It's the clothing I was given."

"Slaves aren't supposed to wear long *stolas*, just short ones. Someone may mistake you for a free woman. Clarus didn't forget to tell you, did she?"

Valerie frowned, remembering how she had been shown to dress by Clarus. She was supposed to wrap a short *stola* around her so that everything below her thighs would remain bare. The girl wasn't the least bit happy when Valerie had asked for additional pieces of fabric, insisting on covering herself completely. She hoped she hadn't gotten the child in trouble.

"I'm sorry. It's my fault. I insisted on dressing like this. In my time —I mean country—women don't walk around with bare legs."

"Have them both beaten," Gravia huffed. "I will tell you, Christos, these slaves of yours are much too impertinent. You must starve them for a while, then take the whip to their backs. They will be much more obedient."

"Oh?" he asked, an eyebrow raised. "Is that how I should treat *you* then, my dear? Will you mind me better if I have a whip in hand?"

"Perhaps," Gravia answered as she rose slowly. She moved to where Christos stood and rubbed her body against his. She shimmied up and down, spreading her legs and running one hand along her inner thigh. "We shall have to try it sometime." She grabbed Christos head and pulled it down to hers.

Valerie took a step back as Gravia's tongue flitted in and out, licking Christos's mouth. Christos glanced in Valerie's direction. He sighed, pulling away from Gravia. "You haven't yet told me your name. What are you called?"

Valerie cleared her throat. "V–Valerie."

"Valerie," he whispered as his hands cupped Gravia's buttocks, forcing her against him.

Gravia moved away from Christos's embrace and unfastened her gown. Letting it drop to the ground, she revealed her nakedness. Valerie's head swam. She shifted nervously. My God, didn't these people care that she was standing right here? "Please, may I leave now?" she whispered.

Gravia returned to Christos. "Send her away. I want you to myself tonight."

Christos walked away from Gravia and toward Valerie. He grabbed her long braid and pulled her to him. "Please, let me go," Valerie pleaded. Was he going to rape her, here and now, in front of this woman?

He ignored her plea. "You do know you're mine, don't you, Valerie?" Christos lowered his mouth near hers and she was filled with the same feeling of anticipation she had felt earlier with Thomas. "I own you."

She put a hand on his chest, knowing she should fight him. But, for one fleeting instant, she wondered what it would be like to be kissed as she had seen him kiss Gravia—with so much passion.

Christos took advantage of her hesitation and his lips met hers. Slowly, he caressed her mouth with his warm, moist kisses. Valerie tingled where his hands moved over her arms, brushing them softly with his fingertips. His kiss grew more urgent and he forced her lips apart. Just as Valerie had seen Gravia do, Christos now licked her, pushing his tongue into her mouth. The warmth of it filled her and she leaned against him, wantonly answering his need with her own. What was this passion he was bringing to life within her? How could she feel so strongly about someone she had only just met? Someone who now owned her. Why, it was positively decadent.

She opened her eyes slightly and found Christos staring into hers, his half-closed with passion.

"Christos!" Gravia called from where she stood. "I'm growing cold, if you follow my meaning."

Christos raised his head and sighed. "I'm coming." He looked down at Valerie and caressed her cheek with the back of his hand. "Would you like to join us, little Valerie."

Valerie's eyes flew wide open. "J–join you?" she repeated. "Wh–what do you mean? I'm afraid I don't understand."

Gravia laughed bitterly. "She's a stupid crippled child and I don't want her ugly form in my bed. Send her away."

Christos tensed. "Perhaps I should send *you* away, Gravia," he growled. "Your evil tongue wears on my nerves."

Valerie wrenched herself free from Christos's embrace, an angry flush covering her face. Stupid child, indeed. Valerie limped out into the hallway and slammed the door behind her, not wanting to hear anything else the woman may have to say.

For heaven's sake, what was becoming of her? She had been here only a short time, and had already forgotten her morals. She paused at the atrium railing for a brief moment to steady the fast beat of her heart. Heaven help her, but part of her wanted this Christos to chase her down, stop her from leaving him. She wanted him to take her into his arms, send Gravia away, and finish what he had begun…

She wiped roughly at her tears with the back of her hand. She should be angry and disgusted, not desirous of a man she had only just met, a man who had purchased her at a slave market.

I must avoid him as much as possible.

That was the only way to keep safe.

She made her way back down to the kitchen, haunted by the sound of Gravia's laughter as it echoed through the atrium.

CHRISTOS SAT AT HIS DESK, unable to keep his thoughts focused on the household books. How many days had it been since he'd brought the woman from his dreams into this home? Four days? Five? He shook his head. He was usually better at keeping track of such things.

Witch or no, she has bewitched me for certain.

The scent of garlic and onion reached him, and his mouth watered. Christos made his way down to the kitchen and paused in the doorway. There she was, her back to him, washing dishes at the sink. He paused and took in her shape, her slender curves. As if she felt the scrutiny, she turned around.

"Oh my," Valerie said, hand to her heart. "You almost scared the life out of me."

He chuckled. "Apologies."

"No need." She dried her hands and lifted the heavy lid from the pot on the stove, picked up a large wooden spoon, and started stirring. The movement magnified the delicious aroma. "Hmmm. I wonder if this is what brought you to the kitchen?" Her eyes twinkled.

"If you would be so kind, I fear I'll perish from hunger if I don't have a bowl of whatever that is."

"Laundry." Valerie stared at him. "It's laundry."

"Excuse me...?"

She laughed and the sound filled the room. "I'm teasing you. Of course, I'll fill you a bowl."

He scanned her body as she worked. The bruises were fading and her ankles were healing nicely. "I was concerned for a moment that the household linens had set my mouth watering. I feared I'd be forced to figure out how to make them into small enough pieces to chew."

Valerie handed him the food. He stared at her.

"What?"

"I'm grateful you're healing. In truth, I was concerned whether or not you'd recover. Physically and mentally."

"Well, we Britannians are made of stronger stuff than you Pompeians can throw at us."

He took a bite of the thick stew. "Oh, this is good."

"I'm glad you like it. It's the first thing Stella has allowed me to cook on my own."

"Where is our Stella? Is she treating you well?"

"She's at the market. As far as treatment, she hasn't hit me, though she often threatens to." Valerie shrugged. "I can't imagine she could do any worse than I've already experienced, so I don't worry about it so much."

Christos leaned in conspiratorially. "Tell her I said this, and I'll deny it, but she's mostly all show. Just don't get on her bad side. She does have a temper."

"So, I've seen with Clarus and some of the field slaves."

"Ah, our little Clarus. She's taken a liking to you, I've noticed."

Valerie smiled warmly. "She's a good girl. Reminds me of my little brother..." Tears misted her eyes. "Back home."

He touched her cheek, his thumb brushing away a tear. His heart was near to bursting with sadness for this one; everything she'd suffered, including the loss of her family.

I will keep her safe.

"Your stew," she said softly.

"Hmm?" He was tempted to kiss her—not like that first kiss with Gravia watching—he should not have done that—he wanted to kiss her with tender passion. Valerie was different from the other women he knew. She was his slave and yet he could not get her out of his mind nor out of his dreams.

"Y-your stew is getting cold." She stepped back the color high on her cheeks only made her more appealing. "You should eat and I should get back to work."

"You do know I'm in charge, right?"

"You just like to think you are, Master Christos." Stella walked into the room, Clarus behind her with her arms loaded with their purchases. "We all know this is my kitchen and I'm the boss here."

Christos laughed. "You are one impertinent slave, Stella." He patted her shoulder. "If you hadn't raised me since I was a boy, I'd put you out into the fields for certain."

Stella laughed. "And it's much appreciated." She turned to Valerie and Clarus. "You two, put this food away and start getting ready for the evening meal. She took the bowl out of Christos's hand and wagged a finger at him. "You'll ruin your dinner. Now off with you."

He glanced at Valerie. She had her hand over her mouth, but he could see the smile she was trying to hide. It was good to see that.

I was grieved to think she might never smile again.

"Until dinner then." He bowed with a flourish and left the room, but not before his eyes met hers one more time.

CHAPTER TWENTY

Valerie rose earlier than usual, before the other servants. She quietly made her way to the bath, her bare feet lightly padding against the tile floor. Here, she hoped to have a moment to collect her thoughts before the day began.

Three weeks had passed and still she had no clue as to how she could return home. If only she knew what the catalyst was that launched her back in time? Perhaps she could figure out how to replicate it. Even if she did find the key, she still needed to escape the house, but Stella and Julius rarely let her out of their sight, let alone allowed her to go outside.

Not to mention, Christos baffled her. He was kind to her and greeted her warmly each morning and bid her a good night each evening, but she sensed an unleashed tension in him. Something she could not fathom nor define.

She served his meals and he was polite, even smiling at her. He asked how she had fared and when she told him, he nodded. Luckily, since that first night, Gravia had not returned. She didn't dare ask Stella or Julius why, and she certainly wasn't going to ask Christos.

Just stay away from him as much as possible.

Easier said than done, even when she wasn't around him, she couldn't stop herself from thinking about his smile, or his ebony eyes, or how he ran his fingers through his dark, curly hair when he was distracted…

Reaching the bath, Valerie placed her tunic for the day on a stone bench next to the tub. She had conceded to wearing the shorter garment in order to avoid further confrontations with Christos. And she was amazed at the newfound freedom the clothing afforded. With no corset or crinoline to bind her, she could move with a grace and ease she had never known.

Valerie shrugged off her robe and let it drop to the floor. She lowered herself into the tepid water and, with a sigh, leaned back and closed her eyes.

In her mind's eye, she saw Mama and Papa having their morning tea and biscuits with strawberry jam. Every morning, it was the same. She smiled to herself, remembering the day Reggie had discovered her romance novel. Mama was so cross at first…

It seemed like a lifetime ago, and she knew deep down that it truly was. But she was determined to return to her time again, no matter the risk.

She half-dozed in the warm, soothing waters of the bath, her thoughts lazily floating to Christos. "Do not forget that I own you now," he had told her almost every day since her arrival. He was arrogant, but she couldn't deny there was something in his arrogance that spoke of self-assuredness rather than conceit.

She squirmed. Thank heaven he hadn't tried to kiss her after that first night with Gravia. The man completely unnerved her. There were times when she was gathering herbs in the garden, or washing the kitchen floor, she would sense his presence. Those dark eyes on her. Watching her…

What did he hope to discover? That she could still do her job despite the fact she was lame? No, it was more likely he wanted her unsettled. Whenever her eyes met his—she *did* feel unsettled…One moment he was kind when their paths crossed; another, he was distant, his mind obviously some place else.

Absently, Valerie touched her lips. That one kiss had sent fire racing through her veins with such intensity—a feeling she had never experienced—certainly not with Thomas.

She shifted in the bath, her legs restless, a tingling began to flutter in her core.

Here I go, feeling unsettled again.

"*Salve*, Valerie," a deep masculine voice called out softly.

Valerie's eyes flew open. She instinctively crossed her arms over her breasts. Christos stood at the foot of her bath. "How can you still be modest?" he chided. "Put your arms down. I would see again that which you guard so mightily."

She shook her head. "It isn't right."

"Ah, now, what isn't right about the human body? What evil lies there we should hide it away in the darkness and behind our hands and arms?" Without making a sound, he stepped closer to the tub and sat down behind her. Lazily, he let a hand drop, lightly fanning the water with his fingers. "You've been avoiding me, haven't you?"

"I'm afraid you overestimate yourself, sir." She shifted nervously. "I believe you know I've been busy in the kitchen with Stella, learning my duties." But even as she spoke, she sensed he knew she was lying. He was handsome, this master of hers, with his thick curly hair and flashing dark eyes. She feared greatly the emotions he had awakened in her. She feared even more what her response to him would be if he took her in his arms again.

"Julius tells me you don't like to be ordered about. That you act like a regal queen when he tells you to do something," Christos commented, his voice casual.

"Please know that I'm trying very hard to do as I'm asked. But some of the things he orders me to do are beyond reason."

"I seek no explanation. I can see you're not used to this work or station in life." He reached across her shoulder and lifted her hand, examining the palm and fingers. "See? There are no calluses or scars to show you have labored in the past."

"I won't deny what you say." Valerie pulled her hand away and pulled her knees up to her chest.

"You were gently bred for finer things, weren't you? Like love, perhaps? I could order you to come to me, you know. But I am a man who prefers his women to come willingly with their arms open wide." He raised his hand and let warm drops slide down Valerie's spine. She shivered despite the heat of the water. "Tell me, Valerie, were you married in your native land?"

"No," she answered. "Why do you ask?"

"I didn't think you were, especially since no one claimed you from the jail." He lightly touched the back of Valerie's neck. Long tendrils of her hair fell from where they were piled on top of her head, and he twisted them around his finger.

"Would it make a difference? Would I still be your slave?" Valerie held her breath, waiting for his answer. If she could somehow recant her story, maybe he would let her go.

"Of course, you would. I bought you in a legitimate transaction. I only sought to make certain there would be no jealous husband coming to hunt you – or me – down."

Valerie's spirit fell. It didn't matter to him whether or not she was married. Christos let his hand drop back into the water again. She peeked at him out of the corner of her eye as he took a bottle of scented oil from the ledge and poured it into his hands.

"I understand from the other servants that you were married once," she said. She knew it was none of her business, but she could think of nothing else to say. Christos's presence was maddening. Why didn't he go away?

He raised an eyebrow. "Do you now? What else have they been gossiping about?"

"N-nothing, really. I–I'm very sorry about what happened to your wife and child."

"They both died, but the child was not mine."

Valerie looked over her shoulder. "I'm so sorry. I didn't know."

"Well, you must have been the only one in all of the empire who didn't. Five years ago, I was away on campaign – in your Britannia. Segis took a lover, became pregnant, and died in childbirth before I returned." He slipped the glass stopper on the oil bottle and put it down. "The gods are ironic in their justice."

"And you've never remarried?"

"I need no more pain in my life."

Christos answered far too quickly. After all those years, his voice still carried hurt and bitterness. Some instinct deep inside her stirred, and she wrestled with the urge to reach out to him.

"So, tell me, Valerie, how do you like being here so far? Is it as bad as you imagined?"

She cleared her throat, acutely aware of how his hands were now massaging her shoulders and working the scented oil into her skin.

"You've a pleasant house and, from what I've seen, you treat your servants well. But I'd still prefer to be home."

"Home? This *is* your home."

"No, this is your home. As I told you before, mine is far away from here." She looked up into the brightening sky. "As far away as the moon and stars."

"I would not have guessed a poet's heart beat in your breast." Christos leaned forward, and his lips brushed against her ear. "You are like a flower, dear Valerie. Open up to me. Let me sample your sweet nectar."

Without even realizing it, Valerie leaned into his kiss as his mouth moved over her jaw and down her neck. Slowly, his hands slid past her shoulders and forced her arms away. He cupped her breasts, lifting and kneading them. His touch sent pleasurable waves through her body as he teased her into responding.

"You cannot deny me, Valerie. Remember, I own you."

Valerie jerked free from his embrace. "How could I forget? After all, you see fit to remind me at every turn." She grabbed her robe and, standing, yanked it on.

Christos's expression grew dark and forbidding. He rose and laughed harshly. "You like this little game we play, don't you? You pretend to be the virgin and me, the satyr. Tell me something. When you sacrifice yourself to me, will you enjoy it as much as I will?"

Valerie rubbed her temples, the aggravating tension of their encounter growing within her. What did he mean 'pretend?' "What are you talking about? Didn't you say you wouldn't force yourself on me?"

"I won't have to. You were made for the pleasures of the flesh. Can you deny this?" He shook his head. "The way you lean into me so freely when I touch you –your body yearns for the enjoyment I can give." He ran a wet finger down the side of her cheek and whispered, "Perhaps you should pay attention."

"Never!" Valerie thumped her cane on the floor. At the same moment, a low tremor shook the room.

Another earthquake!

Frantically, she glanced about. A heavy clay vase tumbled from its pedestal and crashed to the floor.

"Come with me." Christos scooped her into his arms and rushed out into the open garden, away from the structure of the house. He held her tightly against his chest. Then, just as quickly as it had begun, the rumble subsided. He let her slide out of his arms and took a step backward, his eyes never leaving her form. "How did you do that?"

"I didn't do anything," Valerie answered as she straightened her robe with shaky hands.

He shook her, sending her hair tumbling down her back. "This walking stick of yours. You hit it against the floor, then the earthquake came. What magic is this?"

"It's not magic, I tell you." Valerie pulled away from him. Then, a sudden shattering thought lanced through her.

My God. Have I been transported to ancient Pompeii only to meet my death?

"Tell me, please, what day and month is it?"

"Augustus. I believe it's around the third day." Christos looked at her closely.

Valerie's eyes grew wide. "What year?"

Christos regarded her with confusion.

"I mean, who is the emperor and how far are you into his reign?"

"Titus is emperor. His rule has only just begun." He ran a hand through his hair and his eyes narrowed. "What are you about, woman? Tell me what you know."

Valerie quickly calculated what year she was in. "In three weeks' time, Vesuvius will destroy Pompeii," she choked out.

"How can you make this claim? Do you have the gift of sight?"

"No." Valerie shook her head. She turned around and studied the hunting scene painted on the wall. Several tall cypress trees were planted on either side of it and a vine of ivy was beginning to creep up and over the artwork. Could she convince him of the coming eruption without giving herself away? What would he do with her if he knew her secret? She ran a hand through her hair and leaned wearily against her cane.

"I'm a student of history." She took a deep breath. "Particularly Roman and Greek history."

"But what you're saying about Vesuvius, if it's true, is part of the future. It hasn't happened yet." Christos turned Valerie around and forced her to look at him.

"I know this sounds incredible and far-fetched, but you must believe me." Her eyes met his.

Christos rubbed his forehead and smiled slightly. "You know, it was those green eyes of yours that caught my attention when the people dragged you through the streets… Those same emerald jewels that haunted my dreams before you ever appeared before me in the flesh."

He leaned forward, and she was burned by the intensity of his gaze. "If you say you can predict the future, then you must truly be a witch."

Valerie pulled away from him, her head swimming, her breath coming faster at the sensual intensity in his gaze.

I haunted his dreams?

She shook off her desire to explore his admission and focused on the earthquake. Christos obviously didn't believe her, so why did he insist on perpetuating this idea when she had so resolutely denied it? She had to laugh. A witch? Well, why not? She bowed before him. "Yes, my lord Christos Campanius Marcellus, you've guessed my innermost secret. I *am* a witch and I can control the elements." Her eyes narrowed. "I can control you, if I so choose."

It was Christos's turn to laugh. "Show me."

Valerie hesitated for a moment. Did she dare? She took a step forward and dropped her cane. Lacing her arms around his neck, she pulled his face close to hers. She brushed against him as she had seen Gravia do. "Kiss me," she bade, her voice low and seductive.

Christos gathered her into his arms and pulled her tightly to his body. With a groan, his mouth melded with hers. "Ah, sweet, sweet, Valerie." His hands moved in a heavy caress down her sides and over her buttocks. He pushed against her and his hardness pressed into her through the toga he wore.

Hekate's prophecy flashed through Valerie's mind…

You must travel to find your love. Travel through the mists.

Could Christos be that man?

I'm being foolish.

To him she was only a slave, personal property. Her mind raced and, suddenly fearful, Valerie pulled away from Christos.

He looked at her, askance.

"Did I not say I could control you?" she whispered, her voice shaky.

Christos smiled crookedly. He ran a hand along her bare arm. She shivered in response to his touch. "Tell me truthfully, witch. Who controls whom?"

CHAPTER TWENTY-ONE

"Take the master his midday meal and be quick about it," Stella ordered. She slowly moved her bulk to a small stool and Valerie was amazed it didn't give way under her weight.

"When you get back, we'll need to go to the market." She stopped talking for a moment, catching her breath. "We must finalize the selections for tomorrow night's banquet."

Valerie nodded, biting her tongue to keep from crying out in joy. They were going to the market! Finally, she was going to be let out of this house. If she were lucky, she might even find a chance to escape.

Her heart tugged at the thought of leaving Christos and sweet Clarus. What would become of them? She needed to convince them to leave Pompeii, to save themselves. But she could not go with them.

I need to get home.

She couldn't stay in the past, especially with a man who only saw her as his property and not as a woman.

I certainly can't stay when the entire city is bound for destruction in less than three weeks.

Valerie arranged a hunk of fresh bread, goat cheese, and a carafe of warm wine on a bronze tray. She looked closer, then realized it was the same tray she had carried to Christos's room her first night there. She grinned as she pictured whacking the same tray over the head of a certain dark blonde-haired woman.

"What are you smiling about over there?" Stella asked, her voice sending Valerie's mental image scattering.

"Oh, nothing really." Valerie hoisted the tray up to rest on her shoulder. "I was just thinking, that's all."

"Well, stop it!" Stella stared hard at her. "You don't fool me, you know. You think you're too good for this work. I've seen your hands. They've never done a hard day's labor."

Valerie carefully placed the tray down on the table. With deliberate movements, she pulled a stool up opposite Stella. Their eyes locked. "I've never lied to you, Stella. I came from a wealthy family where we had our own servants. I told you my first day here I didn't know how to prepare a meal, but I am trying."

"Trying to make your way right into the master's bed, as near as I can tell." Stella laughed and her whole body shook, the stool creaking in protest with the motion.

"Please understand, Stella, that I have no argument with you, and I'd prefer to keep it that way." Valerie stood and placed the tray on her shoulder once again.

Stella grabbed her by the wrist just as she was picking up her cane. Valerie stared down at the woman's hand, then wrenched her arm free from her grip. Her voice was low as she spoke. "Don't touch me again, Stella." Valerie grabbed her cane, then turned to leave the kitchen.

"I've seen it before," Stella called after her, shaking her head. "He buys a pretty young thing like yourself, uses her for his pleasure, then sells her off."

Valerie followed the sound of clanking metal out into the back atrium. She was surprised to find a pair of heavy wooden doors ajar, revealing a small workshop. As she approached, the hammering stopped. She found Christos bent over a hot fire built in a heavy stone container. Beads of sweat ran down the sides of his face as he held a sheet of gold in the flames. She put the tray down on a nearby marble bench, and approached him. "What are you doing?" she asked, fascinated.

"Working," he answered as the metal turned a glowing molten red. At the exact moment it threatened to turn to liquid, he dropped the hot sheet over a wooden mold. Valerie watched, captivated, as the gold formed itself around the carving, creating a woman's image.

Christos put down the heavy iron tongs he had been holding and sat down next to the tray of food. "Simple fare for a working man," he commented as his gaze swept over the bread and cheese.

Valerie shrugged. "Stella said you weren't to fill yourself up today.

She said you needed to save your stomach for tomorrow night's feast." She leaned over the jeweler's bench and explored its contents with her eyes. Vials of colored powder, faceted and cabochon stones, gold, silver, and copper covered the surface. She paused when she found a pair of pink tourmalines carved with delicate intaglios resting near the edge.

"Did you make these yourself?" she asked, running a finger gently over the concave surface.

"Yes, I did," he answered as he broke off a hunk of bread. "I thought a setting of granulated gold would display them nicely."

Next to the tourmalines Valerie found a golden serpent armband, its eyes glowing red with rubies.

"Go ahead. Try it on," Christos urged.

Without hesitating, Valerie slipped it over her hand, pushing it into place above her elbow. She held her arm out and admired the handiwork. He hadn't missed a detail in designing the piece, right down to the scales along the creature's back.

"It's beautiful. I saw one like it once at the museum in London."

Could it be the same one? Did our paths already cross?

Christos glanced up from his food. "I beg your pardon? Museum?"

"Did I say museum? What I meant was, my father once told me of one like it he had seen in dealing with traders." She slipped off the armband and placed it back on the workbench. Desperate to change the subject, she asked, "Is this how you support yourself? By creating jewelry?"

"Hardly." Christos laughed. "My family has been in Pompeii for generations and I inherited my wealth from my ancestors. The jeweler's art is more of a pastime, something I learned to do from an uncle when I was very young." He patted the bench where he sat. "Come, sit by me."

She didn't move, recalling their game of one-upmanship after the earthquake a few days ago. Who controls whom? Well, she would not be ordered about so easily by this man. "I'm quite comfortable standing, thank you."

"You're an obstinate one, aren't you?" he observed. "Whatever am I to do with you, dear Valerie? I'm trying to be patient with you. As I've said before, I know you're not used to this kind of life." He picked up the simple clay goblet and took a drink. "But you are still a slave in my house. And I am still the master. The sooner you accept this simple fact, the happier you'll be."

"I won't be happy until you set me free," she murmured.

Christos snorted. "And where would you go? You've forgotten too soon the good citizens' reactions to your presence." He leaned forward and rested his elbows on his knees. "Why else do you think you haven't been allowed outside of the house these past weeks?"

"You mean to say you've been protecting me?"

Christos smiled. "I wish you no harm. Surely you know that by now."

"No harm?" Valerie slowly walked over to him, a tight smile playing about her lips. "The same as you would wish no harm to come to, say – your house or furnishings?"

"Mmmm, I suppose you could put it that way," Christos answered, the hint of a question hanging in his tone.

Valerie leaned down and pointed a finger in Christos's surprised face. "To the bloody devil with you, *Master*. While you may consider my body to be one of your personal possessions, you'll never own my soul!"

She straightened and looked to the heavens. The sun was high in the sky and beat down on her face, heating it to the point where she felt consumed by a great fever. Valerie shook her head and returned her gaze to his. She remembered what Stella had said. "I actually feel sorry for you and your need to purchase women. You'll never know true love."

Christos rose slowly, his eyes were dark and threatening and never left Valerie's. "You don't know what you're talking about."

"Oh, I know only too well. I've known men like you. You seek only pleasure and the woman be damned."

Thomas' snide comments ran through her mind.

You're undesirable.

The words taunted her. "No wonder your wife took a lover." But even as the words tumbled out of her mouth, Valerie realized she had gone too far.

Christos grabbed her shoulders, digging his fingers into the tender flesh. "You need to learn to curb your tongue, woman." He spun Valerie around and ripped the back of her short tunic down the middle, exposing her bare skin. He untied the leather belt he wore and folded it in half. With a quick snap of his wrist, he cracked the belt loudly in the air.

Valerie cried out in surprise and struggled to get away from him. Christos grabbed her by the hair. "You will stay and receive your punishment!"

No matter what, she would not give him the satisfaction of hearing her beg. She twisted out of his grasp, with all the strength she had, the momentum causing her to stumble and fall.

She lay there for a moment, dazed, expecting to feel the sting of leather against her exposed back at any moment. Instead she felt strong hands lift her and help her sit on the bench.

"Please forgive me," he whispered. "I would never hurt you. I'm sorry. I'm so sorry."

Valerie's gaze met his and it shocked her to see the shimmer of tears in his eyes and something more —something she hadn't seen before — remorse. Was his arrogance merely a facade? What manner of man would she find beneath…?

No! He threatened to beat you.

She recalled Stella's warning that Valerie was only his latest conquest, that he would sell her when he was bored with her …

Valerie's chest constricted as she fought her inner turmoil, her compassion for this complex man from a different time who could make her feel such passion one moment and then anger the next.

She fought her instinct to offer comfort. She could not allow herself to be used so by this man, by any man. Yes, she might be his slave, but her feelings still belonged to her.

Besides, what would it change?

I need to escape, to find my way back to my own time…

Valerie leaned forward, resting her hands on her cane to steady herself. They looked at each other in silence for a moment.

"I'm sorry," he repeated, his voice a ragged whisper.

"Go to Hades." She straightened and went back inside.

CHAPTER TWENTY-TWO

"Hand me that bowl over there," Stella instructed.

Valerie absently picked up the clay bowl and passed it to Stella, the image of Christos and his tears still etched in her memory. The pain of his wife's betrayal had shone brightly in his eyes and she understood now it was Segis he'd wanted to lash out at and not her.

But did it really matter what she thought of him and he of her? They were from two different times—two different cultures. She was planning to escape in any case. Pompeii was on a path of destruction. She wouldn't allow herself to think about Christos and what would happen to him after that...

Valerie had started to let go of the bowl before the other woman had hold of it. She grabbed it just in time before it crashed to the ground.

"Pay attention to what you're about, girl, or I'll have Julius discipline you! Would you like that?" Stella shouted.

Valerie gave her a sullen look.

"I thought not. Now, put some wood in the fire before it goes out."

Stooping down, Valerie picked up a sizeable log and placed it inside the stone stove. She poked at the glowing embers with a long stick, sending flames up through the gravel covered top. A large pot of water sitting on an iron grate began to boil.

"Is there anything else you'd like me to do, Ma'am?" Valerie stressed the last word, heaping it with sarcasm. If she didn't escape this house soon, she would not be held accountable for her actions where Stella was concerned. The woman seemed to live for the chance to make Valerie's life a hell on earth. Emotionally drained after her encounter with Christos, she didn't have the patience to deal with the older woman.

Stella eyed her. "Hand me that box over there. And this time, try not to fumble." She shook her head. "You'll never make a kitchen maid, as clumsy as you are."

Valerie sighed and counted to ten. As she passed Stella the box, she smiled sweetly. "So, tell me, when are we leaving for the Forum?"

"Not for a while yet. We need to prepare a few items first," Stella explained.

She didn't dare ask. If she risked angering the cook anymore, or even acted as if she were anxious to leave, Stella might forbid her to go. "What are we going to cook first?"

"These." Stella dipped her hand into the small wooden box and extracted a brown mouse. Its nose twitched in fear as it wriggled in her fingers, trying to get away.

"Mice? You're going to cook mice?" Valerie gasped. "You can't be serious!" She reached for the creature, recalling all the dear little mice Reggie had collected. He had given each and every one of them a name and paperboard nest.

Stella pulled her hand away and, with one quick motion, broke its neck between her thumb and forefinger. She dropped it into the boiling water and grabbed another one.

"For heaven's sake, how could you do that?" Valerie's hand flew to her throat.

"What's the matter with you? Never had mice to eat?"

"Of course not!" Valerie was beside herself. "Who ever heard of eating mice, unless of course you happen to be a cat. Besides, I can't imagine there's even enough meat on them to bother with."

"Mice are a delicacy. We always serve them at dinner parties. It's a tradition with the Romans," Stella explained, her voice growing more and more impatient. "But I don't suppose you'd know that, would you?" She dropped another into the water.

Valerie knew she'd have to continue to adapt to her new environment until she could escape, but eat mice? She shuddered. *Not bloody likely.* "What do you do with the poor things after they're boiled?

Surely you don't eat the fur as well?" She raised her eyebrows in question.

"Of course, you don't eat the fur." Stella tossed the last of the mice into the hot water and wiped her hands on her apron. "They only cook for a moment, then you scoop them out. The fur will slip off nice and easy." She handed Valerie a small wood strainer with a handle attached. "Here, you try it."

Valerie shook her head, her stomach roiling. "I couldn't."

"You'll do as I ask, or will I have to call Julius." Stella hoisted herself onto her favorite stool and crossed her arms, her eyes fixed on Valerie. "I can't imagine you'd want a beating, but maybe you're one of those girls who like to be abused. I'm sure Julius would be quite accommodating."

Valerie didn't doubt for a minute Stella would bellow for help. If she had a run-in with Julius, he could forbid her from going to the market as well. And she might not have another opportunity to plan an escape route before the eruption. With a grimace, Valerie dipped the spoon into the pot and extracted one of the mice.

"I thought you might change your mind. Now, grab the fur back by the tail and give it a good tug." Stella smiled, obviously pleased.

Valerie closed her eyes, composing herself. When she opened them, she took a deep breath and lifted the mouse out of the spoon by its tail. She held it at arm's length and pulled the fur. She was surprised to find that it did indeed slip off easily, just as Stella had said it would. "Now can we go to the market?" Valerie asked, her stomach churning as she dropped the small pelt to the floor.

Stella laughed, obviously enjoying Valerie's discomfort. "Not until you finish." She handed Valerie a bowl of honey. "Now, dip it in here."

Still holding the creature by its tail, Valerie let it sink into the sticky amber liquid. As soon as it was completely covered, she pulled it out, letting the excess drip back into the bowl.

"Over here," Stella waved her hand.

Valerie took a step forward and stumbled, a wave of dizziness washing over her. She leaned on her cane. It was so unearthly hot in this kitchen. It felt like the room was closing in around her. Was there never a slight breeze to cool the day? "Haven't we tortured this poor creature enough? Surely there isn't anything else that can be done to it."

"Shows how much you know," Stella sniffed. "Here, roll it in these poppy seeds, then lay it out straight to dry."

Valerie swallowed hard, then rolled the honey-covered animal in the small seeds until it was barely discernible as a mouse. Next, she laid it out straight as an arrow on a tray.

"Good." Stella grinned so wide, it disappeared into her heavy jowls. "I'll be in the atrium preparing the benches. Come and get me when you're done, then we'll go to the marketplace."

Valerie watched as Stella left the room, her dress caught between the folds of sweaty flesh. A sudden impulse came over Valerie and she stuck her tongue out as far as she could in the direction the woman had just gone. She giggled. Poor Lucy would have surely been beside herself if she had witnessed Valerie pulling such a stunt. Reggie, on the other hand, would've enjoyed it quite immensely.

She wiped the sweat from her brow and peered into the kettle of boiling mice. The smell was hideous, like the pair of Reggie's moldy stockings Aunt Mabel had once found stuffed under the kitchen counter.

Valerie closed her eyes again and took a deep breath, steadying her nerves. She made another face, then went to work, praying her breakfast wouldn't erupt from her belly.

CHAPTER TWENTY-THREE

She could not stay with Christos. Not after their last encounter. Already her feelings for him were becoming too confounding, too maddening…

I have to leave. I have to get back to my own time.

Valerie followed Stella and Clarus outside. She looked first one way, then the other. The whitewashed buildings glowed brightly in the late morning sun and the accent colors of red, blue, and gold used on the doorways and trim seemed to vibrate against the starkness. The area surrounding Christos's house was fairly deserted and she relaxed a little. Perhaps no one would bother her today. Or, maybe curiosity seekers had all forgotten about her.

The trio stepped across the rocky street and the full force of the sun bore down on Valerie. She was thankful for the short gown, which allowed what little breeze there was to flow through the folds of the light fabric.

"What's that smell?" Clarus asked. She raised her nose in the air and sniffed.

"I don't smell anything," Stella answered, her reply curt. She waved a pudgy hand. "Keep walking. I want to finish up as fast as we can. We have a lot of work to do for tomorrow night."

"I think it smells like rotten eggs." Clarus sniffed again. "Yes, that's exactly what it smells like."

Valerie inhaled deeply. Clarus was right. A faint odor permeated the air. Only she recognized it from Master Hobbs' science experiments to be sulfur, not rotten eggs.

Valerie looked off into the distance. There, silhouetted against the azure blue sky, sat Vesuvius in all its glory. It wasn't flat and misshapen, like she had seen it in her own time. Here, in this time period before the eruption, the cone was fully developed into a full mountain peak. She squinted and could see a thin trickle of gray steam escaping through the top. Valerie raised her hand to wipe the sweat from her brow and it was shaking. She wiped her hand on her gown.

"What's the matter?" Clarus whispered beside her. "You look as if you've seen the dead come back to life."

"And so I have," Valerie murmured. She realized she had very little time before the volcano would release its fury on the unsuspecting city.

"What in Zeus' name are you two yammering about?" Stella huffed as she stopped to catch her breath.

"You wouldn't believe me if I told you." She looked down into Clarus' face and saw a flicker of fear in her large brown eyes. There was no need to alarm the child. She patted her on the head. "At least it smells better than boiling rodents. Don't you agree?"

Clarus smiled, nodding. "Most anything smells better than that!" With a hop and a skip, she ran off toward Stella.

Valerie hurried along to catch up with the pair, her cane making a hollow thumping sound against the stone pathway. "I was wondering, Stella," she called, "what will we prepare next? Earthworm stew?"

Stella drew herself up as they continued down the street. "I've heard enough complaining from the two of you. Behave yourselves or I'll have a talk with Julius. He'll straighten you both out."

The woman was constantly holding the threat of a beating over their heads.

How can people slip into cruelty so easily?

She thought of Christos and realized that in his case, his wife's betrayal had had a lasting impact.

I'm sorry…I would never hurt you.

She had to stop thinking of Christos and concentrate on escaping.

A small child ran past, giggling. Unconsciously, Valerie braced herself for an attack. The girl kept going, though, oblivious to her presence. She let down her guard a little and continued to watch the child for a moment. The girl's long black hair flew behind her, so wild and carefree.

Valerie sighed, reminded of all the summers spent with her family at her Grandmother's country home when she was young and still able to run. Before the accident, she had felt as free as a flying bird when she raced through the bright yellow and green meadows of the hills and through the purple beds of heather. She shook her head. She was being ridiculous again. None of that mattered now.

Lost in her thoughts, she didn't notice the dark shadow the sunlight cast on the wall behind her. It approached steadily, then lunged, jarring her with a sharp jab to her back. Valerie stumbled, grinding the tip of her cane into the dirt. Ready to defend herself, she turned around, expecting to find a threatening crowd. Instead, she found Julius.

"Just wanted to let you know you're not alone. In case you thought you'd be able to get away with anything."

"And, pray tell, what do you suppose I'd be trying to get away with?"

He studied his fingernails. "Mmmm, maybe escaping."

"And where did you get the idea I would even want to escape?" Valerie asked, feigning innocence. "Especially considering how well the Pompeiians have treated me." She turned to follow after Stella and Clarus. Julius grabbed her arm.

"Stella's right. You do think you're too good. I'm thinking you need to be taught a lesson." He raised a hand and Valerie steeled herself, ready to dodge, but he simply rubbed his chin.

She let her breath out slowly.

What am I turning into?

Every time a person came near, she expected some sort of attack. She needed to be strong if she were going to get herself out of this mess.

Taking a deep breath, she drew herself up. "What gives you, or anyone else for that matter, the right to judge what I need? I've had enough of you men and your little lessons." Valerie stared hard into Julius' eyes, exasperation filling her. "I'm not a schoolgirl who needs a nanny to make her behave." She waved her hand and started walking after Stella and Clarus. "Please. Why can't you just leave me alone?"

"Because I don't like you." He shook a meaty fist in the air. "You'll pray to the gods for mercy before I'm finished with you. I promise you that!" Just then, a wagon came speeding down the street. With a yell,

Julius jumped back and landed in the drainage ditch on the side of the road. Red-faced he got back up.

Clarus glanced over her shoulder at the commotion. Her eyes grew wide as Valerie caught up with her. "You're in trouble for sure. Look what happened to Julius."

Valerie turned around. She was certain Julius considered himself to be a great and noble warrior, but the sight of him wiping mule manure from his backside made her giggle. "Perhaps Sir Julius should be more careful where he sits."

"That's enough, you two," Stella interrupted. "Julius is a fine man and I won't listen to you making fun of him."

Clarus and Valerie glanced at each other and the child rolled her eyes. "I think Stella has feelings for Julius," Clarus whispered. "I've seen him climb the stairs to her loft many a night."

"You can't be serious!" Valerie exclaimed. The image of the tall, burly guard and the wide, sweaty woman just didn't fit in Valerie's mind. She shrugged. Perhaps some things were beyond understanding.

Like traveling through time...

The trio turned a corner, leaving the tightly set houses of Christos's *insula,* and entered the wide expanse of the Forum market. On both sides, booths with brightly colored awnings were situated, proudly displaying each of the vendor's wares.

"How about a nice scarf for your mistress?" one of the merchants shouted.

"They don't want your trash," another man yelled. "Come over here. I sell only the finest garments."

Valerie ignored the vendors, intent on keeping up with Stella and Clarus. She tried to hurry, but they moved much more easily than she over the rock-paved streets and had already gone on ahead to the food stalls.

"How about a fortune? I could tell your fortune, you know."

Valerie froze. That voice! Slowly, she turned around. An old woman approached her from the depths of an alley. It couldn't be, could it? "Hekate? Is it really you?"

"Who else would it be?" Hekate chuckled and her cloudy brown eyes sparkled. "A ghost?"

"How did you get here?" Valerie's head swam, and she leaned against a stuccoed stone wall for support. "Were you trapped in the earthquake, too?"

"Course not." Hekate waved a gnarled hand. "I knew it was coming."

"But how?"

"I have my ways…" Her eyes glinted into Valerie's. "I see something in your eyes I don't see last time. You meet someone?"

Valerie blushed.

"Ah, I knew it would be so. This is good. Maybe young lady never go back to her world. Maybe she want to stay in Pompeii forever?"

"I can't stay forever. You know what's going to happen within a week. The city will be destroyed, thousands of people killed." Valerie grabbed the old woman's hand. "Tell me, how do I get back to my own time? How do I find 1865 again?"

Hekate pursed her lips, the motion serving to accentuate the heavy wrinkles lining her tanned face. "I cannot tell."

"You can't, or you won't?" Valerie watched the other woman closely, her eyes narrowed. "You must travel back and forth all the time, from the looks of it. How do you do it?"

"I don't like your tone." Despite the heat, the old woman pulled her tattered shawl close around her shoulders. "As I say, I have my ways. Problem is, they can't be yours. The traveling is different for everyone. You must find your own path."

"My own path?" Valerie ran her free hand over the roughhewn cedar of her cane. "How do I find it when I haven't the faintest idea how I got here?"

"Ah, now, it's like I say before, too. You starting to grow up now. It's good for you to be on your own. Have faith. You'll figure it out." She tapped her chest and raised a finger to the heavens. "The heart lead the way for you, but you got to pay attention to what it says."

"The heart? My heart?"

"*Si.* The path of the heart." Hekate touched Valerie's cheek, then turned to leave. "I go now. Just so you know, your family is good."

"Please. Don't leave me!" Valerie tried to hurry after her but she stumbled and fell to the hard, stone pavement. By the time she got back up again, the old woman had already disappeared into the shadows of the alley.

"Follow your heart," Hekate's voice floated to her from the darkness. "It get you home."

Valerie leaned back against the wall. Tears welled in her eyes. "Please Lord," she whispered, a heavy ache filling her soul. "I want to go home. Please show me the path." Still leaning against the wall for support, she drew herself up and, spotting Clarus in the distance, headed toward the girl.

ANOTHER FIGURE EMERGED, unseen, from the shade of a covered entryway. Gravia's eyes were wide as she stared after Valerie. The heat must have gotten to the poor stupid girl. What was it she had said? The city would be destroyed next week? And where exactly was this 1865 place? She had never heard of it before.

"What do you make of it?" she asked the man standing next to her.

Julius walked out onto the street, straightening his tunic and tying his belt. "Who knows? Something isn't right about any of this. Did you see where the old woman went?"

Gravia craned her neck around the corner, but there was no one to be seen. "She must have turned into one of those buildings." She tapped a short finger against her chin. "The girl wants to escape."

"Of course, she does. Every slave dreams of freedom." Julius laughed and made a grab for Gravia's breasts.

She pulled away and slapped his hand. "Stop it! Someone might see you and tell Christos!" She crossed her arms. "I think perhaps we should help her get away."

"What? Have you gone mad?"

"Of course not, but I want her out of Christos's house. Maybe you could let her think you want to help her." She smiled prettily at Julius and caressed his arm. "After she is away from the city, you can do with her whatever you like."

"What makes you think she'd believe I'd want to help her? She knows I don't like her."

"You underestimate yourself. You can be quite convincing when you try."

"I think you're jealous, Gravia. You've seen how Christos looks at the girl, haven't you?" Julius shook his head. "Tell me, would you kill for him?"

"I would stop anyone who would take him, and his wealth, away from me. Besides," she continued, "I think you might enjoy taking care of the slave." She raised her eyebrows. "Am I wrong?"

Julius laughed. "Not much goes by you, does it Gravia? I'll tell you what. I'll see if I can 'help' the slave tomorrow night. With the dinner going on, Christos will be too busy to notice she's missing."

Gravia clapped her hands together. "Perfect. I knew I could count on you, dear Julius." She smiled again. "Come by in a few days and I will give you your reward."

CHAPTER TWENTY-FOUR

"Hurry, everyone! The guests will be here soon!" Stella bellowed to the kitchen staff. Six slaves scurried in circles around Valerie as she filled several heavy clay pitchers with hot spiced wine. The pitchers would be placed on one of several portable iron and stone stoves throughout the garden.

"I don't think I'll let you serve tonight," Stella said, as Valerie picked up one of the clay pots to bring to the garden. "I'm certain you'll spill something or knock a platter onto a guest's head." Stella shot a pointed look at Valerie's feet. "I want you positioned near the entry to the dining area. You'll be washing the visitors' feet as they arrive. Maybe later I'll let you near the garden."

Valerie placed the pitcher down on the table with a thud. "Did you say I am to…wash feet?"

Stella crossed her arms over her chest. "That's exactly what I said. That way you'll be on your knees and won't cause any embarrassment to Master Christos."

"Was this the master's idea?" Valerie asked, trying to keep herself from trembling.

"No, it was mine." Stella tapped her chest proudly. "I won't have you bringing disgrace upon the House of Campanius with your pitiful display of limping."

Valerie took a step backward. Her eyes widened as if she'd been slapped.

Clarus walked up and slipped her small, rough hand into Valerie's. "She'll call Julius, Val. It's not worth the punishment to argue," she whispered as tears welled in her eyes. "Please, just agree with her."

Val…

Clarus had called her Val. Her vision clouded as she was transported home. Reggie standing in the doorway of her bedroom as tears ran down his freckled cheeks…

Don't pay any attention to those mean ladies at the park, Val. You don't have to take me there anymore to play…

Valerie bent down and embraced the child, hugging her close. She straightened, her arm still around Clarus' shoulders, her eyes locked with Stella's. "I trust someone will demonstrate exactly what it is I'm to do?"

"I didn't think you'd give in so easily. Hmph. Maybe you're smarter than I thought," Stella conceded. "Clarus here will show you what to do." She stuck her chin out and glared at the child. "Don't think you're going to do the work for her, either," she instructed the girl. "She'll do it herself."

Valerie pulled Clarus in close to her chest. It was one thing to take Stella on herself, but Clarus didn't need to be in the middle of their disagreement. "May we leave now, Stella? Or do you need to call dear Julius and ask him his approval first?"

Stella sputtered, but before she could form a single word, Valerie and Clarus were out of the kitchen, giggling as they rushed out of harm's way.

"Welcome, my friends. So good to see you again." Christos stood just inside the front entry, his stark white toga glowing in the lamplight, as he bid his guests enter. Friends and acquaintances arrived in a steady procession, wearing their brightest clothing, the ladies' intent on showing off the finest of their jewels.

After Christos's greeting, Clarus led the visitors to a spot just outside the garden dining area. Everyone marveled at the decorations as they walked down the long corridor. Laurel wreaths hung over each doorway, scented petals were strewn on the floor and the finest of linens were draped over the marble dining couches.

"I see he's added another mural," one lady commented as she adjusted her gold armband. "The 'Dance of Dionysus' is an old classic and suits this house well. Christos has the most refined taste I've ever seen in a man."

"Ah, yes. Quite exquisite. I believe it to be the work of Marcus Apollos. He does create such handsome art," her companion replied.

"Here we are." Clarus directed the ladies to where Valerie waited on her knees, near a large column by the garden. She was surrounded by the array of items she had assembled – a stack of linen cloths, soft leather slippers, and a bowl of warm scented water.

"Please, have a seat," Valerie bid, directing one of the ladies to a stool positioned in front of her. She was careful to keep her eyes lowered as she had been instructed, lest they think her insolent. Insolent, indeed. They should all have the pleasure of meeting Lucy then they could see what insolence in a servant really meant.

Valerie desperately tried to hide her distaste as she removed first one sandal, then the other. The Romans bathed regularly, but the dust of the streets seemed to cake itself between their toes. Her eyes ran over the woman's foot as she rinsed it. She could not be expected to clean their toenails as well, it would take her hours. Stella could call Julius and he could beat her all he wanted, but here she had to draw the line.

Quickly, Valerie slid a pair of comfortable leather house slippers onto the woman's feet, hoping she wouldn't notice the missed spots. As the lady stood, Valerie bade her enter the dining room, "Right foot forward." Clarus had said something about it being bad luck to walk into a room with the left foot in the lead. She shrugged. A superstitious lot, these Romans were. Not unlike a few Englishmen she knew.

Valerie was in the midst of washing the other woman's feet, when she felt eyes on her. She glanced up from under her long lashes. Standing off to the side was Christos, in conversation with an older man, but his eyes were fixed on her.

Valerie pushed back a stray strand of hair, feeling self-conscious. Did the man always have to be so close? Did he always have to watch her so intently? Hekate's words reverberated in her mind.

I see something in your eyes. You meet someone…?

No, she hadn't met someone. Christos was definitely not the man for her. They were from two different times and cultures. Besides, she hadn't spoken to him since their altercation in his workshop.

Lost in her frustrating thoughts, she accidentally splashed the water too high and spotted the green silk *stola* of the auburn-haired woman sitting before her. The woman jumped to her feet, kicking the bowl over. Valerie grabbed a handful of linens and began frantically wiping up the water.

"What in the name of the gods are you doing, girl?" The woman raised her arm and cuffed Valerie on the ear, sending her reeling to the right. In the next moment, Christos appeared at her side and knelt down. "Are you all right?" he asked, his voice a rough whisper.

Valerie nodded as she rubbed the side of her head, still dizzy from the blow.

"Come now, Petronia. You can see it wasn't done on purpose." Christos helped the woman sit back down and placed the slippers on her feet himself.

The anger left the woman's eyes and she seemed appeased for the moment. It was a great honor for the head of the household to adorn a visitor's feet.

"There now, go on ahead to the dining room. And remember, right foot forward."

Petronia gave what Valerie assumed to be a smile, but the woman's lips were so tight they threatened to split open. "You're much too solicitous of your slaves. I'd beat her if I were you," she offered before leaving.

"But you're not me, are you?" Christos replied. His voice stiff. Anger flashed in his eyes. He turned his attention to her. "Are you certain you're all right?" he asked quietly.

"You needn't worry after me," Valerie replied, her voice shakier than she would have liked it to be. Did he honestly believe he could just run to her rescue and she would immediately forget he had almost beaten her? She glanced up. Everyone was standing around, watching them. Now was not the time or place to talk to him. "I'll finish now, if you like."

Christos smiled as his eyes swept over her figure. "I like very much. But as you suggested, we can finish our conversation later."

She blushed at his perusal.

Why does he have such an effect on me?

He waved his arm. "Everyone, come. Let's offer a prayer to the *lares* for a fine and entertaining evening."

The guests clapped their hands together and murmured their approval as Christos approached the shrine of the household gods.

Carefully, he opened the heavily carved and gilded doors of the tall wooden cabinet, exposing the small altar contained therein. A servant appeared and offered a tray containing bits of grain, cinnamon, and salt. Christos lit the sacramental oil lamp and adjusted the flame until it glowed with a yellow heart. He took the cloth the servant carried as well and positioned it over his head, covering the curly black locks. His lips began to move in a silent prayer as he sprinkled bits of the offerings into the flames. The pungent aroma of cinnamon filled the room and wafted out into the night air.

Valerie wished she could just as easily float away, over the roof, past the rows of houses, and into the dark August night. She hugged her arms around her, watching in fascination as Christos concluded the ceremony.

As he finished, another servant led the guests to their assigned seats. She knew Stella had taken great care in making certain the most influential and important people were at Christos's table. The least important ones were scattered in less conspicuous places about the garden. Valerie watched with amusement as the Pompeiians reclined on the couches, shoulder to breast against the person next to them. How in the world they could maintain any level of comfort eating this way was beyond her. Of course, they'd probably think the same of her dining habits.

"I would make a toast to our esteemed host." One of the guests, a patrician-looking, fair-haired man, raised a goblet of wine that had just been poured. "May this evening be free of lustful glances, coarse conversation, and foul language."

"Felix, you take all the fun out of having a party." Everyone turned in the direction of the voice. Making her entrance into the garden was

Gravia, her bright red *stola* billowing behind her. Her blonde hair was piled high on her head, gold thread and jewels strung through the curls.

Valerie started to step away, but Gravia spotted her before she could escape. "Is it not your duty to wash my feet before dinner?" she asked, her eyebrows raised.

Valerie considered the woman. Gravia was much too smug to suit her. "You mean to say you haven't bathed properly today?" Valerie asked, arching a fine brow. Those nearby gasped and leaned forward, eagerly awaiting Gravia's reaction to the insult.

"Of course, I have!" Gravia stomped her foot on the mosaic tile floor. She plopped herself down on the stool. "You will do me this courtesy," she said, her eyes narrowing, "or else."

"Valerie."

Valerie turned toward the voice. Christos was standing near the entry. "You will please honor my guest." He looked directly into her eyes and she noted the exasperation in his gaze, and something else —remorse.

She didn't want his remorse. She wanted…

What do I want?

"You plead with a servant? What has become of you, Christos?" Gravia asked, her voice high. "Are you growing soft in the head?"

"Perhaps." He laughed and it broke the tension in the room as everyone joined in.

Valerie couldn't help but smile herself. What did it matter? She would be gone from this place soon enough. Carefully, she lowered herself to her knees and washed Gravia's feet. When she was finished, Christos took Gravia by the hand and led her to his table. She pushed another blonde-haired woman out of the way so she could be the one to lie next to Christos. Valerie rolled her eyes. The woman was so obvious, it positively turned one's stomach.

As Valerie stood to the side with the other servants, a drum began to beat behind her. Several slaves marched past, playing instruments the likes of which Valerie had only seen in history books. The musicians situated themselves behind a sheer pink curtain at the opposite end of the garden, the melody from their playing, lulling and ethereal.

"What do you think you're about?"

Startled, Valerie jumped and turned toward the woman. "You told me to stay out of the way, Stella, and that's exactly what I'm doing." She smiled. "Is that all right with you?"

"Of course, it's not all right." Stella puffed herself up and thrust her ample chest out even farther. "One of the slaves has turned up ill and I'll need you to clean away the dirty plates and goblets. Drop even one and I'll ship you to the fields for the rest of your life. Is that understood?"

"How could I help but understand, dear Stella, when you ask so nicely?" Valerie offered a stiff curtsy, then turned and walked through the peristyle and into the garden, her cane tapping out a steady beat against the tiled floor.

CHAPTER TWENTY-FIVE

Clarus motioned to Valerie as she entered the garden. She stepped carefully over a row of low growing shrubs dividing the sitting area from the rest of the house and took her place at the girl's side.

"Now what?" Valerie whispered.

"We wait until they have finished each course, then we will remove the soiled dishes to the kitchen," Clarus whispered back. The music grew louder. "Look." She motioned with a nod of her head. "The first course is arriving."

Valerie watched as several slaves carried in large bronze and silver platters piled high with appetizers. Sardines, sea urchins, and lobster claws adorned one tray, while another held nightingale tongues and the mice rolled in honey and poppy seeds. She covered her mouth and looked the other way as a guest downed one of the poor creatures in a single bite.

She grimaced. "I still can't believe people actually eat those things."

"Did you try one?"

"Of course not." Valerie pulled at her short *stola*, straightening it.

"Then I do not think you should be criticizing." Clarus' eyes met hers. "If we are lucky, there will be food left over and we will dine as well as the guests tonight."

Valerie glanced down, her cheeks growing red. "You speak with a wisdom beyond your years, Clarus. I'm sorry. I've never been very good at keeping my opinions to myself."

"So I have noticed. It is hard for me to believe slaves in your country are allowed to speak so freely."

"We don't have slaves in my country, only paid servants," Valerie explained.

"You mean you were given money for your services?"

Valerie shook her head. The past few weeks had taken their toll and, as she thought of home, a great melancholy overcame her. "Dear Clarus, I wasn't a servant. I'm the daughter of a knight of the realm. A banker by profession who employs his own servants."

Clarus silently considered her companion for a moment. "I do not understand what it is you say. You speak so strangely."

"I know." She patted the girl on the shoulder. "Tell me, can you keep a secret?"

Clarus squeezed her hands together. "I am the best! Please tell me one!" She leaned forward, eager to listen.

"Well, I know of someone who lives in Pompeii. She's not certain how she came to be in this place. She misses her family very much. But, somehow, she traveled here from the future and doesn't know how to return. She just wants to go home."

Home.

The word tugged at Valerie's heart and she swallowed the lump in her throat.

"You are telling me a story, not a secret!" Clarus exclaimed, stomping her foot. She stuck her bottom lip out. "I thought you trusted me."

"I do trust you. This is a secret and it happens to be true. She honestly doesn't know how she got here."

Clarus looked at Valerie closely, as if judging her and the content of the secret. "You are this person, are you not?"

Valerie nodded slightly. "I am. Do you believe me?"

Clarus stared at her and then nodded back. "I do."

The music grew to a frenzied pitch, the rhythm of the beating drums reverberated through Valerie. Two slaves arrived in the midst of the sound, carrying a roasted wild boar. The animal was adorned complete with a shield and helmet of some foreign army. Another slave ran after them, brandishing a Roman sword. As the tray was placed in the center of Christos's table, everyone clapped. The servant with the sword attacked the meat, slicing it into huge chunks for the guests to enjoy.

Gravia passed her plate to Christos, nudging him gently with her shoulder. Her lips brushed against his jaw as she requested a piece of the thigh. "Just a small one, dearest Christos. I cannot risk too much as I fear I would grow too fat and lazy here on your couch."

A man named Felix laughed from his position across the table from the pair. "Since when, Gravia, do you worry about such matters? Why, at my party, you consumed more food and drink than any man there."

Gravia drew herself up. Her eyes spat venom at the man. " I cannot believe you would say such a thing about a lady."

"I wouldn't say it about a lady, but I would certainly say it about you."

Valerie giggled from where she stood near the table and a few nearby guests turned to look at her. Quickly, she covered her mouth and dissolved into a coughing fit. Once composed, she went to Felix's side. She felt an immediate kinship with this fair-haired man and his honesty where Gravia was concerned. "May I remove this plate for you, sir?"

Felix smiled and nodded. His blue eyes swept over her figure as she leaned across the table. "Where did you find her, Christos?"

"At auction." Christos answered easily enough, but the cold stare of his eyes betrayed a deeper emotion.

"Of course. I remember now. She's the one the townsfolk were calling a witch. I would guess she could cast a spell on any man, with those green eyes of hers."

"I do not see where the attraction lies," Gravia said with a pout of her lips. "She is a cripple, after all. How can any man find her attractive?"

Valerie stepped forward, her eyes blazing. She opened her mouth to reply but stopped short when Christos's eyes locked with hers.

"It makes no difference what form the body may take, Gravia," he stated quietly, his eyes never leaving Valerie's. "What is important is the heart that beats within. If it be a strong and true heart, one of courage and unyielding love, then it is attractive no matter the outside." He smiled and Valerie's resolve to be angry with him began to slip away. "Of course, a pleasant face and well-rounded shape doesn't hurt."

"A toast to that, dear friend!" Felix raised his goblet high and tipped it slightly to Valerie. "To the witch in our midst. Though a slave in body, may her soul travel to the heights of ecstasy and freedom in a man's embrace." He leaned toward her and whispered, "I could be that man."

Valerie's cheeks heated in a blush and she hastily retreated to the kitchen with Clarus. So many flowery words she had never heard before, even from Thomas who considered himself an expert in the art of seduction. She would do well to keep her distance from this Felix.

"Careful, Felix," Christos admonished, his voice low. "I would remind you she is mine."

"And you would not allow her to offer comfort to your oldest and dearest friend?" He motioned with his hand toward Gravia. "Why, even Gravia here has deemed me worthy of such compassion as you would not allow a slave to give."

Christos's eyes met Felix's. He regarded the man coolly. "Gravia is a free woman and can do as she pleases. There are no words between us that would bind her fidelity to me."

Gravia pushed her plate away and rested her breasts on the table. She ran a finger over Christos's cheek. "You do not really believe Felix, do you, my love? You know how he likes to carry on."

"Do you think me the fool, Gravia?" He shook his head and chuckled. "I know you too well."

"But I love only you," Gravia purred.

As Gravia spoke, a bright flash of lightning streaked against the moonless sky. On its heels was another, followed by the low rumble of thunder.

"It seems the gods would argue with you." Christos picked up his goblet to take a sip but stopped when the mixture began to shake of its own volition. On the table, the plates jumped and rattled as the ground moved. Several platters slipped and crashed to the ground. One of the small wine warmers toppled over. The clay amphora split in half as it hit the hard tile. The blood red wine soaked into the crevices between the stones, staining the mortar.

From the other side of the garden, a woman screamed. Her cry was followed by another. The guests clutched the edges of their couches, their faces stark with terror.

Then, just as quickly as it had begun, the quake subsided.

"This does not bode well," one of the diners commented. "The gods are angry."

"We have done nothing to anger them," another reasoned.

"I would guess it is just a tantrum," Felix observed. "You saw the lightning. Perhaps Zeus himself is having a fight with his lady love." He looked pointedly at Christos. "The same as our dear host."

Christos signaled the musicians and they began to play again. Slowly, the tension in the room began to ease as the debris from the earthquake was cleared away. He grinned as another course was brought into the room. Dear Stella, she wouldn't let anyone, even the gods, interfere with her dinner.

ANOTHER LOW RUMBLE filled the air as Valerie was making her way back to the garden to continue her duties. She had been in the kitchen with Clarus when the earthquake had hit. She calmed the girl and hugged her tight as they huddled in a safe corner as every dish and clay pot rattled.

Like an army general, Stella ordered everyone to get back to work as soon as the shaking had passed. Valerie had whispered to Clarus to sit while she went back to clear the dishes.

Along the darkened path to the garden, Valerie kept working Hekate's riddle about finding her path, over and over in her mind.

I don't have much time left. Oh, Hekate, why did you have to be so mysterious? Why couldn't you just tell me the truth of all this?

A strong hand from a shadowy alcove halted her.

"Come with me," a deep voice ordered.

She turned toward the voice, her eyes narrowed. "No, Julius. Leave me to my work." She pulled her arm free and started back in the direction of the garden.

"They are foolish! The house will collapse on all of their heads." He gestured to the side door. "Come, or you will die with these people."

Valerie hesitated. Were her calculations wrong? Would Vesuvius destroy Pompeii tonight? "I need to find Christos."

He grabbed her arm again. "Christos sent me after you. He said he'd meet us outside."

The sky gave an ominous rumble. "All right," Valerie relented. "I'll come with you."

As Valerie and Julius stumbled out into the street, another figure stepped forward and ran after them.

"Valerie! Wait!" Clarus yelled. "Don't go with him!"

Valerie turned her head to Clarus, but Julius pulled her along.

"What about Clarus?"

"Christos will bring her."

"Why are you being so nice to me?" She tried to discern his expression, but it was too dark.

"I'm following Christos's orders. Now come along."

Her thoughts were all muddled as Julius dragged her deeper into the dark night. She had to trust that Christos wouldn't allow any harm to come to her...So why did she feel a sense of trepidation that had nothing to do with the earthquake?

CHAPTER TWENTY-SIX

"Where's Christos? You said he was meeting us, didn't you?" Julius glanced around. "Just a bit farther…"

Valerie tried to pull away. A shiver of fear scurried up her spine. "We should go back, maybe something happened to keep Christos from meeting us."

Julius didn't answer but urged her along.

"Julius?" She ground her heels and cane into the dirt, pulling herself and the man to a halt. "Did you hear me? I said we should go home."

"Of course, I heard you." He yanked on her arm, and she tripped over a raised stone in the road. He steadied her. "It won't be necessary."

"Why is that?" she asked. Apprehension twisted in her gut. She glanced over her shoulder. The streets were deserted. There was no one around who might help.

He patted the center of his chest. "Because I've decided to give you your freedom."

"I–I thought only Christos could do that." Valerie looked around again, trying to memorize the path they were taking. They hadn't been walking that long, they shouldn't be too far from the house. She could get back on her own if she had to.

"Christos is a fool." He stopped and shoved her against a doorway. "He doesn't understand your spirit, like I do. You shouldn't be a slave." Julius ran a callused hand down her cheek. His fingertips were icy cold. "I offer you freedom. Will you turn it down?" With a quick motion, he gripped her neck and squeezed ever so gently. "Will you?"

Valerie dropped her cane as she tried to shove him away from her. "Stop it!" She choked out the words.

He leaned forward, and she could see clearly every pore and scar that covered his face. His tepid breath reeked of wine. "Beg me to set you free," he rasped.

"Julius," she whimpered as he squeezed her throat tighter.

"Say it!"

"I–I want you to set me free."

"Say, *please.*"

"Please. Please." Valerie watched as the crazed glow in his eyes mellowed into a smile. What demon has possessed the man? How was she going to get away from him?

"Good." He loosened his grip on her. "Let's go." Julius bent down and easily scooped Valerie up into his arms.

"I can walk." She pushed against him, but he held her firmly. "Just let me get my cane."

"You won't need it where I'm taking you." Julius stepped from the shadows and into the street again. As he hurried down the road, a laugh erupted from him, echoing along the empty street.

UNABLE TO FIND Valerie and Julius, Clarus walked back into the house. She should have told Valerie what she'd heard Julius tell Stella last night. Clarus couldn't sleep from the heat so she'd gotten out of bed to seek a cooler place to pass the night. As she tip-toed by Stella's door, she heard a man's voice from within. She shouldn't have done it, but she stopped and placed her ear to the wood, listening to Julius whispering with Stella.

"Soon, I'll have her out of your way, my love."

Stella replied with a deep throaty chuckle. "She's been a thorn in my side since the day she arrived."

"I'll enjoy getting rid of her. And I'm doing it all for you."

Clarus didn't listen to the rest of their conversation as they began to make low guttural grunts and moans.

Why didn't I warn Val?

She didn't have the chance to tell her, with all the preparations for the banquet and then she completely forgot when the earth began to shake.

She wrung her hands in agitation. She needed to help her friend. But how…? *Christos!*

She squared her shoulders and headed toward the garden.

"WHERE IS that lovely slave of yours, Christos?" Felix asked. "I have a pile of dirty plates I'd like her to take away." He gestured toward the center of the table. "I haven't any room left for a dish of dessert, and I was so looking forward to Stella's pomegranate cake."

"I think I saw her going out the front door during the disturbance." Gravia flicked a crumb of bread from her arm. She raised her eyes to Christos. "She probably took advantage of the diversion to escape. What do you think, my love?"

Christos ignored their comments. They might be his oldest friends, but that definitely didn't mean he trusted them.

He excused himself and walked about the garden, chatting with his guests, while covertly inspecting every corner and niche as he did so. Concerned by her absence, he called to Stella, who came lumbering out of the kitchen at his command.

"What is it, Master?" she asked, her breath coming in short gasps.

"Where is Valerie?"

"I thought she was out here, sir, where I told her to be." She looked nervously about. "I fear my cake is going to burn, Master. May I please return to the kitchen?"

"Have Julius go looking for her."

Stella bowed her head. "Yes, sir."

With a wave of his hand, Christos dismissed the woman. He walked back to his dining couch. Turning his attention to Gravia, he asked, "If you saw her leaving, why didn't you say something?"

"Why, Christos, I was so terrified by the earthquake, it took all of my strength to hold on to you." She glanced at him again through her lashes and smiled. "I'm certain she will return in the morning. After all, how far can she get, considering she is crippled?" Gravia patted the empty space next to her. "Come, finish dining with us."

"Please do, friend," Felix bade. "If the girl doesn't show up by morning, I'll go with you myself to fetch her home."

A frown creased Christos's brow as he lowered himself to his seat. Gravia had been through plenty of quakes to be so frightened. And Felix was being too damned accommodating. They knew something and there was no way to find out at the moment without creating a scene. He could hardly leave his guests to run off in search of a slave, especially after just telling Stella to send Julius out after her.

Valerie was foolish to think she could be rid of him so easily. She was his, after all.

His eyes wandered about the garden, not focusing on anything in particular, when the lamplight glinted against a woman's emerald necklace. It brought to mind a pair of emerald-green eyes...haunting his dreams for months...pleading for help as she was dragged through the streets...smoldering with sensuality as she bathed...glowing with tears after he'd raised his hand to her...

His chest constricted as he thought of Valerie.

I gave her every excuse to run away, and none to stay...

"Christos, I asked if you would like a piece of cake." Gravia licked her dark red lips as she offered him a bite with her own hand.

Absently, he opened his mouth and accepted the offer. Everyone at the table cheered and applauded. He shook his head as if to clear it, then realized what he had done. "Forget it, Gravia. It won't work."

"But you just accepted my proposal of marriage, did you not?" She waved her arm in a wide sweeping motion. "And I have all of these witnesses."

"Perhaps his feet are already growing cold," Felix offered.

Gravia smiled, triumphant. "Do not worry, my love. I will warm them for you, for the rest of our days."

CHAPTER TWENTY-SEVEN

Clarus scurried down the walkway and into the garden. She tripped over the shrubs and fell, face first, at Gravia's feet. She raised herself to her knees, panting.

"Why are you in such a rush?" Christos asked, an amused smile playing about his lips. "Are there demons chasing you?" He looked over her shoulder, a mock frown creasing his brow.

"It's Valerie," she gasped.

"Ah yes, the missing slave with the emerald eyes," Felix said. "Have you come to tell us she's run away? We already know that. Now, why don't you clear these plates away for me. When you're through, you can fetch me some cake."

Clarus opened her mouth to speak, but Gravia interrupted her. "Do what you're told, girl, and be quick about it!"

Clarus looked at Christos, tears welling in her eyes. "Let the child speak, Gravia," he said. "Felix's belly can wait a moment longer." Christos leaned forward, smiling again. "Now, what is so important that you must interrupt this dinner?"

"I–I'm sorry, master. It's just that I know Valerie did not run away."

Christos's smile faded. "And how can you be so certain?"

"She is an escaped slave," Gravia stated flatly. "She deserves no further attention from us." She studied her long fingernails. "Julius is going to take care of her."

Christos's head swiveled to Gravia. "What do you mean, 'Julius is going to take care of her?'"

"Julius is the problem!" Clarus said taking a step closer.

Gravia stood. "This slave girl is impertinent!" With one swift motion, she backhanded the girl across the mouth. Clarus fell and slammed her head with a sickening thud against one of the portable stoves.

Christos jumped to his feet and rushed to the child's side. He lifted her and cradled her limp form in his arms. When he pulled his hand away, it was stained bright red with blood. "You are truly a cold woman, Gravia, to attack a child so viciously." He ground out the words as his eyes bore through her.

"She is not a child. She is just a slave, for the love of Zeus." She shook her head. "Really, Christos, I think you grow too attached to these servants of yours." She straightened her gown. "One would think you exhibit, shall we say, an unnatural affection for the girl?"

Christos's eyes narrowed. "Your games grow tedious, Gravia. You will take your leave now." He stood with Clarus in arms. The remaining guests milled about, as if they weren't certain what to do next. Christos sighed and turned to his guests. "My apologies, dear friends.. It would seem as if the gods were playing a hand against our having a good time tonight. Please take your leave, we shall enjoy each other's company once more, in the near future."

As the guests left, Christos climbed the stairs to the loft above the kitchen. Gently, he laid Clarus's still form on her bed. He put an ear to her chest. Thank the gods. She was still alive. He poured water into a clay bowl and began to bathe her wound. "Please, little one, you must awaken. I need to know what has happened to our Valerie."

"Julius! You can't leave me here!" Valerie screamed as she clutched at the wall, of the damp, dark cave, to keep from falling over. The floor of the cave was on an incline and it was all she could do to stay close to the entrance so that she wouldn't slide farther down.

"Don't fret. I'll return soon enough." He grinned, the firelight from the torch he was holding distorted his face like a demon of hell. He stuck the torch into the cave opening, sending a thin shaft of light flickering inside. "Now, tell me you'll miss me."

He's mad. I am dealing with a mad man.

The only way out of this was to convince Julius she wanted him. Valerie shuffled toward him. "I – I will miss you very much. I don't want us to be apart." She reached out to him with one hand, her other hand sliding down the damp wall of the cave. "Please, take me with you."

Julius grinned again and ducked back out of the cave. Valerie could barely make out his shape as he began to roll a heavy stone in front of the opening.

"What are you doing?" She tried to make her way to the entrance but lost her footing and slid to the bottom, landing in a heap. "No!" she screamed again as the last bit of light from the torch disappeared from sight.

Her chest heaved and her body shook with sobs as her thoughts raced in panic.

Oh, dear God, how am I going to get out of here?

The tears ran freely down her cheeks. Did Christos know? Had he ordered her to be punished because of her behavior at the party?

Valerie sneezed as the moistness of the cave worked its way into her bones. She took a deep breath and the smell of salty sea air filled her. She reached down and felt the ground, scooping up a handful of the substance that covered the rocky floor. It was sand. The cave must be located somewhere near the water, if not right on the shore.

Something scurried by, and she pulled her legs up as best she could, tucking them beneath her. She shifted as she tried to find a halfway comfortable position where she sat in the rocks and sand. Valerie took another deep breath. She reached out to the sides, feeling the rocky walls of her dungeon. They weren't more than an arm's length away, all around. Valerie swallowed hard. She must be at the bottom of some sort of natural well. Considering she was so close to Vesuvius, it might even be a lava tube.

"Help!" she shouted. "Is anyone out there?" The sound bounced off the walls. Valerie covered her ears. There was no way out, except up.

She sat up on her knees and, feeling around with her hands, searched for any crevices to help her climb back up. Locating one of the footholds that Julius had used, she gripped it tightly and pulled herself up, slipping her good foot into it. She found the next one and grabbed hold. Raising her impaired foot, she forced it into one of the openings. She put her weight on it slightly, testing it for support, but the lack of strength in her foot caused it to slip from the foothold and she fell back down to the cave floor.

"Bloody hell," she cursed and drew herself up on her elbows.

Valerie tried again and again to no avail. Exhausted, she scrambled to a rock and climbed up on its surface. She ran a hand through her hair and nestled back into a small niche in the side of the cave. She hugged her arms around her waist and closed her eyes, forcing herself to remain calm. There would be no way out of her prison, at least not until Julius returned.

"JULIUS, MY LOVE," Gravia purred. "Tell me again how you got rid of her." She rubbed a hand along his thigh and he moved closer.

"It was quite easy, really. The earthquake was the perfect diversion. I simply told her she would be safe with me." He shrugged his shoulders. "Can I help it if I'm so convincing?"

Gravia laughed and clapped her hands together. "I love it! But for now, you must return to Christos's house. They think Stella sent you in search of the girl." She cast a sidelong glance at her companion. "Will the woman lie for you?"

"Stella? Of course, she will." He nuzzled her neck. "She thinks I got rid of Valerie for her, the silly woman." Julius lowered himself between Gravia's legs. "If she only knew."

CLARUS SHIFTED and Christos sat up. He groaned, stiff from spending the night on the hard floor. The bright light of morning had worked its way through a crack in the roof and touched the girl's eyelids. She swiped at it, as if she could make the disturbance go away.

"Clarus?" he whispered her name. "Are you awake?"

"I'm thirsty," she murmured, the words slurring together.

Christos's face broke into a smile. "I'm so happy to hear that, little one." He helped her sit up so she could drink from the goblet of water he offered. He frowned as he felt the large bump on her head. Gently, he lowered her back to the pillow. "How are you feeling?"

"My head feels as if it is on fire." She slowly opened her eyes. "What happened? Why are you here in my room?"

"I was too worried about you to let you sleep alone." He smiled again. "I hope you don't mind."

Clarus started to nod, then stopped as the pain became unbearable. "I remember. Mistress Gravia. She hit me." Tears rolled down her pale cheeks. "Why, master? Why?"

"I cannot answer your question, little one. Everyone is ruled by their own conscience and it appears that Gravia lacks one." He wiped her brow with a cool cloth. "Last night, you started to tell me something about Valerie. Do you remember?"

Clarus scrunched up her face as if deep in thought. Suddenly, she tried to get to her feet. Christos carefully pushed her back down. "Please, I must find her."

"I wish to find her as well. Do you know where she has gone?"

"I only know what I heard yesterday, before the party. Julius told Stella he was going to get rid of her." She took a deep breath. "During the earthquake, I saw him push Valerie out the front door."

"But when Gravia said she saw Valerie leave, she didn't mention Julius." He eyed her intently. "Are you certain of what you heard?"

"Valerie would not run away," Clarus whispered.

"How can you be so certain?"

"Because she can't get home from here."

"That I know, dear Clarus. Valerie used to live across a great sea and would need a boat to travel home."

"No, that is not why. She is from another time. She told me her story. She came from the future and does not know why she's here or how to get home." Clarus's voice trailed off as she drifted back to sleep.

Christos leaned back on his heels and wiped the damp cloth over his own forehead. The future? Impossible! But then, he remembered their conversation in the garden. What was it she had said? She was a student of history. And she knew of the earthquakes. Slowly, he stood. She had also said Vesuvius was going to destroy Pompeii.

He leaped up and rushed down the stairs. The front door opened and Julius entered just as Christos reached the atrium.

Christos approached him casually, knowing he had to be careful if he was to find Valerie. "You look terrible, my friend. Where have you spent the night?"

"That's just it. I haven't slept at all."

Christos rubbed his chin, considering the man. "Really? I thought you would have found time to rest. Or, at the very least found, a pair of willing arms to offer comfort."

Julius grinned. "Well, under the usual circumstances, perhaps. But when Stella said you wanted me to find the runaway slave, I was so intent on my duty that I searched all night." He stomped his feet, knocking off the sand that still clung to the inside of his sandals.

Christos nodded toward the floor. "It would seem your travels took you quite a distance from here. I would have thought the girl would not be able to get far, given her foot."

"Well, she might have had an accomplice..." His eyes skittered away. "But I did my duty to you, did I not?"

"Ah, Julius, you are truly a friend." Christos clapped the larger man on the back. "And I want you to know your loyalty will not go unrewarded."

Julius coughed and pulled away. "You know, I'm starving. Do you mind if I go to the kitchen to break my fast?"

"Of course, I'll walk with you." He kept his hand on Julius's shoulder. "So, where's the girl?"

"Oh, didn't I tell you?" Julius coughed again. "I, uh, I haven't found her yet." He glanced at Christos. "I'll head back out as soon as I have something to eat. If that is your wish."

"Of course, my friend." Christos smiled, giving Julius a hearty slap on the back. "Enjoy your breakfast, so that you will replenish your strength for your search."

CHAPTER TWENTY-EIGHT

Christos leaned on the railing of the atrium, waiting for Julius to finish his breakfast. Just as Julius was leaving the kitchen, he made a point of stretching and yawning.

"Did you not sleep well?" Julius asked him.

"No, I didn't. Too much excitement last night. I do believe a nap may be in order." He gestured toward the door. "Are you going back out to look for the slave?"

"Yes, that's exactly what I thought I'd do, unless you've changed your mind."

Christos rubbed his eyes. "Of course not. The girl's much too arrogant to think she can escape. She thought too highly of herself all along, didn't she? Do me a favor and bring her back in one piece so I can give her a sound lashing."

"I'll do as you wish," Julius replied, with a low bow, taking his leave.

A few moments later a heavy sigh escaped Christos as he ventured into the street. He caught sight of Julius's bulky form, rounding a corner. He hurried to catch up, careful to keep out of sight.

What evil had driven this man to betray his trust? How could this person he called friend, the man whose very life he had saved innumerable times on the battlefield kidnap Valerie?

By the gods, if he harms her, I will send him to Pluto myself.

He kept his hand on the hilt of his sword as he hurried through the city of the dead, his mind swirling with images of long, chestnut-brown hair and emerald-green eyes. Her beauty had haunted his dreams before he'd even met her. Was Valerie truly from the future? If so, how could he convince her to stay?

JULIUS PICKED his way over the black volcanic rocks lining the shore. He stopped and rubbed his chin.

Now, where did I leave the girl?

Hearing a faint call for help, he chuckled, and headed toward the cave's entrance. The tide was coming and beginning to reach the opening to the cave. He spit on his hands and grabbed the heavy stone. Rolling it to the side, the well was bathed in sunlight.

"Julius?"

"*Saluto,* my pretty witch," he called down the steep incline.

"Help me out of here. Please."

"I can't do that." If only he wasn't so enamored of Gravia, he might have taken the pretty witch to his bed, maybe even left Pompeii with her. She wasn't much use for anything else with her lame foot, but she would make for a most pleasant bed mate.

He sighed and shrugged his shoulders.

What's done is done. Gravia will be pleased and she'll reward me amply for my troubles.

Besides, no woman had ever come close to Gravia's wanton charms in bed…

He leaned over the edge of the opening and rested his chin on his hands.

A RUSH of cold water spilled into the cave, splashing Valerie across her face and soaking her tunic. She stumbled against the wall, her hands sliding over the slippery surface. "What's happening?" she shouted. "For heaven's sake, why are you pouring water on me?"

Julius laughed. "I'm not. Nature is. If you are truly a witch, you should be able to fly out of there, now that the opening is clear." He crooked a finger. "Come on, little witch. Fly to me."

"I'm not a witch nor can I fly!" Her hand found a groove in the cave wall and she started to pull herself up again, when another rush of water came. A steady stream followed it and the cave began to fill at an alarming rate. Valerie glanced down. The water was up to her knees. "Julius! Why are you doing this to me?" she screamed. "Get me out of here! Now!"

Julius looked down at her, a benign expression on his face. "I would cleanse Christos's house of your witchery—"

No sooner had the words left his lips than his expression changed to anger. Julius stood and began to argue with someone. Angry male voices resounded from above. Valerie craned her neck to see. "Help me!" she yelled, hoping whoever was up there would hear her over the rush of water.

A loud clanging rang out along with grunting and cursing. The stranger, whoever he was, had confronted Julius and the two were fighting.

The water reached her waist. Frantic, Valerie grabbed another handhold and pulled herself up. Soaking wet, her tunic was now plastered against her skin, weighing her down.

A gurgling scream floated down from the entrance. A flash of steel blinded her as a heavy object splashed down beside her.

Valerie's mind registered a thatch of dark hair, bulging eyes, a gaping mouth, and blood oozing from the stump of a neck.

The lump bobbed up and down, taunting her.

Julius!

She screamed, her hand clinging to the crevice for dear life.

"Valerie?"

She looked up. "Christos! Oh, thank God! Hurry!" she sobbed. "The water is up to my shoulders."

Christos began a steady descent into the blackness of the cave. Valerie's breath caught in her throat when Christos slipped. She breathed again when he regained his footing. He reached down to her and wrapped his strong hand around her wrist.

"I'm going to pull you up, but you've got to hold on tight to me."

Valerie nodded. "Please, just get me out of here."

Christos smiled through the dark tangle of wet curls that hung over his eyes. "As you wish."

Valerie held tight to Christos, her arms wrapped around his neck and her legs around his waist, as he climbed out of the cave.

Exhausted, Valerie let go and collapsed when they reached solid ground.

"You saved me…" she whispered, fighting to stay awake.

Don't let go…

It was too much to bear. Too much pain. Too much fear. Too much confusion. The only thing that felt right was Christos's strong arms around her.

She closed her eyes as his lips touched hers and slipped into blessed unconsciousness.

"OH, Mama, this is the best Christmas present ever! *A Tale of Two Cities* by Charles Dickens! How did you know?" Valerie beamed, hugging her mother close.

"How could I not know, when you reminded me at every turn?" Jacqueline kissed Valerie's forehead. "Just be certain your studies don't falter."

Valerie hugged the book to her breast. "I promise they won't." She kissed her mother on the cheek. "I love you, Mama."

I love you too, Valerie…"

"…Valerie. Valerie?"

Another voice entered her dreams. A man's voice, deep and strong. Comforting. A hand caressed her cheek. "*Pulcher.* Beautiful."

"Mama? I didn't know you spoke Latin."

"To what ghosts are you speaking your strange language? Awake, that I might help you keep them at bay."

Slowly, Valerie opened her eyes. The room was black as pitch, the only light offered by the crescent moon. "W-where am I?"

"In my room."

Valerie turned her head toward the man's voice. "Christos?" she whispered.

"*Ita.*" He ran his hand over her brow, pushing back her damp hair.

Valerie lay back down. "I was dreaming. I thought—I was home." She closed her eyes. "My mother was there." A tear ran down her cheek. "I'll never see my family again, will I?"

"Hush, you need to rest." He continued to caress her face. "We can talk of your home later."

She didn't want to rest. She missed her family, she missed home, and time was running out. She sat up, pulling her legs up and hugging her arms around her knees. The soft cotton coverlet fell away revealing her bare shoulders. Christos leaned forward and kissed the side of neck, leaving a trail of warm, moist kisses down her arm.

Valerie continued to cry, sobbing silently.

"Shall I stay with you tonight?" Christos asked, his voice as soft as his kisses. His eyes met hers. "The decision is yours…"

So much had happened since the day she stepped on the ship bound for Italy. She'd lived an entire lifetime, had suffered many hardships, and yet she had also come to know another side of herself. A strength she didn't know she possessed. Valerie had no idea what the future held for her, or if she'd ever find her way back home. It seemed as though this moment in time was all that mattered.

She gazed into Chritos's eyes and what she saw made her heart catch.

Eternity.

"P–please hold me, stay with me tonight. I'm frightened."

Christos smiled. "Ah, now, there's no need to fear. I've slain the demon who would do you harm." He stood and removed his clothing and sandals. Slipping into bed beside Valerie, he scooped her into his arms. He held her close, his arms locked tightly about her. Her smooth back pressed against his strong furred chest. They lay together, and for the rest of the night, Valerie allowed herself to feel the comfort of Christos's embrace.

CHAPTER TWENTY-NINE

Christos awoke just before dawn, when the first glowing rays could be seen at the edge of the horizon. He smiled and nuzzled the neck of the woman at his side, not knowing when last he had slept so well. The comfort and peace he'd found in the soft form beside him was one he hadn't known for years, if ever. He pulled Valerie closer, and she sighed, her breath a soft caress against his arm.

How had it come to pass that he could feel so strongly for a slave? But he knew in his heart that she would never be slave to any man.

The words she had spoken to him were true...

You may own my body, but you will never own my soul.

Would she someday give herself freely? After all, hadn't she told him in his dreams that she was his all those months before they'd even met?

I dreamt of you every night. And now, you are here...Have the gods fated us to be together?

Christos smiled to himself again. "I will be *your* slave," he murmured in Valerie's ear. "A slave of love."

He nuzzled her neck once more and ran his tongue along its base, then licked the lobe of her ear.

Valerie shivered and turned her head, opening her neck to him that he might explore. Gently, Christos ran his hand down her back, massaging lightly. Her skin was as soft as down. He took a deep breath.

May the gods help me—I have been bewitched by this woman.

His lips trailed the same path his fingers had just taken. Kisses as light as the touch of a butterfly's wings were gently scattered on Valerie's back.

Still sleeping, she sighed and pushed against him. The full round-ness of her buttocks fit snuggly into the curve of his lap. Valerie turned slightly, allowing Christos a partial view of her bare bosom.

He had to remind himself he'd undressed her and put her to bed only because he was worried about her. He rested here now only because of her plea for comfort.

Would you take advantage of her when she sleeps so peacefully in your care?

Valerie stirred and half-opened her eyes. "I was dreaming again," she whispered.

"What was it about?"

"I dreamed someone was touching me." She looked at him through thick lashes, a faint blush covering her cheeks. "Everywhere."

Christos smiled. "Not everywhere," he whispered into her ear. Gently, he rolled her onto her stomach and massaged her buttocks. His hand swept over her hip and down her thigh, forcing her legs apart.

She started to pull away from him. "Christos. I don't know …"

"There's nothing to fear, no need to doubt," he said as his hands continued to move up and over the back of her thighs. "Ah, my sweet Valerie, would you deny me your love?"

V ALERIE SIGHED AT HIS TOUCH.

You will travel through the mists of time to meet your true love.

Hekate's words floated through her mind…

No man had ever made her feel so alive, so in tune with her own body, and yet so light—as though she could float on air with just one kiss.

Is this fate? Am I meant to be with Christos?

She lay her head on the pillow, her breath growing ragged as his hand moved back down to her thighs. His movements were slow and seductive, sending a delicious ripple of excitement through her.

Christos squeezed her buttock, then ran a finger between her legs.

He pushed one finger inside her, penetrating her growing wetness. Gently, he moved in and out, caressing her from within.

Valerie gasped. "What magic are you working?" Her body pushed toward him, encouraging him to continue his explorations.

"The magic of love," he whispered as he began to kiss her neck once again. He rolled onto his back, pulling her with him. "Please, let me love you." Christos ran his hands under her hips and urged her forward until she was kneeling over him on her hands and knees. He slid down and caught one breast in his mouth. He licked the nipple, then gently blew on it until it grew hard. He licked again.

Valerie groaned and felt the dampness between her legs begin to spread. As he kissed her, Christos slipped a hand between her thighs and massaged her softness. Again, he ran his hand over her, circling until his thumb rested on her most sensitive spot and his finger was inside her. Valerie lowered her head, then raised it, arching her back. She was overcome by one wave after another of aching desire.

Christos continued to touch her and she pushed against him. "It's not time yet, my love."

"Time for what?" she murmured. Valerie sensed there had to be something else, something that would take this sweet ache from her, but what?

"Ah, my sweet innocent." His finger pushed deeper inside, touching her tightness. "There is much to learn."

"Teach me," Valerie whispered, her voice husky. She lowered herself so she lay fully against his chest, the dark hair tickling her skin.

"Come." He gently urged her mouth to his and the tantalizing movement of his tongue was too much to bear. She would disintegrate into the half-darkness that surrounded her if there were no release from the magic he was working on her body.

She pushed against his fingers, harder this time, then began to buck wildly as the endless, delicious tension Christos had built within her came to a peak and released itself in a burst of pleasure.

As Valerie sighed with languid contentment. Christos gently pushed her onto her back and lay above her, bracing his weight on his elbows. His lips captured hers in another fiery kiss. Valerie groaned and ran her fingers over his back to his buttocks.

He took her hand and placed it on his manhood, directing her movements up and down.

She reveled at the power she held over him, the way he closed his eyes and moaned at her touch.

He opened his eyes, gazing into hers and positioned his hips between her thighs.

"Will you open yourself to me?"

With a delicious shiver, Valerie spread her legs and rested her heels on his back. Probing gently at first, he entered her. Then, with one swift movement, his lips met hers as he pushed forward. Valerie cried out with the sudden rush of pain.

Christos kissed her face and neck, lying unmoving inside her and after a few moments, she began to feel the sweet ache build inside once more.

"We aren't finished, are we?" she asked, uncertain.

Christos chuckled. "No, my love. This is just the beginning." He started to move within her again and once more his touch made her wanton, urging him deeper and deeper.

She ran a finger down his cheek, and he took it into his mouth and sucked on it. "Christos," she murmured.

Every time she moved against him, a jolt went through her. She moved her hips, meeting his thrusts in a timeless rhythm. Faster they moved until she could no longer contain the throbbing within her. She arched her back in a feverish release as he continued to thrust inside her, until the heat of his own release surged into her.

After a few moments, he eased out of her and drew her into his embrace.

Christos pushed the damp strands of her hair off her forehead and kissed her brow. She gazed at him in wonder. "If only I had known," she whispered.

CHAPTER THIRTY

"My, my. This is quite an interesting scene."

Valerie's eyes flew open. She clutched the coverlet to her breast and sat up.

Clarus ran into the room on Gravia's heels. "I am sorry, master. I told the mistress you were not to be disturbed."

Christos stretched, then stood, heedless of his nudity. "What are you doing here?"

Gravia's brow arched at the blood-stained bed linens. "I see the slave has left her mark. I would not have thought her to be a virgin. She shifted her gaze to Valerie. "I hope you know I will not tolerate you in his bed after we are married."

Valerie's eyes flew to Christos's. "Married?" She repeated the word in a whisper, stunned.

Christos slipped a white tunic over his head. "Gravia has grand designs for me and my wealth, but they are all in her head."

Gravia sauntered up to Christos. She looped her arms about his neck and pulled his face close to hers. "Did you not eat the cake from my hand?"

"It doesn't matter."

"See, he does not deny the action." She dropped her arms and smiled. "We have wedding plans to make, my love. Get rid of the slave."

Valerie tugged at the cover and wrapped it around her. "That won't be necessary." She stood, then stumbled. Tears stung her eyes. She grabbed the headboard and steadied herself. Why did she have to be without a cane at a time like this? "Clarus, would you please help me?" she asked, mustering up every last vestige of dignity she possessed.

Clarus hurried to her side. Valerie placed a hand on her shoulder, allowing the child to help her toward the door.

"Valerie, wait." Christos pushed Gravia aside.

"There is nothing for you to say." She glanced over her shoulder. His gaze was full of tenderness, making her knees wobble.

How can he look at me like that, after what he did?

"I do trust the good master has enjoyed the use of his slave?" she said in a broken whisper.

"Our night together wasn't about slave and master. You know it and so do I."

Valerie shook her head, her eyes swimming with tears.

"I almost lost you once," he rasped, reaching his hand out to her. "I will not lose you again."

Gravia stepped in front of Valerie and with a quick movement, released the fastener at her shoulder and dropped her *stola* to the floor, exposing her nakedness beneath. Her hands on her hips, she gave Valerie a feline grin.

Valerie's heart twisted as the tears began to slip down her cheeks. "Do you honestly believe you can keep both of us?" she asked. She covered her mouth, stifling a sob, as Clarus led her from the bedroom.

CHRISTOS TOOK a step toward the door. Gravia grabbed his arm. He spun around, his face dark and forbidding. "Tell me, Gravia, was Julius as good in bed as Felix?"

Gravia's eyes grew wide then she smiled and shrugged her round shoulders. "I do not know what you are talking about." She turned and sauntered to the couch. Sitting, she patted the spot next to her. "Come, sit by me."

Christos remained where he stood. "Julius is dead." He continued to stare at her, waiting for her reaction.

Her face paled. "I–I did not know that. Wh–when did this happen?"

"Yesterday." Christos moved until he was standing directly in front of her, he crossed his arms over his chest. "I killed him myself."

Gravia jumped to her feet. "You did not! I do not believe it! Julius was your friend!"

"*Was*, Gravia. He lied to me. He kidnapped Valerie and sought to harm her."

"You call her by name as though she is my equal!" she turned and stalked to the balcony.

Christos leaned down and grabbed her arm. "Why did you help him?" He shook her. "Tell me now or I'll see you dead as well."

Gravia yanked her arm free. "I do not know you anymore. That slave must be truly a witch for she has tainted your brain and turned you against me."

"No, Gravia, you did that all by yourself." Christos shook his head. "I knew I couldn't trust you, but it didn't matter when all you did was play at your flirtatious games. How many men have you manipulated and bent to your will. Your vile machinations? Julius, Felix, and countless others I would venture."

"What I do with my body is my business. If you cannot appreciate me, then perhaps we should not marry after all." She studied her fingernails. "I have received countless love letters from heart-broken men who despair about our engagement.

"You should see the graffiti that covers the wall by my house." Her eyes flashed. "There are many men who would die to have me, Christos. Does that not make you jealous?"

"No, Gravia. It makes me pity you." He grabbed her *stola* from the floor and threw it at her. "If I find out you've been near anyone in this house, or harmed anyone in my care, I'll kill you." He shoved her out the door.

"You and that cripple deserve each other," she spat as she pulled the garment over her head. "May the gods bring down the heavens on both of you!"

Gravia's curses echoed throughout the house with each thumping of her sandals down the stairs, punctuated by the slamming of the front door.

Christos blew out a breath and ran his hands through his hair. From the washstand in the corner of his room, he splashed cold water on his face. "Venus Fisica, forgive me," he sighed. "By the gods, I've made a mess of things." He finished washing and went in search of Valerie.

THE SUN HAD LONG AGO REACHED its apex in the sky and was now beginning its gradual descent. The last rays shone down through the atrium and into the garden. Valerie sat on a marble bench near Christos's workshop, staring at the rendered scene on the wall before her. Diana, goddess of the hunt, appeared to be giving bow and arrow instructions to Minerva. Off to the side of the pastoral landscape, Jupiter aimed a thunderbolt at one of the women's hearts.

"Strike me instead, dear Jupiter," she murmured. "Take this pain from my breast."

"I would not wish it to be so." Christos said from the doorway. "I would that he take me instead, for I deserve the punishment."

Valerie stayed with her back to him, afraid to look in his eyes, lest she crumble in a heap of tears.

His sandals made a soft slapping sound on the stone floor.

Don't turn around, or you'll lose yourself in his beautiful ebony eyes, and then what?

The heat from his body enveloped her. She ached to feel that heat on her skin once more…

"Please, turn around and face me," he whispered.

Sadness and pain and anger filled her being. She'd been such a fool, believing that he could care for her. She was his slave, his property, after all. In this world, he had every right to use her as he deemed. She rested her forehead in her trembling hands.

Christos sat down next to her. He placed a hand on her shoulder. She pulled away.

"I have a gift for you. Won't you accept it?"

She turned slightly and he held up a new cane for her to see. It was crafted of fine ebony – ebony as dark as Christos's eyes. The handle was the same woman's head she had seen him casting a few weeks ago, in the garden.

"It's beautiful. Thank you," she murmured as he placed the object in her hand. She rolled it between her fingers, and the wood was warm and smooth to the touch.

Christos let his hand fall to his lap. "I've been wrestling my demons for weeks now. That day out here, you stirred up a past I thought was long ago forgotten, long ago healed." He sighed. "Little did I know it would take a woman such as yourself, a woman from another time, to make me see the truth."

Valerie looked at him, her eyes wide. "What did you say?"

"I know the secret you keep close to your heart. I'm not certain I believe it, but how else can I explain your existence? Either that or I am in Elysium."

He took her hand in his and dropped to his knee. "I lost my soul and you have restored it to me. For that I am ever grateful."

Her breath caught as a flutter of hope began to unfurl in her chest.

He kissed her hand, looking up at her, his ebony eyes glimmering with tears. "For that, I give you your freedom."

She pulled away and looked at him. "Do you know what you're saying?"

He nodded. "I would let you go with the hope in my heart that would choose to remain with me."

She studied his face. "What of Gravia?" she asked, not sure she wanted to know, but unable to leave the question unspoken.

"She is a vile, cruel woman. I've banished her from my home and my life. She won't disturb us ever again."

Valerie caressed his cheek. A sadness lingered in his eyes that tugged at her heart. She ran her thumb over his brow, smoothing the deep furrows. He kissed her palm. She sighed as he took her into his arms once again. His lips met hers in a hesitant kiss.

"If it be God's will, I will stay with you for always, my love," she whispered against his mouth. "But I swear to you, Vesuvius will erupt. You must promise me we'll leave the city."

Christos stood and scooped her into his arms. Gently, he placed her on a thick cushion behind the curtain where the musicians had played during the banquet. "Soon," he repeated, running his hand over her bare arm. Carefully, he unwound the fabric from her body and lowered himself to her open embrace. "Soon."

CHAPTER THIRTY-ONE

A low rumble followed by an ear-shattering blast tore through the tranquility of the new day. Jolted awake, Valerie and Christos were still abed when a second blast shredded the air.

Christos yanked back the curtain. Though it was now morning, the sky was as dark as the sea at midnight. Another explosive roar and the earth rolled beneath their feet. Valerie was tossed against the garden wall. Dust and dirt sifted down over her head as she struggled to maintain her footing. Beyond the curtain, ash and pumice began to rain down on the city at an alarming rate.

"My God." Valerie choked back a cry. "How could I have miscalculated? I swear I thought we still had a few days." She turned to Christos. "It's Vesuvius."

Christos took her by the hand. "Come. I've been through an eruption before when I was young. If we can reach the sea, we should be safe."

Valerie shook her head. The ash was already close to a foot deep and still falling. Visions of plaster cast bodies and excavated buildings ran through her mind. "I'm so sorry. It's too late. If we were to survive, we should have left days ago."

Christos picked up Valerie's cane and robe and handed them to her. "Take these. I won't sit here and wait to die."

He held Valerie close to his side as they dodged the falling debris and hurried into the house. While they rushed down the long corridor past the kitchen, several of the slaves appeared and ran to Christos.

"Come. We need to head for the sea," he called out as he and Valerie approached the front door.

"It is only another mild eruption," Stella observed as she walked into the vestibule. "It will do us no good to panic."

Clarus tugged at Christos's toga. "Take me with you. Please."

Christos smiled at the child as he patted her head. "Of course, little one. We would not have left without you."

Valerie took hold of Clarus's hand and offered the child a smile of comfort.

The staff looked to Stella. She crossed her arms over her full bosom. "I'm staying," she stated flatly.

"How about the rest of you?" Christos asked. "We have to leave now if we're to have any chance of escaping the volcano."

A few hedged toward Christos, but most of the servants chose to stay with the cook. After all, she was the one whose direction they trusted above all others, even their master. "We will stay and prepare dinner for your return."

"You'll die here," Valerie warned. "Please listen to Christos and save yourselves."

Stella glared at Valerie, then turned to the servants. "You're being ridiculous. All of you."

Christos released the latch on the front door and tried to push it open, but the door stuck. He shoved his body against it and the force opened it just enough for them to pass.

Hot ash had fused to the wood. A thick layer of the cooling material, now at least knee deep, had fallen over the city and into the street. And still it continued to come down. He motioned for Valerie and Clarus to follow.

Once outside, Valerie looked off in the distance, in the direction of Vesuvius. A bright red-orange glow illuminated the black sky as sparks flew through the air. Half of the volcano had blown away. A heavy cloud the shape of an umbrella pine suspended upside down hung in the air. Fiery lava ran along the mountain's side and off in the direction opposite of Pompeii. Heavy wet pumice still fell through the air, coupled with noxious sulfuric fumes.

People were running to and fro, screaming or shouting through the streets.

Others sat, huddled together, in doorways and under eaves, praying to the gods.

"Christos!" Valerie screamed over the din as she tripped and fell to her knees in the muck. "I'm sorry, I cannot run."

"Hush, my love." he kissed her forehead. "You are as light as a feather."

He picked her up and, with Clarus firmly gripping his toga, headed for the gates. Fires were sparking up in homes and buildings, debris was falling all around them.

It seemed the farther they walked the more dead bodies littered the streets. There was nothing they could do. Who could stop the march of history? *But I am here and that makes it different. At least for Christos and Clarus.*

She began to pray. *Please let us find the right path out of here.*

Trudging slowly, Christo's foot hit an object in the ash and he stumbled. He put Valerie down, when he saw a familiar form buried in the ash. Bending over, he turned the body over. It was Gravia, still clutching a purse full of gold tokens and jewels.

"It would seem Zeus has brought the heavens down on your head as well, Gravia," he whispered.

Valerie swallowed back the bile that rose in her throat. Gravia's mouth, nose, and eyes were caked with the wet ash. "I'm so sorry." She squeezed his shoulder.

"So am I."

Another violent quake shook the ground. Christos looked up and shouted a warning, pushing Valerie and Clarus out of the way, just as huge stone slab of building from a building tumbled down where they were standing.

"Christos, are you all right?" Valerie called over the thunderous din of the volcano.

He raised his head and shook the ash from his hair. "Don't worry about me." He yanked off his belt and tied it tightly above his knee. A deep gash beneath it bled profusely.

"You're hurt!"

"I'll be fine. Let's go."

The trio trudged onward as fast as they could get through the ash, crumbling buildings, and panicked crowds. Those still able to move seemed to be heading in the same direction, to the sea.

Lightning lit the sky and Valerie saw the gate where she had first entered the city. They ventured past the tall columns that lined the passage and hastened into the Necropolis. Again, the ground shifted and rolled beneath their feet. Unable to see clearly now as the ash continued to pelt them, they walked close to the tombs, feeling their way along.

"Christos! Look out!" Valerie called as a tomb collapsed, sending a column into their path.

Again, he shoved Valerie and Clarus out of the way. Only this time, he didn't move fast enough through the disarray of stone and volcanic rock that littered the graveyard. The monument came crashing down, knocking him to the ground.

"No!" Valerie screamed. She stumbled through the now almost thigh deep ash as if she were wading through a vat of glue.

Damn this foot!

It took what seemed like an eternity to reach him.

Christos opened his eyes when she cupped his cheek. "Seek shelter, my love," he rasped.

Valerie shook her head as Clarus whimpered, behind her. "I won't leave you."

"You have to," he gasped.

She shook her head and coughed. The volcanic fumes were so dense, Valerie could barely breathe.

He reached for Clarus's hand. "Take care of Valerie, little one. Take care of each other."

Clarus nodded through her tears.

"Remember, Valerie, in you I will continue to live." With a shudder, he closed his eyes.

Valerie grabbed his shoulders. "Christos!" she screamed. A sob escaped her when he didn't respond. "Please! I love you! You can't leave me!" Valerie cried.

She clutched his hand to her heart and brushed the ash away as it began to cover Christos's body.

"Valerie." Clarus touched her shoulder. "We can't help the master now. You have to come with me so I can take care of you, just like he said."

She looked up through her tears and gasped. A few feet away was the tomb she had hidden in during the previous quake when she was catapulted back in time. "Over there," she motioned with a nod. "It has a roof. We can be close to Christos."

Clarus helped her and together they made their way to the tomb. A sense of *deja vu* came over Valerie as she brushed the ash and pumice from the opening with her cane, clearing it for them to enter. Crawling on her hands and knees, Valerie climbed through the opening first. She turned and reached for Clarus but the child, succumbing to the fumes as well, had collapsed.

"Clarus!" Valerie screamed. The child didn't stir, she just lay there as the ash continued to fall.

Valerie's eyes burned as her lungs filled with the gases unleashed from the volcano. She retreated into the recess of the niche. Coughing and choking, she stared off into the distance, toward where Christos had fallen. Was there someone near, standing over him? She squinted, but his still form had become lost to her in the downpour.

"Soon, I'll be with you, my love," she whispered.

Closing her eyes, Valerie gave herself over to the fumes. Even her foreknowledge couldn't save them.

Vesuvius had won.

CHAPTER THIRTY-TWO

"Valerie? Are you in there?"

Valerie raised her arm, shielding her eyes from the straight thin ray of bright sunlight.

"Papa?" she whispered. Was she really hearing his voice?

"Val?"

"Papa!" She shouted the word this time. "I'm in here!" But no sooner had Valerie spoken the words than panic gripped her. If he stayed, he would perish! "Get away from here, Papa! You'll die if you stay!"

"She's safe," Valerie heard him call. "I'm not going to die today, daughter. And neither are you."

"But the volcano! It's erupting!" she cried out.

"I don't know what you're talking about. There's nothing dangerous out here, except of course for Lucy's temper." He chuckled and moved away from the opening.

One by one, the heavy stones covering the entry fell away as the men continued to dig. Dirt and dust sifted in and Valerie shut her eyes. A breeze blew in through the opening the workmen were creating. She took a deep breath of air. Fresh sea air! Where was the sulfur? The ash? The blackness?

Am I…home?

Finally, an opening large enough for her to slip through was made. Frederick's strong hands reached in and pulled her out, carrying her to flat ground. Gently, he helped her sit. He squatted down beside her and took her hand in his. Then retrieving a handkerchief from his pocket, he lightly dabbed at the moisture gathering in his eyes.

"You had us terrified, young lady," he admonished through his smile. "Goodness, it's wonderful to see you."

Valerie reached out and hugged her father. "It's good to see you, too," she whispered through her own tears.

When she released him, he stood and looked down at his daughter.

He whistled through his teeth as he removed his jacket. Placing it around her shoulders, he said, "Out and about without your undergarments again, eh? I'm sure your mother will have a conniption fit when she sees you dressed like this." He winked. "That is, after she's done crying a bucket of tears and holding you in her arms for at least two days.

Valerie looked down at her clothing. Disappointment filled her. She was dressed in her long dark charcoal skirt and white blouse, exactly as she was when she left her own time.

Did any of it happen?

Or was it all a dream stirred up by her overactive imagination and being stuck inside the tomb? She glanced around her. The Necropolis was just as it had been when she first arrived with her family.

"We'd better get back to camp so you can clean up," Frederick offered.

"Yes, Papa," Valerie replied, her head bowed. It had all seemed so real. She touched a finger to her lips. Christos had seemed so real.

"Excuse me, sir." One of the workmen motioned for Frederick. "Here. Your daughter forgot this." He pulled his hand out of the opening and handed Valerie's cane to her father.

Frederick raised his eyebrows as he handed the ebony walking stick to his daughter. "Say now, where did you come by this?"

Valerie stumbled as she grabbed the cane out of his hand. Catching her balance, she turned it over and over in her hands. It was the one Christos had made for her! That meant she hadn't dreamt him!

Dear God in Heaven!

If the cane was in there, maybe Clarus was too! "Please," she called to the workmen. "Is there anything else in the tomb?"

After a few moments of searching, they returned to her empty handed. "Sorry. Nothing else."

Valerie let out her breath, her heart aching. Clarus didn't survive either. But she had been real. Christos had been real, too. She had the cane to prove it.

The last time she saw them, they had both fallen in the ashes of Vesuvius, suffocating to death. She began to shake, as tears spilled down her cheeks.

"What is it, child?" Frederick asked, his voice threaded with alarm.

"Oh, Papa." Valerie wiped at her eyes. "I wish there was a way I could tell you." She took a deep breath to compose herself and forced a smile. "I'm just overwhelmed with emotion. I'm so happy to be home."

Frederick smiled and nodded as he took Valerie by the elbow and led her from the Necropolis. "Fill in that hole so no one else gets trapped in there!" he shouted over his shoulder to the workmen.

Valerie held tight to the beautifully wrought handle on her cane, and began to cry again.

She *had* traveled through the mists and found her true love...

But he is forever lost to me.

"YOU SHOULD HAVE SEEN HER, MAMA!" Reggie exclaimed as he tossed a stick into the fire. "When she walked into camp, she wasn't wearing that birdcage under her dress and was as filthy as a gutter dog."

"You will watch your language, Reggie," Jacqueline scolded. "It isn't polite to call your sister a gutter dog." She put her arm around Valerie's shoulders and pulled her close. "I was so worried about you when you didn't come home yesterday. We were all frightened for your safety. I only wish I hadn't been with the other search party looking in the opposite direction when they found you today."

Valerie pulled away from her mother. "Yesterday? What are you talking about, Mama? I've been gone for almost two months."

Jacqueline exchanged a worried look with her husband. "I promise, dear. It's been only a day." She caressed Valerie's head. "You must have taken a worse bump than we imagined, though, for the life of me, I can't find a single lump."

Lucy appeared from out of the shadows. "Here's a nice poultice fer ye."

Valerie tugged at the strings of her dressing gown. No sooner had she returned to the campsite, than she was being fussed over like a baby chick in a hen house.

Lucy had seen to it she had a hot bath and a change of clothes. Then went to work on her poultice. Lucky clucked as she tied the heavy cheesecloth around Valerie's forehead. It reeked of mud and soured herbs.

"I'm all right, Lucy. I don't need a poultice." Valerie pinched her nose, trying not to breathe in the smell.

"Nonsense. I been carin' fer ye since ye was little and I think I know what's best." She patted Valerie's shoulder.

Valerie shook her head and couldn't help but smile. What a contrast her life here was to the one she had just experienced in the past—she had to do the pampering in ancient Pompeii, and now she was the one being coddled.

She watched her father for a moment as he moved about absently in his seat near the fire. He leaned forward and twisted and turned, trying to face his book just so in order to read by the firelight. He must have felt her looking at him because he glanced up and smiled. All was right in his world once again.

Valerie smiled back at him. "I love you, Papa. And I love you too, Mama." She hugged her mother tightly.

"My goodness." Jacqueline laughed. "Whatever brought that on?"

"I missed you both so much. If you only knew how badly." Ever watchful, Lucy handed her a cup of tea. She sipped the warm, honey-sweetened liquid and stared into the campfire…

In her mind's eye, she saw Christos once more, knocked to the ground, ash covering his body. Would her family believe her story? Dare she tell them? At the very least, they'd probably think her mad… "I think I'd like to go to bed now, if you don't mind."

"Of course not." Jacqueline stood and offered her arm. "You never did tell us where you found that beautiful new cane."

Tears welled in Valerie's eyes. "You wouldn't believe me in a thousand years." Overcome with sadness, she looked off in the distance as she spoke. "Nay, nearly two thousand."

Lucy clucked and fussed the next morning as she packed the trunk at the end of Valerie's cot. "Things never seem to fit back in as well once they're taken out," she muttered under her breath.

Valerie rubbed her eyes and sat up. "What are you doing?" she asked, following the woman's movements.

"We'll be leavin' this day." She sniffed. "And none too soon, I don't mind tellin' ye."

"Leaving? But haven't we only just arrived?" Valerie swung her legs to the floor and stood. Gripping her cane tightly, she walked to the opening of the tent. She pushed back the flap and peered out into the campsite.

She watched the workmen pass baskets of dirt to one another down a long line and dump them into a pile. Once empty, they handed them back along the same line to be refilled.

"Yer father and his lordship Smythe aren't getting' along. He kept makin' noise about the investment and here you were missin.' I thought for sure Mr. Brooks was going to punch him in the nose," Lucy said closing the trunk. The lid popped up again. "And yer mother and father are worried over ye and anxious to get ye home to a doctor in England." Blowing out a breath, she plopped down and, with a quick flip of the wrist, she fastened the lock. "There, now. I left ye some clothes over here fer the carriage ride back to the ship."

Valerie crossed her arms and leaned against the rock and canvas wall. "I'm not leaving."

"I beg yer pardon?" Lucy took a step toward her. "Ye took a harder blow to the head than I thought." She motioned at the cot. "Lay yerself down and I'll fetch ye some nice hot tea and another poultice."

Valerie shook her head. She walked to the chair and slipped off her nightclothes. "I don't need tea or poultices. Will you help me dress, please?"

Lucy hesitated for a moment. "Well, I suppose ye'll have to dress sooner or later." She scooped up the heavy corset and held it out. "Ye know the routine."

Valerie held her arms up over her head and held her breath. As Lucy fastened it tightly into place, she slowly let out her breath, recalling days of short, comfortable *stolas*. She definitely hadn't missed this piece of torture while in ancient Pompeii.

Next, Lucy placed the crinoline on the floor and Valerie stepped into it. *The bloody birdcage*, she cursed silently as the older woman laced it into place around her waist. Then came her stockings, blouse, skirt, and jacket, followed by a pair of ankle high shoes.

She sighed.

"Lucy, what did you do with the dress I was wearing yesterday when Papa found me?"

Lucy wrinkled her nose. "It was disgustin', all covered in dirt and ash. I threw it away."

"You what?" Valerie stomped her foot on the hard ground. "Where did you put it?"

"What's the worry, girl? It's not as if you don't have plenty of cloth-ing." Lucy finished buttoning Valerie's shoes. "If you must know, I tossed it into the dirt pile out back."

Valerie grabbed her cane and headed out the tent in search of her clothing. Christos had touched the skirt and blouse. He had held it close and retrieved it for her after he bought her at the slave market.

Venturing into the street, her heart skipped a beat and she forgot all about rescuing her skirt and blouse. Last night, when it was dark, the town hadn't seemed quite so empty. Now, in the light of day, the past came back to haunt her…

The streets were deserted, when only a few days ago they were bustling with activity before Vesuvius erupted.

"Valerie. Come here, child," Frederick called.

Wiping the tears from her eyes, Valerie walked to where her father was standing near one of the buildings.

"Look what I found. Signore Fiorelli said I could give this to you. A gift for all of your troubles he said. I thought they'd make lovely earrings." He smiled. "What do you think?"

Valerie held out her hand and her father gently placed two stones in her palm. She turned them over and brushed the dirt away with her thumb. They were pink tourmalines, the exact same ones she had held in Christos's garden. Carved intaglio with a woman's head, they had survived the volcano intact.

Her vision blurred and her breath came in short gasps. The world was closing in around her. She clutched at her throat. She couldn't breathe.

"Whatever is the matter?" Frederick took her hand. "Come. Sit down."

Valerie shook her head. She looked up at the building standing before her. She took a step, stumbled, and caught herself against her cane.

"Christos," she whispered. Leaving her father to stare after her, she entered the ruins and traced the path to the garden at the back of the house. Here, the fragments of Diana and Athena's hunt scene were still visible. Valerie dropped to her knees and dug her hands in the ash that had yet to be excavated. She raised her eyes to the heavens.

"Why didn't he live?" Her shoulders sagged and she dragged her hands through the dirt. *Why didn't I die?*

She glanced up at the sound of children's laughter. Looking down the corridor, she spotted Reggie and a local boy running in the street, playing a game of tag.

Life has a habit of marching on even when those you love are gone.

Valerie slowly stood and walked back down the corridor, moving her fingertips over the mosaics still clinging to the wall. A pain shot through her breast and she clutched the cane to her. Leaning her forehead against the wall, she gently traced the outline of the cool tiles as tears ran freely down her cheeks.

Without looking back, she left the remains of the once noble home and made her way through the street toward the Necropolis, taking the same path she had taken during the eruption. Valerie stopped again as she spied one of Signore Fiorelli's plaster casts. She crouched down and studied the facial expression. A faint outline of a purse could be seen clutched in the figure's hands.

"Gravia," she murmured.

Valerie wiped at her tears furiously and stared at the sky. Having known the past, having known love, how could she face the future?

She stood and stumbled down the uneven pavement until she reached the gates. Slowly, she picked her way toward the tomb where Papa had found her. Would she find her love among the casts of the other bodies? She searched the area nearby. There it was. The heavy column that Christos had fallen next to.

Terrified of what she'd find, but unable to stop herself, she approached the scene before her. Several people had been uncovered. But, to her amazement, none lay under or even close to the column. She dug frantically in the scattered rocks until her fingers were torn and bloody. Where had his body gone?

"*Buongiorno, Signorina* Brooks. I am very glad to see you are well and moving around."

She looked up, glaring. Fiorelli took a step backward. "Tell me what you have done with him!" she demanded, her voice raspy.

"With whom?" He leaned over and followed her digging movements with his eyes. He considered her for a moment. "Perhaps I should take you back to camp so that you may lie down for a while."

"No. I'm not going anywhere until I find Christos." She looked wildly from side to side. "He was here. I know he was. Right near this column."

"If you are speaking of the bodies, *Signorina*, some did not survive the casting process. We had difficulty in the beginning, when we were perfecting our methods, and lost several of the forms."

"You mean he's gone forever?" she whispered.

"I don't think you will find what you are looking for among the statues of the dead, *Signorina*."

Valerie got to her feet, tears running freely down her cheeks. "How could you destroy him?" she sobbed. "He was my love!"

Fiorelli gripped Valerie's arm. "You must come with me, *Signorina*. Your mother will be worried about you."

Suddenly exhausted, Valerie fell against the older man. Fiorelli steadied her and she followed along next to him, moving numbly. She ventured one last slow look at the debris at her feet then allowed Fiorelli to lead her out of the Necropolis and back to the city.

CHAPTER THIRTY-THREE

Valerie watched in silence out the window of the carriage as it pulled away from Pompeii and headed north to the harbor. After visiting the Necropolis and finding no trace of Christos's body, she had decided it *would* be better to leave. She couldn't live with the ghosts that haunted the site. Besides, Christos would always be in her heart, so it didn't really matter if she was in Pompeii or London, did it? At least, that's what she tried to tell herself.

Valerie's eyes met Jacqueline's. She read the concern on her mother's face. She'd overheard her parents whispering about her, how pale and drawn she was. How they had hoped this trip would do her some good, not push her further into melancholia. But, after everything that had happened with Thomas Smythe and then being trapped in the tomb, it probably would have been for the best if they had all stayed home.

"Tell me, Val, what are you thinking?" Jacqueline asked.

Valerie shrugged and looked back out the window. "Nothing," she murmured.

"The expression on your face tells me otherwise. Is it Thomas?"

"Heavens no."

Jacqueline leaned back as the carriage bumped and swayed over the dirt road.

Valerie returned her attention to the passing countryside, but her ears were still attuned to her parents' conversation. Jacqueline patted her husband on the shoulder and whispered, "I tell you, Frederick, she's not right. Something's terribly wrong with her. It's almost as if she's pining away."

"She's had a terrible fright," he answered, keeping his voice low. "Trust me. She'll be fine in a few days."

"Well, I think she's gone crazy!" Reggie declared loudly. "And I think she should be locked up until her mind comes back!"

Valerie glared at her brother for a moment, then relented with a smile. She ruffled his hair and tweaked his nose. "You know something, brother? I missed you, even if you are a little lizard." Valerie leaned back into the padded leather coach seat.

Reggie grinned and went back to working on his sailor's knots. "I want to be ready for our trip home," he said. "Just like a real sailor." While he worked, he glanced out the window. "Papa! I think that other carriage is going to hit us!"

Valerie and Jacqueline both ignored him, but Frederick closed his book and leaned out the window. The driver of the other coach waved at him. Frederick sat back into his seat and tugged at his jacket to straighten it. "Nothing to worry about."

Reggie poked his sister in the side. "Take a look, Val! I say we're going to wreck for certain!"

"No, we're not because I know who it is," their father reasoned. "And because I know who it is, I know precisely where they'll be stopping so there's no chance of an accident."

Valerie opened her eyes, her curiosity piqued for the moment. She looked at her father. Always one for a good mystery, he was. "All right, Papa. How about you share your information with the rest of us?"

"Yes, Papa," Reggie chirped in. "I demand to know what's going on." He slammed his fist into his thigh, imitating his father.

Frederick chuckled. "A friend of Fiorelli's, one of the locals, asked if her nephew and his daughter could travel with us. Seems the man has business in England but has never been there. She was hopeful we'd show them around." He shrugged. "So, I agreed. Seemed harmless enough to honor the old woman's request. Besides, I understand the man's something of an expert in Roman antiquities. Should make for some interesting conversation for you, daughter."

Valerie nodded slightly and closed her eyes. Let the man talk all he wanted to, she wasn't about to have anything to do with him. Once she got on that ship, she was going to lock herself in her cabin for the rest of the journey home. She struggled to rein in her emotions. Her parents would follow Reggie's suggestion and lock her up for sure if she didn't stop weeping at the drop of a hat.

Jacqueline smiled and patted her husband's hand. "Your father does have a soft spot, you know, hidden beneath all that gruff."

Valerie opened her eyes as their coach drew to a halt, having arrived at the shipyard. It listed to one side as the driver stepped down and opened the door. Frederick eased out the narrow door and helped Jacqueline disembark, then Valerie. Reggie hopped out last.

"We should greet our new traveling companions," Frederick announced.

The driver was assisting a small woman, bent with age, down the steps of the other carriage.

Frederick greeted her warmly and introduced her to Jacqueline.

Valerie froze. "Hekate?" she whispered.

"Did you say something?" Jacqueline asked.

Valerie nodded toward the old woman. "I – uh – I believe I know that woman."

"And how do you know her, Val?"

"Yes, Val. How do you know her?" Reggie echoed.

"I, um, I met her at the site, before the accident." Valerie's next thought escaped her as a tall, dark-haired man stepped out of the carriage after the old woman.

Her breath caught. It couldn't be!

Oh, please let it be!

Valerie's free hand flew to her throat. Her vision blurred and she struggled to keep from fainting.

Christos!

He smiled and inclined his head in greeting…but his eyes—those beautiful ebony eyes—were full of love.

Hekate clapped her hands together. "Ah, Valerie. Nice to see you, again." She patted her chest and winked. "You listened to the heart, eh?"

"You two have met?" Frederick asked.

"Around the site. I see your daughter. She give me water." The woman smiled. "She's a good girl."

Before Valerie could say anything, Hekate motioned to the man standing beside her. "This my nephew, Christos Campagna." She pointed to her carriage. "And his daughter, Clare. They gonna travel with you to England." Just then, Clarus climbed down, smiled, and offered a shy wave.

Clarus!

Valerie's eyes flew to the girl and then to Christos. She fought back the urge to throw herself into his arms. Her thoughts tripped over themselves.

How did they get here? Vesuvius claimed them. I saw both Christos and Clarus die!

Silent tears swept down her cheeks. She pulled her eyes from Christos's dear face and looked off into the distance, where the remains of the great volcano loomed on the horizon. After almost two thousand years of eruptions, it didn't look nearly so terrifying to her anymore.

"You are thinking of the volcano?" Christos asked in a heavy accent.

Numbly, Valerie nodded, as she realized he was speaking English. It must have been Hekate's magic.

"My aunt tells me marvelous tales of lovers whose fate Vesuvius has sealed. Perhaps, if you like, I will share these stories with you on the ship?"

Valerie smiled through her tears. "Your aunt is a very wise woman with a talent for the improbable."

Frederick cleared his throat. "We should be going now, young lady."

Valerie nodded. "Please, Papa. Just a moment with Hekate before she has to leave."

Frederick glanced at Christos, then the old woman. "Don't take too long. We're on a schedule here."

"I won't Papa," she said. Turning, she wrapped her arms around Hekate and hugged her tight. "Thank you," she whispered. "For everything."

"Love always survive everything, even the mists of time," Hekate whispered.

Valerie looked back to Christos and her voice quivered when she spoke. "Yes, it does, my friend. Yes, it does."

Valerie remembered the figure bent over Christos's body after he had fallen. She realized what had happened. "It was you, wasn't it?"

Hekate smiled, her dark eyes sparkling. "Everyone needs a little help, sometimes, when facing a crossroads."

VALERIE HOPED Lucy wouldn't make a fuss and insist she take a nap. But Lucy surprised her. When Valerie told her she was going to join Reggie on deck and take a stroll, Lucy beamed and nodded in agreement, saying she was going to take a stroll herself with Johnny.

Valerie trembled with anticipation as she made her way topside. She had so many questions for Christos but there would be time enough to ask them.

A lifetime.

Christos was leaning against the railing looking out to sea. The rush of emotions of the last few days hit Valerie hard as she approached him, and she stumbled. Christos's strong arms caught her before she fell to her knees. He took her hands in his. "Ah, my love," he murmured in his ancient dialect.

"How?" she asked, the words barely a whisper. She studied his face. "And you're not hurt."

Christos shook his head. "I don't know how it happened. After you left, I heard someone calling my name. I opened my eyes. It was Hekate. Just like the goddess she's named for, she took my hand in death. The next thing I knew I was surrounded by the ruins of the city. She took me into her home and dear Clarus was there asleep on a bed." He nodded at Clarus who was sitting on a bench beside Reggie, patiently nodding as he instructed her on tying sailor's knots. "Hekate told us she'd know where to find you."

"I am so glad she did." Valerie's eyes filled with tears. "I thought I had lost you forever."

"Ah, Valerie, you are my life. I will go to this England of yours and do whatever is necessary to make you my wife." Tears filled his eyes. "By the gods," he rasped, "I swear to you that nothing will ever separate us again."

Valerie nodded through her own tears. "That day when I went to the market with Stella and Clarus, I met Hekate in the street and she told me to have faith, that all I needed to do was to listen to my heart and I would find my way home."

"And did you?" he whispered, his hand caressing her cheek.

"Yes, I did."

EPILOGUE

Christos stood against the stone railing of the large wrap-around porch of his new home and looked out over the countryside of his adopted country. This place was not the Britannia of his memory, but a civilized country of cities filled with all manner of people. Almost twelve months had passed since he'd arrived, and he was still learning. He glanced over at Valerie, where she sat in a rocker with her morning tea, moving rhythmically back and forth. Drawn to her, he crouched next to her chair.

"How are you, my love?" One year in wedded bliss and he was still amazed she was his.

Valerie ran a hand over the swell of her belly. "I am well." She touched his cheek. "I've never been happier."

He took her by the hand and helped her stand. They embraced and she giggled when he jumped back, the baby soundly kicking him.

"Val!" Clarus came running from the back of the house. "Look! Grandmama and Grandpapa are here!" She bounded onto the porch and pointed at the carriage coming up the cobblestone drive.

Christos ruffled her hair. "You best go clean yourself up before Lucy spies you."

Clarus giggled. "Lucy is all bark and no bite."

Christos shook his head as his gaze met his wife's twinkling eyes. Clarus had taken to life in England like a duckling to water.

"I bet Lucy has a basket of your favorite cinnamon scones," Valerie said, tapping Clarus' nose.

"They're the best!" Clarus said. "I'll be back in a jiffy," she called over her shoulder as she bolted for the door. "Don't eat them without me."

"We won't," husband and wife said in unison.

"Will she ever slow down?" Christos moaned.

"I hope she never does," Valerie said. "And neither will we." She slipped her arms around his shoulders and smiled into his eyes.

Christo's breath caught at the beauty in the emerald depths.

He bent his head and kissed her soft lips.

"You have bewitched me since the beginning of time," he whispered against her lips.

"Is that a complaint?" She giggled into his neck.

"Never." He tilted her chin up for one more lingering kiss. "You are my past, my present, and my future."

"The future is ours as long as we follow our hearts," Valerie said as she placed his hand on her swollen belly. "Forever."

"Forever."

A NOTE FROM THE AUTHOR

I hope you enjoyed *Through the Mists of Time,* Book 1 in the Oracle Dreams Trilogy. If you'd like to leave a review, please visit Amazon.com.

I love to hear from readers! You can contact me through my website at www.teribarnett.com. While you're there, please go ahead and subscribe to my newsletter so you can stay up to date on new releases, special offers, and giveaways.

And, for a special treat, keep reading for a Sneak Peek of *Shadow Dreams*, Oracle Dreams Trilogy: Book 2!

SNEAK PEEK
SHADOW DREAMS
ORACLE DREAMS TRILOGY: BOOK 2

Near Paran
The Plane of Keilah

"We have a visitor, Ma'am."

The High Priestess Liazar licked her lips in anticipation as the guest was ushered into her chambers. She moved quickly to her simple, carved wooden chair, and sat down. "My, my. What have we here? Come, stand in front of me child. I'd like to have a better look at you." With long, thin fingers, she motioned to the girl, her pearl and garnet ring glistening in the candlelight. "How old are you, Cherub?"

"Seven, Ma'am."

Liazar openly displayed her pleasure with a wide smile, her teeth shining in the candlelight. Seven! So young! Surely, the little one had many years ahead of her. She looked the girl over, admiring the sweet rosy cheeks and long silver-blonde hair.

"What do they call you?"

"Sarah, Ma'am," the child answered solemnly. "Sarah M'Doro."

"And you have no kin here in Paran?"

The girl wrinkled up her forehead as she thought. "Well, there is my mother. And my grandfather. Papa died long ago. I don't remember much about him."

Liazar looked sharply at her maid, Esther. "I told you to bring only orphans, didn't I?"

Esther glanced down, studying the squat shadow she cast onto the floor. "I'm sorry, Ma'am. When I found her playing in the woods, I assumed she belonged to no one. Who would let their child run free like that?" She rushed over to the girl as quickly as her bulk would allow and knelt at her side. "But she is a pretty one, isn't she? Just look at the life in her eyes."

The High Priestess shifted in her chair. This was a dilemma. If there were relatives to miss the child when she didn't return home, there could be trouble. She looked again at Sarah, feeling her need growing. Of course, the absence of one child could be easily explained, particularly if she were left to run alone. Perhaps wild animals might have dragged her away. Liazar smiled again. She leaned forward, her long red hair spilling over her shoulders.

"Come nearer to me, Sarah M'Doro."

Sarah hesitated for a moment. Esther gave her a little shove from behind. "Go on, girl. You don't want to make the High Priestess angry now, do you?"

Sarah shook her head. Slowly, she took a step toward Liazar. She stopped, the candlelight casting deep shadows around her slight form. "I'm afraid. Please let me go home."

"Now, now, Cherub. There's no need to fear. I only want to give you a hug before I send you on your way." Liazar reached for the child. "Is that all right with you?"

The girl shrugged her shoulders. "I suppose that would be all right. As long as you promise."

"I promise I will let you go as soon as I've hugged you."

Sarah moved to stand directly in front of Liazar. She held her arms out, innocent, waiting for the embrace.

Liazar sucked in her breath as she noticed the downy softness of the child's skin and the long lashes that brushed her cheeks. She raised her hands and placed them on either side of Sarah's head, the thumbs resting over the girl's eyebrows. Murmuring quietly, she closed her eyes and uttered an ancient incantation.

Suddenly, Sarah swayed and fell with a soft thud to the thickly carpeted floor. Liazar opened her eyes and took a deep breath. "Put her form with the others, Esther," she bade. "Take care she's kept safe."

As the maid carried the child away, Liazar eased back into the chair, smiling. She lifted her hands, feeling the flushed warmth of her face and the firm, smooth skin. Blood pounded in her temples and her heart raced. The transference was complete. She now possessed the little one's soul and the years it had left to live.

Soon, she thought, *soon I will be immortal!*

I hope you enjoyed this sneak peek of
Shadow Dreams
Oracle Dreams Trilogy: Book 2

Visit Amazon.com to purchase your copy!

ABOUT THE AUTHOR

In addition to her Oracle Dreams Trilogy, Teri Barnett is the bestselling author of the Bijoux Mystery Series and the upcoming Lac Voo Mystery Series. Both cozy mystery series are set in sleepy tourist towns on the Lake Michigan shoreline. She's also the creator of Cats & More: Adult Coloring Book Series, a Reiki Master Teacher, and has written numerous non-fiction books about the practice and teaching of Reiki. Other non-fiction works include *How to be a Kickass Goddess: Twelve Steps to Owning Your Life* and the accompanying *Kickass Goddess Journal*, because you always need to journal when you're a Kickass Goddess.

All of Teri's books can be found on Amazon.

And if being an author isn't enough, Teri is also an award-winning artist and nationally recognized commercial interior designer who brings a lifetime of learning and exploration to her writing and workshops. Born and raised in Michigan, Teri currently resides in Indiana where she writes books, does cool art, crochets too many shawls and blankets, and hangs out with Black Cat Lou, her bossy black cat. BCL is the inspiration for Griselda, Morgan Hart's rescue cat in the Bijoux Mystery Series, who makes her debut in Book 2, *Mystics are Murder*.

When Teri isn't busy working on her next book or redesigning the world, you can find her doing the artist thing in her studio, tromping through the forest, hanging with her kids and grandkids, or riding through the corn tunnels of Indiana on her motorcycle.

You can visit Teri online at www.teribarnett.com to learn more about her books, subscribe to her newsletter, and/or just to drop her a line to say hello.

TERI BARNETT
COMPLETE BOOK LIST

ORACLE DREAMS TRILOGY

Historical/Paranormal Time Travel Romance Trilogy

Through the Mists of Time: Oracle Dreams Trilogy Book 1

In 1865 London, Valerie Sherwood Brooks embarks on a tour of Italy where she is catapulted back in time to the ancient city of Pompeii and into the arms of a mysterious man who will alter her very destiny.

With a romantic heart and yearning for adventure, Valerie is overjoyed at the prospect of leaving London for the excitement of Italy, even if it means traveling with her overly protective parents and rambunctious little brother. Despite a childhood accident that has left her in need of a cane, Valerie is determined to explore the ancient ruins of Pompeii on her own. But when an earthquake shatters their visit to the Old City, Valerie is hurled back in time to 79 A.D.

Thrust into a world of intrigue and danger, Valerie is forced into servitude in the grand home of the darkly handsome Christos Marcellus. As Valerie tries to keep her wits about her, she is torn between her complex feelings for Christos and her need to get back to her own time.

Knowing the coming eruption of Vesuvius will mean doom and destruction, Valerie is faced with a life and death decision. Will she make the right choice in time?

Shadow Dreams: Oracle Dreams Trilogy Book 2

In the village of Paran, in the peaceful realm of Keilah, Bethany M'Doro embarks on a voyage to the Earth plane, to the year 1875, in search of a man who has the power to save her or destroy her.

Widowed with a young daughter, Bethany M'Doro possesses a unique ability to see into the past and her clairvoyant gifts make her invaluable on archeological digs. Her team's most recent discovery—an ornate comb buried under a pile of charred bones—sparks a vision of the ancient evil cult of Eitel, known for stealing children's souls. Although it was believed the cult was destroyed centuries ago, Bethany senses it has been resurrected by a diabolical new leader.

Bethany returns home from the expedition, to discover her worst fear has been realized. Her daughter Sarah has gone missing along with several other children from the village. It can only be the evil cult Eitel. Desperate to find them, Bethany's visions guide her to the Earth plane, to Devil's Gate, Nevada in 1875. There she encounters Connor Jessup, the only man who has the power to help her. But Connor is tormented by his own personal demons and a tragic past that continues to haunt him.

Bethany now faces the greatest challenge of her life. Can she heal Connor and convince him to travel back with her to Paran to find Eitel's lair and save Sarah and the other children from certain death? Or will her daughter be lost forever?

Pagan Fire: Oracle Dreams Trilogy Book 3

In 883 A.D., in a secluded convent in Great Britain, Maere cu Llwyr embarks on a journey back to her home of Tintagel, Cornwall with a powerful warrior who claims to be her long lost betrothed.

Dylan mac Connall survived the slaughter of his family by a traitor to their clan. A young boy at the time, he was rescued by a wise woman who taught him the ways of magic and warned him of the perils that lay ahead if he chose a path of revenge. But Dylan can no longer heed the advice of his foster mother and is determined to avenge his family and find the spirited girl he loved in his youth.

Raised in an abbey by the Sisters of Saint Columba, Maere cu Llwyr is ready to take her full vows and become a nun. But when the warrior Dylan arrives and claims to be her rightful betrothed, Maere is shocked and wary of what her future will bring. A wee child when she was abducted from her village, Maere has blocked the memories of that horrific night. She has no recollection of the powerful ancient magic dormant inside her, or of the handsome man determined to unlock both Maere's mind and her power.

As Maere and Dylan travel back to Tintagel, they must face the mercurial goddess Morrigu, dangerous Viking raiders, and the traitor who destroyed their families. Can Maere and Dylan survive the battles to come and find their way back home and to each other? Or will they be forever separated by forces outside of their control?

BIJOUX MYSTERY SERIES

Romance is Murder: Bijoux Mystery Series Book 1

A dead diva, a rotten romance, and a town full of nosy neighbors…

Morgan Hart is home. A former homicide detective in Detroit, Morgan is back in her old hometown of Bijoux, Michigan to take over the reins of Sheriff from her dad, Able. The town has undergone quite a transformation since she lived here with new, kitschy shops along Main Street and a burgeoning tourist trade. Even the iconic pink Firefly Bed & Breakfast has jumped on the bandwagon and is hosting a romance writers' convention with some of the biggest names in the 'happily ever after' biz.

Morgan hopes to ease into her new job, new cottage, and new life – after all, Bijoux hasn't had a murder in a hundred years. But all of Morgan's plans go up in smoke when the biggest diva of the romance world is found dead.

As Morgan and her deputy, JJ Jones, begin their investigation, the townspeople have no qualms about telling her how to do her job, including Caleb Joseph, owner of the local bookstore who is far too nosy (and attractive) for Morgan's comfort.

With a murder to solve and the town in turmoil, Morgan will have to rely on her big city cop skills to catch a killer harboring a hate for happy endings.

Mystics are Murder: Bijoux Mystery Series Book 2

What do you do when your star murder witness only speaks 'Meow?'

Who could predict it would happen again? Morgan Hart didn't expect her first day as police captain of Bijoux, Michigan, the sleepy lakeside town where she grew up, would include a murder, even though that's just what happened. But with the killer behind bars, Morgan can take a breath and start painting her cozy cottage.

Or so she hopes.

When a fortune-telling mystic is found dead at Bijoux's Walk into the Light Psychic Gathering, Morgan and her deputy, JJ Jones, are called in to investigate. The trouble is Morgan's only witness is Griselda, a black cat with blood on her paws.

While every psychic in town claims to know what the cat 'knows,' Morgan relies on her own instincts to sniff out the suspects while dodging her conflicting feelings for local bookshop owner and town hunk, Caleb Joseph. And with her dad, Able's, upcoming wedding to Zoe Buffet, Bijoux's most famous clairvoyant and coffee cake queen, Morgan is under the gun to figure out which mystic is the murderer before the couple says I do.

Cupcakes are Murder: Bijoux Mystery Series Book 3

A cupcake conundrum, a culinary queen on the edge, and a cold-case killer on the loose…

Morgan Hart is settling into her job as police captain of Bijoux, the quaint and quirky tourist town nestled on the Lake Michigan shoreline. Murders have been solved, kittens have been rescued, and progress has been made in the renovation of her cozy cottage by the beach. Despite her grief and ongoing frustration over her husband's unsolved murder six years ago, Morgan hopes an overdue break in the case will finally lead to justice, even if it means exposing a betrayal that could leave her reeling.

Meanwhile, Morgan needs to keep a sharp eye on the upcoming Baker's Dozen Hometown Cupcake Bake-off and TV special hosted by British baking superstar Sassy McComas, aka The Queen of Cupcakes. Rumor has it, Queen Sass is secretly searching for a fresh face to host a new TV show and the competitors vying for the top spot include Bijoux's own pastry princess, Hannah Bellamy.

But when one of the top challengers in the Cupcake Bake-off turns up dead, Morgan has to sift through the evidence and stop the killer before they strike again and threaten to topple Queen Sass from her throne.

Pumpkins are Murder: Bijoux Mystery Series Book 4

A dead carver, dueling witches, and more tricks than treats…

Bijoux, Michigan is serious about Halloween.

Known as the most haunted town on the Lake Michigan shoreline, Bijoux hosts the annual Pumpkins and Poe Festival—the town's annual homage to Edgar Allan Poe and all things spooky. Pumpkin carvers from around the country flock to Bijoux, slicing and dicing their way into Halloween history. But when one of the carvers turns up dead with a jack-o-lantern on their head and a note with the word Nevermore scrawled in orange ink pinned to their apron, police captain Morgan Hart is called in to investigate.

After solving multiple murders at three previous Bijoux events, the beleaguered police captain steps into the fray once again, along with her down-in-the-dumps deputy, JJ Jones, recently ditched by his girlfriend, local cupcake maven, Hannah Bellamy. Meanwhile, Morgan's own "weak and weary" heart keeps getting tested by Caleb Joseph, owner of the Raven's Nest bookstore. The too-hot-for-his-own-good former Gothic Lit professor has made a hobby out of snooping around Morgan's cases.

It's up to Morgan to thwart various Halloween hijinks around Bijoux while preventing the town from panicking as she tries to catch a killer who's turned "trick or treat" into the darkest diversion of all—murder.

Mistletoe is Murder: Bijoux Mystery Series Book 5

Skeletons with secrets, prohibition pirates, and holiday hijinks...

Morgan Hart is hoping for a boring Christmas. After eight months of murderous mayhem in her hometown of Bijoux, Michigan, she just wants to snuggle under a warm blanket in front of a cozy fire, with a good book, a hot chocolate (extra marshmallows of course), and Griselda purring beside her. She might even work up the nerve to ask Caleb Joseph over for dinner. Cal, the attractive owner of the Raven's Nest bookstore, has become a good friend since Morgan moved back home to take on the job of police captain.

A bestselling mystery author, Cal recently purchased the old Lawrence Mansion on the edge of town and plans to throw a big Christmas Eve bash. But Morgan's holiday plans—romantic and otherwise—go up in smoke when dark and shadowy secrets are revealed during the clean-up of the 19th century-built home. Can Morgan and Cal uncover the ghostly truth or are they destined for a disastrous deck-the-halls?

CATS & MORE: ADULT COLORING BOOKS

Volume 1: Angsty Cats

Volume 2: Snarky Cats

Volume 3: Mandala Cats

Volume 4: Spooky Cats

Volume 5: Jingle Cats

Volume 6: Mystery Cats

Volume 7: More Mystery Cats

Volume 8: Coloring is Murder *(based on the Bestselling Bijoux Mystery Series)*

Volume 9: Cat Facts

Volume 10: Camping Tarot

Volume 11: Cosmic Cats

Volume 12: Crochet & Cats

NON-FICTION

Visit ReikiOne.com, PresenceandShadow.com, and/or SacredPriestess Journeys.com for more information.

How to Be a Kickass Goddess: Twelve Steps to Owning Your Life

What would your life look like if you owned it? REALLY owned it? Who would you be? How would you live? What would you do? In a straightforward, down-to-earth style, How to Be a Kickass Goddess: Twelve Steps to Owning Your Life takes you on a journey directly into You - everything you are and everything you can be. Now, grab this book and get busy. The world needs all the Kickass Goddesses she can get!

How to be a Kickass Goddess: Companion Journal

Beginnings: ReikiOne First Degree Manual

This manual covers the basics of Reiki training and practice, including history, principles, hand positions, and treatment guidelines. Also included is a brief introduction to the chakras and using crystals with Reiki.

The Deeper Journey: ReikiOne Second Degree Manual

The ReikiOne Second Degree Manual includes the three symbols traditionally associated with this degree, explanations and their use, methods of distance healing, sending Reiki through time and space, combining symbols for greater effect, the chakra system, the human aura, and a suggested reading list.

Reiki Master: ReikiOne Third Degree Manual Part A by Teri Barnett, Reiki Master Teacher

This book contains the 4th symbol, its use for Reiki treatments, a discussion of what it means to be a Reiki Master, and how to use crystal grids with Reiki.

Reiki Master Teacher: ReikiOne Third Degree Manual Part B

The Master Teacher Manual contains all the information your students need for stepping into Reiki Master Teacher - A review of the 4th symbol (plus additional data on this symbol), the 5th symbol for attunements, attunement instructions (individual and group), methods and ethics of teaching, getting in touch with your inner teacher, marketing ideas, an extensive reading list, and much more.

The Reiki Teacher's Handbook

A composite of all the ReikiOne Manuals, the Reiki Teacher's Handbook takes your teaching a step further. This book provides you with all the tools you'll need to teach Reiki. Written from the experienced perspective of a master Teacher of the Usui Shiki Ryoho method, you'll find this book adapts easily to other forms of Reiki and can grow with you as you progress on your teaching path.